DREAMS OF FREEDOM

*An Irish woman's
story of love, justice,
and a young nation
coming apart*

DREAMS OF FREEDOM

MARILYN HIGGINS

Dreams of Freedom:
An Irish Woman's story of love, justice,
and a young nation coming apart

Copyright © 2024, Marilyn R. Higgins
Published by: Marilyn Higgins, Publisher.

ISBN Print Edition: 979-8-218-52466-1

Library of Congress Control Number: 2024913565

For permissions and to contact the author, email:
marilynrhiggins@gmail.com

On the web, MarilynHigginsAuthor.com
Website designed by David Gingrich.

Cover design by Lotus Design,
in cooperation with David Hazard | Ascent.

Editorial development and creative design support by Ascent:
www.spreadyourfire.net

For Brady

#Bradystrong

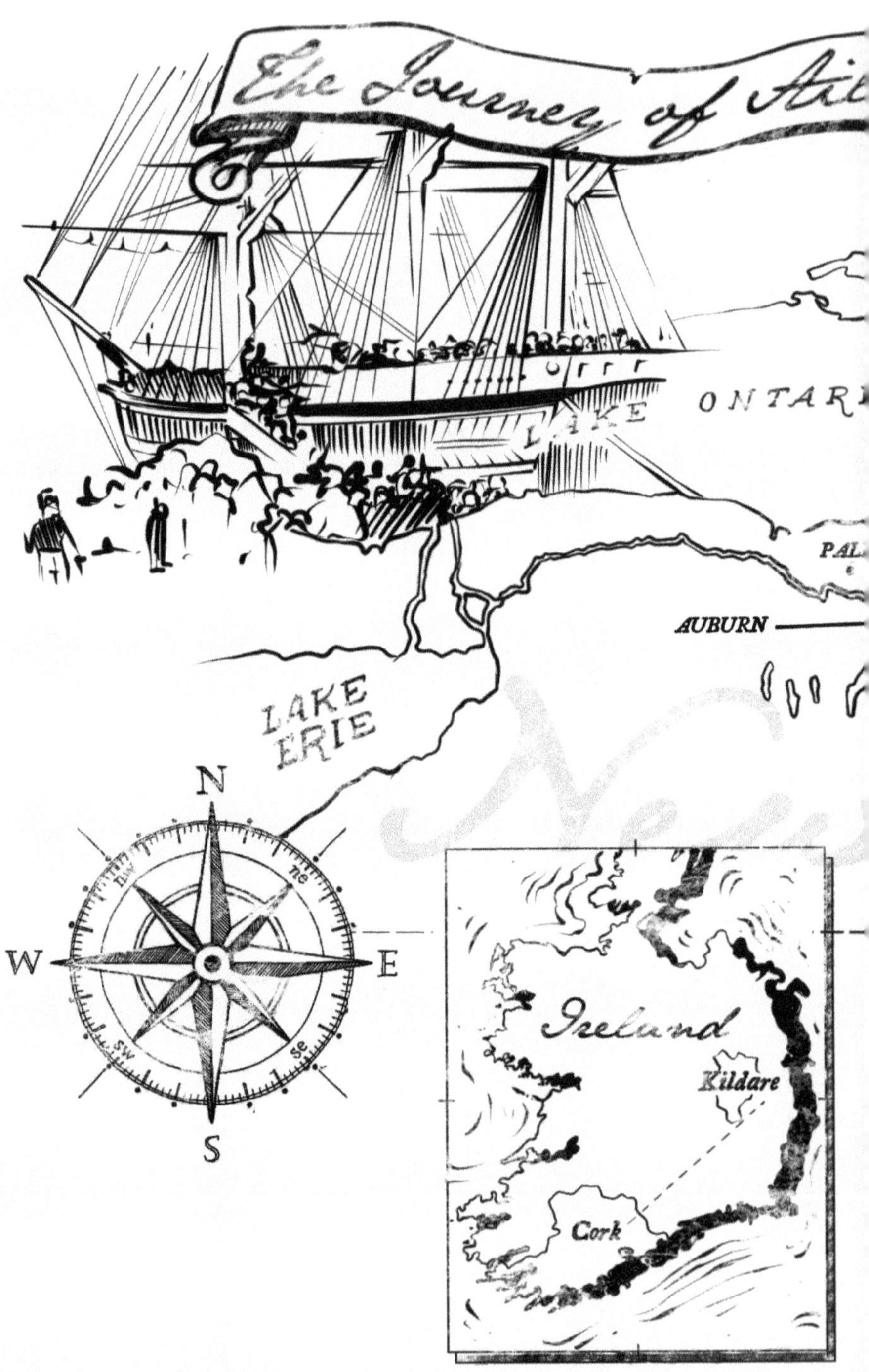

Designed by Sarah Wiley-Joyce, Syracuse NY

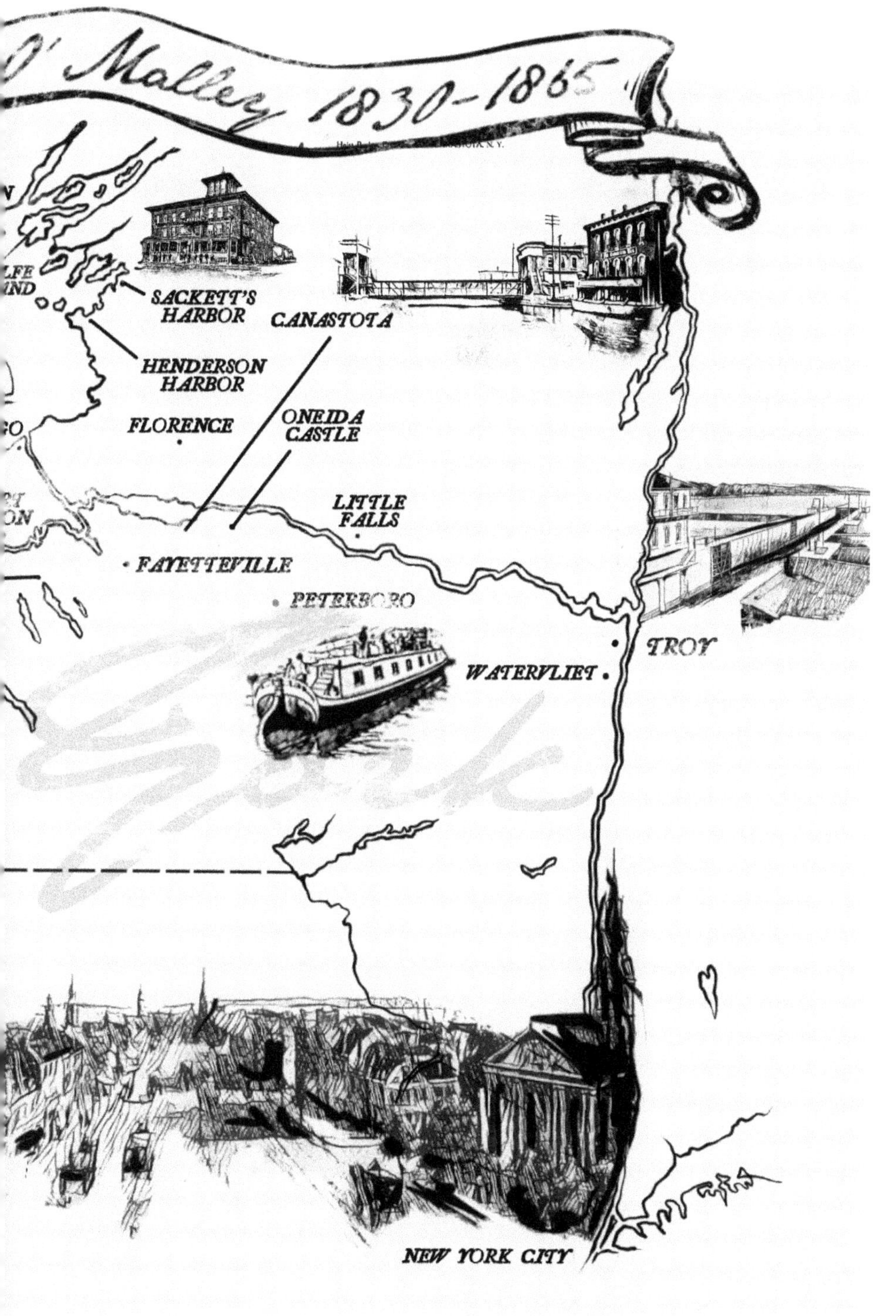

O' Malley 1830-1865
SACKETT'S HARBOR
CANASTOTA
HENDERSON HARBOR
FLORENCE
ONEIDA CASTLE
LITTLE FALLS
FAYETTEVILLE
PETERBORO
WATERVLIET
TROY
NEW YORK CITY

CONTENTS

BACKDROP OF HISTORIC EVENTS

1823—*Oneida Nation begins migration to Canada and Wisconsin*

1825—*Completion of the Erie Canal*

1827—*Joseph Smith finds Book of Mormon plates near Palmyra, NY*

1829—*Catholic Relief Act passes, allowing Catholics to serve in Parliament*

1830—*First edition of "The Protestant" is published denouncing Catholicism in US*

1835—*Mob attacks abolitionist meeting in Utica, NY.*

1840—*World Anti-slavery Convention held in London*

1845—*Frederick Douglass travels to Ireland*

1847—*Gerrit Smith and Stephen Myers organize the Florence Farming Association*

1848—*First Women's Rights Convention held in Seneca Falls, NY*

1850—*Fugitive Slave Act passed by Congress*

1852—*Ulysses S. Grant stationed in Sackett's Harbor, NY*

1859—*Harriet Tubman moves to Auburn, NY*

1861-1865—*The American Civil War*

April 1865—*President Lincoln is assassinated*

To Sail 1st April,

FOR NEW-YORK,

THE WELL KNOWN PACKET SHIP,

FRIENDS,

THOMAS CHOATE, Commander,

400 Tons Burthen, Copper-fastened, and newly Coppered to the Bends, *(lately arrived from Charleston in 21 days,)* has superior furnished accommodations for Passengers; and a Cow on Board to supply them with Milk.

Shippers and Passengers are requested to have Goods or Luggage, intended for this Vessel, at Greenock, by Saturday, the 29th, at farthest.

For Freight or Passage, apply to Messrs. STEVENSON, MILLER, & Co. Greenock; the CAPTAIN on board; or here, to

JOHN FYFE & CO.

GLASGOW, 11th March, 1823.

PART ONE

1831–1835

---

*"Gentlemen, you may soon
have the alternative
to live as slaves
or die as free men."*

**In a speech by Daniel O'Connell,
Mallow County, Cork**

1

A BLESSING

A gray figure was striding along the road, and she hoped it would not be anyone bringing more bad news. Twice this week, someone in the village had died—sweet young Brigid Daley, of consumption, and old Daniel McNeil, no surprise, of the drink. Aileen opened the narrow, northern casement windows first. A cool breeze entered the stone cottage on the hill above the River Liffy and signaled there would be rain that day.

Her grandmother, Betha, ever fearful of thieves, insisted on latching, bolting, and barring every opening of their cottage at dusk. This habit left the bitter smell of peat hovering near the hearth, and Aileen enjoyed releasing it and bringing in the fresh smell of each new day. She opened the southern windows next, ushering in morning scents of moss and malva from the garden. Finally, she climbed onto an old stepstool, pried open the western window above the sink and glimpsed the road to town and a small slice of the river.

It appeared to be a man. She moved to the hallway to crack open the front door for a better look. She hoped that whoever it was—a wanderer seeking a meal or a hired man from the nearby farm in search of a lost sheep—would pass by without banging on the door. Sunrise was the time she reserved to thank the Blessed Virgin for their health and the little bit of prosperity they enjoyed from their own small landholding. Owning property was something few Catholics, and even fewer women, could lay claim to in Ireland. She was grateful to live here with her grandmother and never failed to thank Jesus for the privilege.

She perched on the small tapestry covered bench near the doorway, bowed her head and gripped the rosary in her pocket. She prayed first for the soul of her mother who had died giving her life 19 years ago inside this very home. Closing her eyes she concentrated on her prayers until her imagination suddenly depicted her mother on the lawn bordering their barn, with Willow, the mother of her wolfhound, Brody. A long, blue skirt swirled in the wind and a faint whisper of laughter floated above her mother's image. When she forced her eyes open, her mother's lovely face peered out at her from the tiger oak frame placed prominently on the mantle across the room. Intent as she was on prayer, the ghostly appearances had made it impossible for her to continue. She stood, placed her feet firmly on the floor and opened the heavy wooden door a crack to see who was, hopefully, just passing by.

The person was tall but still unidentifiable. She returned to her bench and willed herself to concentrate on her morning prayers by pressing a jade rosary bead deeply into her thumb. Just as she finished *The Apostles Creed,* Brody rushed to her feet from the kitchen and began barking loudly, threatened, and anxious. "Hush now, Brody," she hissed, and turned once more to her narrow view of the road.

Joseph Ryan's figure was now visible, climbing up the path from where the stone wall at the base of their property met the road to town. The sight of him, angular and determined with a purposeful energy and gait, elicited a tightness in her chest. This was not a visit she wanted.

He was handsome enough and considered a choice catch by the Catholic mothers of Kildare, yet Aileen had never warmed to his advances, and her grandmother had never encouraged her to do so.

"Why don't you approve of Joseph Ryan?" Aileen had asked her grandmother one day as they slung wet clothes over ropes on the windy hillside.

Before answering, Betha brought their work to a full stop. She did this only when she wanted Aileen to take seriously every single word she had to say.

"I know now to keep advice on romance to myself, child. I regret encouraging your dear mother to accept O'Malley's advances, and I'll not make that mistake with you."

"She loved him though. You yourself said as much."

"But he was one for daydreaming and arriving late to work. It made for a hardscrabble life. Be wary of men. All men." Those last six words had been delivered ominously by Betha to Aileen many times before.

She needed no one to caution her about Joseph Ryan.

He's overbearing on his good days.

She closed the door quickly, hoping he might knock once and, if no one answered, leave. To her irritation, he banged the knocker loudly, causing Brody to resume barking. She opened the door and stepped back, allowing him to enter the ancient, low-ceilinged room. Now it began. She knew what he wanted.

He stepped within a foot of her, leaning in close until she could smell the scent of pipe smoke and sweet hay on his coat.

"It's a lovely morning, Aileen, and I've an idea to take you for a walk up Cutty Hill."

She allowed her rosary to fall deep into her pocket and reached for a long brown curl that had fallen loose from her hair weave. As she tucked it back into place, she noticed Joseph staring hungrily at the spot on her long white neck where it had fallen.

"I'm not for walking this morning, Joseph. I've much to get about here at the cottage."

"Surely you can make some time." he stated, smiling broadly, and brimming with confidence. "The Court has granted probate on Father's will. My inheritance is in hand."

"I'm not for walking today."

His stature and blue eyes were undeniably attractive and now he could boast of wealth as well, but still, she wasn't tempted. She had refused his invitations many times before.

What keeps his interest in me alive?

"But I've come all this way," he protested.

"Are your ears failing you, Joseph? Were you sipping too much whiskey last night?"

He winced at her defiance. "My ears work well enough. They work well enough to know that your Da has made haste to America."

The comment was meant to sting, and it did.

Her heart contracted with painful anxiety as she focused, for just a moment, on her father's reason for leaving for America. He had learned that his children, Molly and Michael, from his scandalous second marriage, to a Protestant woman, had been kidnapped and taken there.

"The dock workers saw 'em," he'd explained while fighting back tears, "wrapped in filthy blankets. Kidnapped they were, and loaded on a ship bound for America."

She was aware of the practice of selling and trading Irish children. With poverty growing it was happening frequently in the port cities. The horrid image of Molly and Michael being stolen replayed frequently in her mind and was doing so again now.

She responded defiantly, "What business is my father's travel of yours? He's a good man, my Da, an honorable man."

"If he's such a gentleman, why did he marry a Protestant and leave you here at your Granny's?"

"You'll not slander him! As a child without a mum, he wiped my tears. He sang me to sleep."

Ryan looked away.

"Would you treat a sad little girl with such kindness?"

Joseph stared down at his boots, looking unsure how he should respond.

"I don't expect you to understand. Da and Grandmother were never chums, but he knew she would love and protect me from the whispering vipers in this town."

"I do understand he's your Da and all, but he married a Protestant!"

"He married for love, and I admire him for it."

"But his leaving could bring a breath of relief to you and your granny."

Now he was speaking in a gentler tone. "The whispering in church will stop. You'll no longer be the subject of gossip at Saturday tea."

"The whispering means more to you than me."

"This could be a blessing of sorts."

"A blessing? Children being stolen?—Out of this house with you!"

He caught her by the arms, pressing his fingers in a little too tightly. "Your reputation is important to me. As I've told you, I want you to become my wife."

She was relieved to hear the scrape of furniture in the room above and surmised that grandmother had risen and would soon be eavesdropping on the stairs.

"Why are you so determined about me, Joseph?"

"You're the loveliest lass in Kildare."

"I've told you my mind, and I'm not one for changing it. You can have any girl in Kildare."

With a sly smile he pressed his face toward hers and whispered, "Yes, but I've already kissed most of them."

"So that's it is it? I'm the only one who doesn't swoon when you walk by."

"You're too bold with your opinions, you are. Everyone says so."

"Yes, I have opinions."

"I've a taste for your high spirits, and you are my intended."

She turned again and met his eyes. "I may be your intended, but you are not mine."

He stepped back quickly as if her words were stinging wasps.

At that moment, instinct told her it would be unwise to make this man from such a powerful family an enemy. She lightened their banter. "I don't fear being thought starched and contrary. It may be this part of my charm that you like best."

He took a deep breath to calm himself, walked into the kitchen, sat at the table, and motioned for her to join him.

"You've always got your head in a book. What's to come of it? You can't get into university here. Women simply aren't allowed. You just ignore this."

"And you ignore all the grand changes being made here."

He knew she was speaking of Daniel O'Connell's election to the Parliament and the recent granting to Catholics of the right to vote.

"Things will improve for women, as well" she added. Feeling certain it was only her lack of enthusiasm and his desire to possess her that propelled him to walk five miles to her door, she tried to conclude the conversation.

"I know of all the young lasses you have wooed and bed in County Kildare, and I'll not join the lot."

"We'll see what Father Murphy and your granny have to say. I've made plans for him to visit the two of you tomorrow," he replied in an angry but satisfied tone. "He'll pronounce his opinion, and that will be that.

Her heart sank. If that meeting were to happen, her chances of escaping Joseph's designs on her were little to none. Despite her brusqueness with most people, her grandmother was habitually subservient to men of the cloth, and she might enforce whatever Father Murphy decreed. In a year she could be carrying the first of Joseph's litter of children.

"I thought I heard a man's voice in here." Betha descended the steps and entered the kitchen.

"Oh, Grandmother, you know Joseph Ryan. They've just settled his father's estate and he's come all this way to tell us how rich he is."

"Is that so?" Betha Dooley twirled her skirt to face Joseph and clasped her arms in front of her. "Well, money can be a blessing or a curse. There's plenty of blokes in this parish with coins in their pockets but no brain in their heads."

Joseph tried charming the old woman. "I've got plenty of money, and Aileen has plenty of brains, so we will make a good pairing, don't ye think, Betha?"

"A brain is a lot like money," Betha replied sharply, "it's not how much you have, it's what you do with it that counts, and I doubt it's her brain that interests you."

Aileen's face reddened with embarrassment.

Ryan sighed and turned to leave. "We'll have the priest talk some sense into the two of you then." Watching him depart, Aileen noticed that he appeared uncharacteristically deep in thought. Then she watched him prance down their path to the village road.

Why is he so pleased with himself?

She took notice of the tall shadow of St. Brigid's steeple over the valley on this sunny day and wondered how long she would be able to avoid becoming Joseph Ryan's property.

2

FAMILIES REQUIRE SACRIFICE

That evening, alone in the garden snipping herbs, Aileen thought of her father.

"Will you come?" he had asked, turning his head to look back at her while boarding the ship. "It could mean starting over," he called out hopefully, just before disappearing down to the passenger hold.

At 19, had this been the last she would see of him? She tried to rub the evening chill from her arms and revisited his remark. He had indentured himself to work for three years on the recently completed Erie Canal to pay for his passage. She hoped he would find the children and a way to pay his debt and return soon.

The next day, as she pulled a faded yellow tea-tin from the cupboard in the kitchen, she noticed her own contented smile in the mirror by the front door. This room made her happy. The sounds of Ireland that she loved best echoed within its walls. Laughter and smart conversation were embedded in the grain of the golden oak table that sat proudly in the center of the room. Letters brimming with excitement could be heard when the terracotta bowl on the sideboard gave up its stamped, linen paper treasures. Babies were announced and gossip was exchanged when the hands of their cousins and neighbors were wrapped around the brown tankards that lined the top shelf of the hutch. This kitchen, with memories of all the sounds she loved and its polished stone floors and faded red ceiling beams, cheered her on even the gloomiest of days.

She knew she was leading a life with privileges that few other young women in Ireland could enjoy. The shelves in the hallway carried dozens of brown and red leather-bound books with titles etched in gold. Aileen could delve into these treasures left by her deceased great aunt Kathleen of Dublin as often as she liked. She read voraciously, losing herself in poetry one day and botany the next. Grandmother allowed her to set her own pace in most things, never telling her when to feed the animals or toss the hay. All of the tasks required to keep their home safe and solvent were accomplished by the two of them with very little bickering.

Aileen stared thoughtfully at the swirling water she had boiled to warm the brown pot for tea. She tried uncomfortably to imagine what life without her grandmother could be like. The thought of leaving Ireland both intrigued and frightened her. She calmed herself, settled the teacups on a tray, and wondered why so many of her countrymen were now speaking so longingly of going to America.

She recalled Grandmother describing how a young Father Murphy had convinced the brawling Costello brothers to set sail for America over tea at this very table decades ago. He had convinced them it was their 'Godly duty' to Ireland to fight the insurgent American colonists on England's behalf. The brothers never returned. It irritated Betha when the priest claimed, as he often did, that the

Catholic vote 'was now assured' thanks to clergy like himself and the sacrifices of boys like the Costellos.

From the front hallway she heard the subservient tone her grandmother used to greet Father Murphy at the door. "So kind of you to come to our home, Father, and so good of you. Thank you, thank you."

It was this subservience that could sink her. Becoming Joseph Ryan's wife was an unthinkable punishment for a crime she did not commit. She sensed her grandmother concurred with her dislike of Ryan but did not know why. God would not do this to her she affirmed, calming herself. Grandmother was merely using the same voice that all parish women adopted in Murphy's presence, fawning like hungry puppies for his blessing and approval and later hacking away at his drinking and the unwashed smell behind his back.

Betha Dooley was a force as powerful as any Aileen had known. She admired her grandmother's thick, braided hair, strong arms, and quick intellect. Betha had even convinced Father Murphy to write "tuberculosis" in the parish records as the cause of her husband's death when he was found prone and lifeless on a woman nastily labeled "the loosest woman in the parish." Aileen found it curious that her grandmother went so often to confession and sensed that she had secrets but knew better than to pry. Gaining confidence that the two of them could withstand anything the priest might serve, Aileen rearranged the cups and doilies artfully on the tray and placed a brandy glass on the side.

"Betha!" Father Murphy boomed, ignoring Aileen's entrance to the front room. "I have a most promising proposal for this child you have raised. This concerns Joseph Ryan." He was a small, pale man with thinning gray hair that hung forward and streaked across his forehead. He expected a smile in return for his exuberance.

Instead, her grandmother avoided his gaze. "You know full well I hold no fondness for the memory of his father, John Ryan."

"You still believe John Ryan foiled the united uprising?" the priest asked incredulously. "Such stubbornness."

"I recall it well, and so do you." she snapped. "All of the factions had joined to make Ireland strong and independent. Ryan was a traitor. He threw it all away. He whispered the location of our weapons to the Brits. You know this to be true as well as I."

Aileen's ears pricked up. She understood that Betha had been a spy and weapons smuggler during the uprising but knew little else about those dangerous times. Her grandmother steadfastly refused to discuss her past.

"With his father's probate done, I'd be glad not to hear the name Ryan again," her grandmother added.

Aileen exhaled quietly and began pouring the tea.

Betha continued in an uncharacteristically sharp tone with the priest. "John Ryan almost destroyed our future," she stated, and, nodding vigorously toward Aileen, concluded "Who is to say his son, Joseph, won't destroy hers? Neither man thinks of anyone but himself."

"He's a worthy match for Aileen," insisted the priest, "and neither of you will be selling pies to make a pound in your old age with Joseph at the helm. He came to me and I –," he hesitated for a moment, "—I gave him my blessing for this marriage."

Aileen tried to disregard the shiver that went up her spine when the word "blessing" emerged from his mouth. A blessing from Father Murphy was important. She would have to hold her tongue now and fabricate an objection with her grandmother later.

The priest blew on his hot tea, then continued. "I wouldn't have given my blessing for the marriage if there was any chance that blasphemous father of hers could reenter her life. The Ryan family is far too important to risk wearing any touch of the scandal that Dennis O'Malley brought down upon your own."

"We agree on that, at least."

"The circumstances surrounding his departure were most unfortunate, but God does work in mysterious ways, and it could be seen as a blessing in the end. Before he left for America, there was always a chance he'd start hanging round her and stirring up old gossip."

"Don't be silly, Father. Aileen never sees the likes of O'Malley. She doesn't even know where he lives. You know the good Catholic life she's lead here with me. The rosary's in her hand morning to night!"

Father Murphy turned in his seat and looked directly at Aileen for the first time since he arrived. Her complexion turned a bright shade of pink.

"We will visit this topic once more on another day," said Betha, firmly concluding the conversation.

Her defiance had made the ugly, lingering rash on Father Murphy's neck turn bright red. Frustrated, but with cool deliberation, he delivered his decree. "Betha, you are once more deficient in the eyes of the Lord, Jesus Christ!" he said, blessing himself. "You know why this must be done."

In a moment he was shuffling down the dusty path to the road leading to the rectory from which he ruled over, if not Aileen's life, then so many others.

Relieved and grateful that he was gone, Aileen wondered what moral deficiencies of Betha's he had been referring to.

"I'll have a rest before supper," Betha announced. Clearly

irritated, she began climbing the stairs, then stopped abruptly.

"A blessing! That priest is insufferable. I cannot imagine anyone, let alone a man of the cloth, condoning the kidnapping of children and selling them into slavery. How could that ever be construed as a blessing of any kind?"

"Joseph Ryan also called it a blessing that Father was gone."

Betha stopped, turned on the stairs, and became pensive for a moment. "The two of them are more alike than you realize." Stepping down, she faced her granddaughter. "I saw that look Father Murphy gave you when I told him you had not seen your da, and I saw the look you gave in return that turned your face the color of my June roses. Is there something you're not telling me?"

"Yes. I've hated keeping it from you. I lied to you about seeing my father and the children. I haven't been going to the library on Tuesday and Thursday afternoons. Since the children's mum died, there has been no one to walk them home from school or make them a bowl of soup while Father works the docks. I've tried to help. Sometimes I meet them at the tinker's street wagon or in the gated park behind the square in town. I'm sorry."

"I suspected as much but didn't want to know." Betha rubbed her forehead and sighed "I don't blame you, Aileen. After all, they are your family. I'd not have chosen Dennis O'Malley to be your father but your father he is, and there is no denying his love for you. From the exchange of looks I gather Father Murphy knows about your visits?"

"Yes, I told him in confession. I asked God's forgiveness for lying to you." Aileen's lips began to quiver. "And for guidance on how to help Da."

Betha's eyes became wide and alarmed. "I don't like the sound of this. That priest cannot be trusted. People are not always what they seem, child, even those that wear the collar. I've protected you too much. What exactly did you tell him?"

"I told him everything. He wanted to know how the children traveled about town and where they played when Da was working. He asked all kinds of questions."

Betha took Aileen's hands into her own. "You may have unwittingly sealed the fate of your father and the wee ones."

"What do you mean?"

"The Ryans have kept that priest comfortable and cooperative for decades. It's good for business, don't you know, to have the man who knows everyone's secrets on the payroll. The Ryans' purse is a large one, and now it's controlled by Joseph."

"I don't understand."

"Both of those scoundrels wanted your da out of the picture. Interesting that both consider his departure a 'blessing'."

"But confession is a holy sacrament, Grandmother. It renews us in Christ."

"There is no godly reason Father Murphy would have needed all those details about the children in order for you to make a confession."

Aileen fell silent.

"His purpose was to find out when and where they were alone. He may have passed it all to Joseph Ryan. He may have arranged the kidnapping. The Ryans have connections at the docks. It would be a simple task for Joseph to place some coins in the hands of a napper and find a ship captain to transport them."

"He knew Da would follow the children," said Aileen slowly, recognizing the terrible truth in front of her "and he wanted him gone." Her heart was pounding now. "He would go to all that trouble and expense just to make me his wife?"

"He's his father's son, that one. He gets what he wants and cares not a shilling who gets harmed in the process. He wanted Murphy's blessing to marry you."

"Jesus, Mary and Joseph."

"They may have plotted to get your da, the children, and any hint of scandal, away from you."

Turning to stare out the window above the sink, Aileen's voice lowered to a whisper.

"My confession helped them to sell the children. If he would do that, then he is strangely obsessed and will never leave me in peace."

Just then, the rising wind was interrupted by the clatter of a window shutter coming loose and slamming to the ground. Aileen could hear the cry of a seabird in the distance and felt a heavy weight descend upon her shoulders.

"Last week I had considered, not very seriously, going to America to help my father. Now I have no choice, I must go."

Betha waited several moments before responding. She stared at the floor and quietly considered every possible action that she could take to keep her granddaughter near. Finally, she responded dryly, "I agree. You do need to go. It's the only way to escape Ryan and find your family."

Aileen groaned and began swabbing the tears that were falling from her face onto the bib of her gray woolen dress.

"I've never wandered beyond this town. Never wanted to. I love Ireland, and I love you, and I can't dream how I will go about finding my father in America, much less the little ones."

"You can do this," Betha encouraged her. "You're smart—too smart for a Catholic girl in Ireland. Right you are about not marrying

Ryan, that dreadful lout. You might find America to your liking."

"So many Irish dream of going there. Not I."

"University might be possible for you there. I won't be here forever, Aileen, but Ireland will. You can always come home. This land will be yours when I am gone."

Betha's eyes revealed the terror in her heart. Aileen could not bear the thought of her grandmother spending her final years alone, and she marveled at the strength she had summoned to convince her to leave.

"We'll make a plan. I know people who can help. You'll need money. Captains pay smugglers for children then transport them to the docks of New York."

"It's horrid."

'They sell them to employers in America for three to seven-years' labor."

"That's slavery."

"Yes, child slavery, nothing new. You'll be going against dangerous people who paid good money for those children. They won't be handed over lightly. You'll need money, some reliable help, and a good bit of luck."

This was the fiery determined woman that Aileen adored. She envisioned her grandmother during the uprising—dark braids falling to her waist, a bandana tied across her brow, giving orders and helping prisoners to escape—just as she was plotting Aileen's escape now.

"It's a difficult lesson you're learning, child. Carry it with you always. Families, well, families require sacrifice."

The next afternoon, Aileen curled onto a straw pile in a dark nook of the barn and sobbed, finally releasing the ache that had settled deep down inside her when she first learned of Father Murphy's deception. She reached for her rosary, prayed, and found some relief.

When she returned to the kitchen, Betha was sitting quietly. Shallow rings of old tea were hardened in the cup before her.

"Keep Joseph Ryan at bay in the coming months. Dangle him along with an occasional wink and a pretty dress. We cannot have him suspect you are leaving."

"I understand."

"I'll take care of Murphy. He'll think he's persuaded you to accept Ryan's proposal."

As the weeks passed, Betha wrote to her friends in Troy, New York, rented abandoned acres for extra funds and filled Aileen's travel bags with only the most precious of belongings. The women spent every available hour together, reliving memories and holding hands as they walked the grassy knolls of Kildare. Gradually, they became firm in the momentous decision they had made, even knowing it could separate them forever.

3

DEPARTURE

Without the cloudy smog and smell of coal that permeated most Irish cities, the trading port of Cork presented a fresh, colorful site on the horizon. Peering out of the carriage, Aileen saw the harbor curl gently away from the land, like a bright blue ribbon reaching out into the Irish Sea. The damp breeze made her ringlets tighten and cast a mist over her heart-shaped face and large green eyes.

She was determined to look confident even if she didn't feel it. It helped knowing that her upright posture and fine indigo dress set her apart from many of the women in Ireland who hid their faces in woolen scarves when speaking with strangers. Her grandmother had procured tokens for her use in New York, and this stash, sewn carefully into the lining of her petticoat, gave her some sense of security.

Still, the next morning she found her gloved hands shaking uncontrollably as she walked hurriedly along the pier in search of her ship, The Dublin Packet.

She ignored the smell of pigs and fish and the unwashed

workers on the docks, choosing instead to focus intently on the names of the vessels she passed as she walked along the bustling pier. A man with a red cap was shouting and thrashing at a poor mule that refused to drag a huge crate marked "Mail" even one step further.

Jimmy was just a step ahead of her, hauling her trunk and cursing at anyone who slowed their progress. "You're thick as shite and less than half as handy," he barked at a man standing in their way. The poor fellow seemed confused by the clamor, and Jimmy elbowed him with a grin. "Get over, 'ya senseless block."

"If you were any longer, you'd be late," he had remarked on her height when they first met. He had made her smile, but she was skeptical when the innkeeper insisted that this disheveled, smallish boy with missing teeth could handle her bags. Now she was grateful for Jimmy's brashness and stinging humor. He opened their way through the crowds and drew the eyes of strangers away from her.

Her tall stature and dark-Irish looks were attractive but uncommon and a frequent source of anxiety for her. She towered over most of the boys in the village and was often mistaken for being older than her 19 years. Confused, but never shy, she occasionally fended off unwelcome advances and sexual remarks with a well-placed kick. Many years before she had inquired about her looks while staring at a painting of her mother with her dark-brown curls and full lips. She had asked her grandmother, "Am I pretty, Grandmother? Do I look like her?"

She recalled Betha issuing a decisive "Yes," while lifting the portrait carefully, almost reverently, with her arthritic hands.

"Women and girls that look like the two of you are always told what's best for them, usually by lads thinking only of what's best for themselves."

Knowing that the painting in the tiger oak frame was carefully tucked inside her trunk gave her a fleeting sense of calm as she stepped along the jetty.

The great ships along the pier began rocking noisily, first slowly then boldly. They broke their clanging tempo periodically and came to a sudden, silent halt when the fickle spring winds disappeared. Looking at the dense mass of vessels before her, she felt a twinge in her heart knowing it was possible that she would never return to Ireland and that the exodus of people crowding onto these ships would not soon come to an end.

She thought again of the painted image of her mother as they stopped in front of the Dublin Packet. On her mother's shoulders was draped the exquisite, blue-lace shawl that was among her prized possessions, and in her fingers was a small, deep-red blossom. Aileen recognized it as one coming from Mrs. Shanahan's finest row of tea roses, which it was said her mother adored.

For her entire life Aileen had initiated imaginary chats with her mother whenever she felt anxious or afraid, and she began one now. "I wish I had her hand for growin' roses," Aileen imagined her mother saying as she sat properly on the settee for the artist. "But here's me, an Irish woman, an' I can't grow a decent potato."

Aileen smiled, and as usual, the light Limerick brogue she'd assigned to her mother's voice calmed her. She wondered if her mother had missed her own father as a child, the way she was currently missing hers.

Grandfather was not spoken of in Betha Dooley's home, and Aileen knew from her cousins that he had seldom been present. She wondered if her mother's father was tall and if he had occasionally played ringboard with her mother in the barn.

She recalled the 'scrubbing day' with Grandmother when she first saw a likeness of his face. While searching for cobwebs on the stone floor with her brush and pail she had spied a delicate slip of paper lodged tightly in a crevice behind a heavy wood cupboard. Something made her stretch to her full reach to retrieve the little paper, a drawing of a handsome boy with dark eyes sitting like a prince on an ornate stool of wickers curls.

"This is Grandfather," she had declared, looking up at her grandmother for confirmation, "isn't it?"

"It is he," Grandmother had replied in a much softer tone than usually passed her lips, "drawn by his da. Please put it in the drawer."

That final comment, a command or possibly an understated plea, made it clear to Aileen that her grandfather was not to be mentioned again.

She was shaken from her daydream by the voice of a man with a heavy cockney accent, obviously from across the waters. He was shouting something completely unintelligible at a small, shoeless child who was choking back tears. The man's face was red with yesterday's whiskey, and he barked orders with an authority he clearly did not possess.

The crying child brought her half-siblings, Molly and Michael, to mind.

How frightened they must have been, seized by a stranger and brought to docks like these. May the Lord forgive me and extract a painful penance from Father Murphy if he failed to keep my confession sacred.

She concentrated on clearing away the image she carried everywhere she went of little Molly, her blond curls caked with mud, clinging to her taller, dark-haired brother, their eyes wet with tears.

"There she is, Miss," shouted Jimmy, pointing to the Dublin Packet.

Startled, she stood before the massive wooden structure. The ship was intricately carved, painted and gracefully shaped. The British flag at the rear mast rippled in the wind, and great mounds of thick yellow rope hung from its sides. She turned to Jimmy and smiled gratefully.

"Thanks to you for finding our way. You're a fine lad, and I'd have been lost without you!"

He smiled and stepped onto the boarding platform, managing to artfully balance her trunk along with a tapestry bag full of additional belongings. "This is a heavy trunk you carry, Miss. Full of books, is it?"

"I find books the best of companions, Jimmy!"

She thought about the books she had selected to bring on this journey and of the pages holding pressed, dried buds from her grandmother's tiny, half-blighted garden. Betha had suggested this just before her departure and had run outdoors to select them in a rushed display of emotion.

Before stepping onto the ship, Aileen slipped off her glove and dug her hand deep into her pocket. She searched frantically for the silver broken body of Jesus draped on the tiny cross of her rosary. With relief she found it and pressed her thumb onto its sharp edges until it hurt. She prayed before stepping forward.

"Oh, God, come to my aid and make haste to help me on this journey."

At the foot of the gangway, she was greeted by a bearded man with well-mended clothes and a flashing smile.

"I am Captain Mick. It's to New York, is it? Welcome aboard."

It was clear from the way he studied her up and down that he was quickly taking in her stately manner, the dark, brown curls tucked under her hat, and her fine clothes.

"Thank you, Sir" she replied. She pointed her eyes down to avoid revealing the fear and sadness rising in her chest.

A knot was forming in her throat. She might never see her grandmother again. Aileen had never wanted to emigrate. She knew the Irish would continue to fill these wooden ships, but she did not wish to be a part of it. She understood, though, that the people of her island were simply too poor and too grief-stricken at all their terrible losses to stay. She touched her fingers to her chest and retrieved the letter from her father she had hidden there.

Letters like these will keep driving the Irish to ports like Cork, taking them to places where they are told that rich rewards came from good conduct and industry. I'm just not believing it.

"Might you tell me something about yourself, Miss?" the captain asked. "Where in Cork are you from? Who are your kin? Perhaps we have mutual friends and interests."

"I suspect we have no mutual interests, Sir," she replied, a curt edge in her voice. She would have none of his boldness. She pointed Jimmy to the stairs. Stories of ship captains stealing children and trading the fares of destitute young ladies for the comfort of their favors during the Atlantic crossing were well known. She wanted nothing to do with the captain. She wanted only to arrive in New York safely, continue up the Hudson, find her father, and locate Molly and Michael.

While Jimmy dragged her trunk to the stairway leading down to the cabins, Captain Mick tipped his hat, smiled, and gave her a look that made her uncomfortable.

"Oh, of course. . .Madam."

Too late she recalled her grandmother's last strident instruction. "Keep your eyes down, your mouth shut, and your chin out," she had advised through her sniffles. Aileen missed her grandmother's imperious commands already. Betha's lessons, given over tea at the barrel table in the garden, or as they sat swinging their legs on the low stone wall at the base of their property, made her think deeply and always inspired her to learn.

When they reached her cabin, Jimmy dropped the trunk heavily, narrowly missing Aileen's foot, and readied himself to leave. She stared at him, realizing that she was about to be totally on her own setting out across an ocean to a land she knew little about.

He sensed her fear. "Goodbye, Miss," said Jimmy. "Good luck to 'ya." His words somehow calmed her.

She pressed a coin into his dirty hand and noticed that his eyes held the faint hint of a smile. She wondered what escapade he might be plotting for his return to the wharf.

"Thank you, Jimmy. May God bless and keep you close to Him and smiling. I'll say farewell and give you a touch of the advice my grandmother gave to me. Mimicking Betha, she straightened her back, placed her hands upon her hips and stated firmly, "Carry yourself like you are important, and people will always think you are!"

"Ha! Bless her soul." Jimmy replied. "No trouble for me following your granny's instructions. Indeed, I will be important someday. What else would she say about staying safe and happy in this perilous life?"

Aileen hesitated for a moment. "Well, this one is more for the lasses."

"Go on then, let's hear it."

"The best protection for an Irish Catholic woman is to have the whole town suspect she has a rich British lover."

This broke the tension of their separation, and they both fell into laughter.

"It's true, you know," Jimmy added, still giggling. "I know Irishmen who puff out their chests when cursing and slapping their wives, but whine like sheep in the face of a wealthy Englishman."

"Bless the wisdom of Betha Dooley," she responded quietly.

"Watch out for that Captain Mick," Jimmy said quietly as they walked together back toward the stairs. "He's the type who'd fuck off before buying his 'round at the pub. I fancy he would peel an orange in his pocket to keep anyone for askin' fer a tiny slice of it!"

Then Jimmy was gone, out into the open, salty air. She returned to her cabin and closed the door. Reaching up for the bolt, she found to her dismay that the door had no lock.

She felt decidedly unprotected and wondered how or if pretending she had a British lover would, in these circumstances, do her any good at all. Steadying herself, she surveyed the spare wooden cubicle that would be her home for the next two months while crossing the Atlantic. The space was spare and painted white. It held a narrow sleeping berth, chamber pot, metal bowl and pitcher, and a small wooden locker. Hearing happy chatter up on the deck, she opened the wooden slats on the door and window to let in some laughter and ventilate the musty room.

The narrow, central corridor outside her door held a long table and served as a sort of saloon where she understood meals and drinks would be served. She sat down heavily on her bed and once again reviewed the steps she had taken to assure Joseph Ryan would not foil her escape.

The letter that I left with grandmother should determine him to be finished with me. Betha will feign being shocked to her shoelaces by my stealing off to Cork in the night, and he'll abandon his silly pursuit of me and find someone else. There are plenty of willing ladies in Kildare for him to choose from. Dear Lord, I pray this is not a fool's errand I have embarked upon.

The children's faces, crying and afraid, appeared again, clouding her sight and catching her breath. She reached for the small muslin packet of heather and lavender tied with string that sat prominently on top of the crisp, white linens piled at the foot of her bed. As she lifted the sachet to her nose, she breathed deeply and allowed herself to feel grateful for being one of the sixteen "good" passengers accommodated in the relative luxury of cabin class.

Then the children's faces appeared again before her, and she fell onto her bed and cried.

4

FRIENDSHIP ON THE DUBLIN PACKET

She retrieved and read her father's letter for the fifth time in two days:

Aileen, my darling daughter,

I did not write before now because my time with the work crew made me feel less of myself. They often paid us in whiskey, and I'm luckier than most not to have been put down by it or the murderous mosquitoes in the Cayuga marshes.

My search for the chiselers has made for many gray days, but suddenly a ray of sunshine has crossed the sweat and sadness that is the Erie Canal.

A sailor from the Fortitude told me that boys brought to the wharves of New York from Ireland are often sold by the captains to labor on western farms. So, with the photograph of our darling Michael's face in hand, I inquired of his whereabouts at every blacksmith and farm supply store along the dig. Perhaps it was your fine prayers that loosened the lips of a lovely cook I met yesterday on a barge traveling east. She told me that a young lad resembling our Michael was working in an orchard near a town called Batavia. I am setting out west to find him as soon as I can be released from detail and pay for the voyage.

If you come here, I am afraid you may see a bad dose of fools acting like maggots. Do not be beaten back by the brutal words that are bucketed down on the Irish here in America. There are grand possibilities here and the chance for you to find friends and a future that does not include the barking orders of your grandmother and the priests.

Daughter, I pray for the day I will see your face again. Yes, your blasphemous father still secrets away some time for prayer. When you come to America, you will live your own life, Aileen. Wealth, position, and purity in Ireland mean not a thing compared to a life well-lived on American soil.Da

She refolded the letter carefully and, unsettled by the darker parts of his news, pressed her hand around the rosary in her pocket. She wondered, *why does he not speak of Molly?*

After her first week on the boat, it was announced by the crew that a pending storm would soon drive all of the passengers to their cabins below deck. She understood and was alarmed by the fact that closing up the lower decks and portals would steal all of the fresh air from the passengers in steerage for days.

Two mornings later, loud quarrels and the sound of crying children emerged from the hold along with harrowing screeches from the sight of rats and the stench of bodies without enough water to cleanse their accumulated grime.

Aileen knew there was also terrible hunger in steerage because, despite the daily ration of food, gaining access to the tiny kitchen in the storm was nearly impossible.

Betha had shown her that good Catholic women were bound to ease the hard lives of peasants whenever they could. Here at sea, there appeared to be little Aileen could do to ease their suffering. Unable to harden her soul or discipline her eyes to avoid the misery and squalor in her midst, she tried in vain to concentrate on her books and prayers, but they felt superfluous.

This was the case one morning when she spied a man with one hand leering at an apple being consumed by one of the sailors. As the juice of the fruit wet the sailor's beard, he seemed to take special delight in knowing the one-armed man was licking his lips in envy. Aileen searched her mind for sermons or prayers to help her understand this kind of cruelty. Finding none, she retrieved some figs from her cabin and handed them brusquely to the hungry man. She quickly walked away, wanting no thanks, just the chance of achieving a decent night's sleep in what had become sad surroundings.

As the storm cleared and the ship cut its way across the rough North Atlantic, she fell into a rhythm of daily habits. After her morning prayers, she sat at the long table reserved for the better passengers and dined alone. She was keenly aware and uncomfortable with the knowledge that many of her fellow travelers were more convivial, comfortable with privilege, and well-traveled than she. Periodically she would converse with a thin botanist named Richard Moore. He wore an eye monocle and a tweed jacket and spoke incessantly in a high-pitched voice of how the seeds he would gather on this voyage to America would enhance the University of London's collection. Aileen was able to converse on the subject of botany with him. Soon, however, she discovered that the man was less interested in plants and more concerned about increasing the esteem in which he was held by his university colleagues, and their conversations soon fell away.

Occasionally she spoke with the twins, Megan and Mary Ryan, from Offaly. The sturdy, red-headed girls were good Catholics and very enthusiastic about reuniting with their parents in New York. Their cheerful dispositions often had the effect of raising Aileen's spirits.

"Papa has opened a shop," Megan declared. "Trade goods."

Mary added, "—from India and the Orient."

"No more farming," they said in happy unison.

When Aileen did join the land speculators, farmers, and investors at the saloon table, she listened closely but seldom contributed to the conversation.

Captain Mick inevitably appeared within earshot of any brief conversation she might have with a passenger. Since he had already chosen a young girl from steerage as his cabin mate, Aileen feared he might be interested in something other than her feminine attributes. With Betha's cautions about men never far from her consciousness, she was wary and kept her distance from him.

One evening when the seas were calm, the discussion in the saloon became more animated and wide-ranging than usual.

"No one thought it could be done!" said Ezekiel Walker, a businessman and land speculator from New York. He was discussing the 'Wedding of the Waters' ceremony held by New York Governor Dewitt Clinton to mark the completion of the Erie Canal. Waters from Lake Erie were ceremoniously poured into New York Harbor after his much-celebrated ten-day journey down the canal from Buffalo on a boat entitled 'The Seneca Chief.'

The subject of the canal was always of interest to those around the table as were the rumors of raucous religious revivals and camp meetings occurring in western New York.

"Better means of travel means people are freer to move about as they wish," said an older woman from London, "and that canal will make New York City the most important place on God's green earth."

"Self-reliance. That's the ticket," said a young man from Dingle who was smoking a pipe and clearly optimistic about American progress.

"I think the Americans have taken Ralph Waldo Emerson's essay on self-reliance and personal choice too far," Aileen offered. "The Lord has His hand in all we do."

Heads turned in surprise at the sound of Aileen's voice, then several of the passengers quickly nodded in agreement, bringing a smile to her face.

"Agreed. Religion is not a matter of choice," said the botanist Moore, "it is something you are born to, as predetermined as the color of your skin."

Bolstered by Aileen's courage in speaking out, Mary Ryan twisted her hands in front of her on the table and added, "Americans seem intent on unshackling themselves from old ideas that might hold them back. They plan to shape their own futures." She looked around at all the eyes on her. "And. . . I admire them for it. In America, I'm going to make my own choices."

An older man guffawed. "You'll see what your father has to say about that."

Megan Ryan defended her sister.

"We will both see about that. Our father is happy to have girls that think for themselves."

The older man muttered about open-mindedness and emp-ty-headedness, but no one engaged him.

The evening's discussion was ending, like most, with a collective pondering of the opportunities presented now that it was possible for goods and people to reach the center of the American continent in a matter of weeks.

"What's grown and made in the western territories can now be sent back to Europe at a tenth the cost," said John Wallingford, a businessman from Dublin. "Seed and settlers without a shilling to their name will flow west onto free lands past the Mississippi where the fields are as vast as this ocean we're on tonight."

"You make it sound like milk and honey," said a farmer between puffs of tobacco from his cigar. "I hear there is a cost to those settlers. There are savages on those lands. Nothin's free."

Aileen did not enjoy the frequent "promised land" conversations on board the Dublin Packet. She was cynical about the idea of America becoming an empire of equals, and it was hard for her to embrace the thought that people who did not believe in God could shape their own futures. The travelers, with their unfailingly belligerent optimism, reminded her of Joseph Ryan. She was relieved to have foiled his and Father Murphy's plans for her future.

After the conversation about the Erie Canal and all the opportunities it created, she allowed herself to think, finally, about her last strange conversation with Ryan. She had blocked it.

He had hurried to her side after Mass and whispered in her ear, "I'll have you for myself Aileen, be sure of it."

Not wanting to reveal her plans to escape to America she had remained coy.

"Oh, Joseph, I'll be sure of no such thing. All the girls in this county are smitten with you and another will catch your eye before too long."

His face had taken on a steely look of fury that alarmed her.

"This is not over," he had declared. "You will not know happiness without me. We have family matters to resolve. Mark what I say."

Her stomach churned now as she relived the strange, unsettling incident. Breathing deeply, she drew the fresh salt air into her lungs, and attempted to quell the discomfort that had overtaken her stomach, leaving her in a light sweat.

As if those factors were not bad enough, she again imagined the frightened faces of Molly and Michael, and her inner demons emerged.

I am completely mad to have taken this trip! I am headed to a place that is more a legend than a country. Molly and Michael could be in the hands of savages, and I've only the funds to last a month. Grandmother's friends in Troy may not even be happy to receive me.

That night prayer only helped a little. Something was taking hold of her.

Despite the ginger root she had stowed in her trunk, the vomiting lasted for seven days. She thought at first it was the fish and the fact that the cook was none too careful in cleaning it, but the illness went on and on. Her stomach turned itself inside out.

For days, she lay in head-pounding misery, unable to relate to her surroundings, lift her legs off the bed, or escape the mind-clouds that followed each eruption of cold sweat and bile. She remained in her cabin, clasping her rosary and praying urgently in her misery.

Is this part of my penance?

Every motion of the ship induced more heaving until, with her hair matted and her dress soaked in filth, she fell down upon the cabin floor, curled into a ball, and cried.

So stupid and careless I was. I allowed the children to be taken, sold, and shipped away. Oh, Lord, forgive me and release them from whatever wretched fate they may be suffering.

She also replayed the last saloon conversation over and over in her mind. The farmer's assertion that new settlers paid a high cost in America haunted her.

Visions of strange, emaciated creatures came to her at night, begging her to give them food and set them free from bondage. Raging winds pushed the creatures away in the morning and revealed Captain Mick looking in at her from the door.

"Go away, you," said someone who was pressing a cold compress to her fevered temples. "It's not polite nor decent to look at a young lady in her underthings."

Aileen saw through the fog of fever Captain Mick's gaze moving up and down her body.

For several hours, Aileen was uncertain if the shabbily dressed woman who brought her spirits of mint and softly washed her face was a part of her delirium or a living human being. She prayed for the woman, regardless, in sad, hoarse whispers whenever the woman entered the room.

"May the blessing of light be upon this good woman, light without and light within, and may the blessed sunlight shine upon her like a great peat fire, and may her friends be warmed by it."

"Jimmy sent me," the woman said one morning, interrupting Aileen's prayer by slamming the cabin door behind her as she carried the sick bucket to the stern. Hearing the name Jimmy revived Aileen a bit, and in a few moments, she pulled herself up onto her elbows. She smelled her own reeking body, winced, and reached for the silvered-glass mirror her grandmother had given her when she left the cottage for the last time.

Surveying the dismal reflection of her pale face and deeply sunken eyes, she muttered, "This is a face that would drive rats from a barn."

As her words were spoken, the woman reentered the cabin carrying a clean bucket. She looked at Aileen and replied, "Well, isn't that a fine thing to say. You've a lovely face, my girl."

"Who are you?"

"Neither an angel nor the ship's whore," she replied laughing.

Aileen noted her Scottish accent and a large scar on the woman's left cheek—a red, jagged line—made by what? An accident? A knife blade?

The woman strode to Aileen's bedside and looked down. "I once had fine dresses and attitudes like your own, but now I've the good sense that Jesus saves for his servants. I listen well when a young lad with a big heart asks a favor."

"A young lad? Did you say the name Jimmy?" Aileen whispered in a contrite and respectful tone.

"You might be off in your dreams with that one," the woman answered, "but so you know, my name's Rose." Setting the bucket beside the bed, she turned and left, closing the door firmly behind her.

The instant she was gone, Aileen felt her absence. She placed her hand on her throat over the spot where Rose had just wiped her sweat with a soft cloth and discovered an actual physical ache in her heart. It was stunning that this disheveled woman, probably from steerage, seemed to have more power to make her well than the prayers she had known since childhood.

This dear woman, Rose, God bless her. She's stronger than the rosary in my pocket!

Aileen inhaled tentatively, and slowly released her lungs without the onset of vomit for the first time in a week.

During the ten days that followed, Rose visited Aileen's cabin frequently. Washing clothes and bedding were cumbersome, time-consuming tasks on board the ship, but they accomplished them together. As Aileen's strength returned, they ventured onto the deck, and when her legs proved wobbly, Rose lent an arm to steady her. They breathed in the fresh air and told stories from their pasts and occasionally laughed out loud. Captain Mick's prying glances made them laugh harder.

From the north, Rose was a Protestant. Like Aileen, her mother had died in childbirth. Rather than remarrying, her father, a shipbuilder, cared for Rose himself, frequently bringing her with him on business trips to London and Wales. Her eyes shone when she described the special jokes and games they shared on these childhood voyages.

During one of their afternoon strolls, Rose revealed some of the darker passages in her life.

"My wedding was a grand affair, all in the Scottish tradition." Her light blue eyes sparkled but only for an instant. Her skin was deeply lined and freckled and her hair, thinning on top, was a bird's nest of red and gray strands pulled loosely into a bun at the base of her neck.

"My husband had received the blessing of the vicar. Father knew little of the family."

"Perilous it can be, listening to the vicar or the parish priest," Aileen offered.

"It was the traditional hand-fasting ceremony that bound us together. Women walk along the south side of the marriage wall, out of sight from the men on the north."

"You cannot see one another?"

"No. The young ladies put a hand through a hole in the gate. It's the custom and a man takes hold of it from the other side. All are guided by the will of God."

Aileen stared at Rose's hands, twisted and marked by what had likely been decades of hard labor.

"I was afraid, mind you," Rose continued, "but when I first saw Rory with his yellow curls and gentle eyes, I told my father I thought God had surely looked kindly on me."

She cleared her throat and continued. "It was during the second week of our marriage that he came to banging on our door."

"Who?"

"Angus, Rory's father. A more foul-smelling, mean tempered man you've never encountered."

Aileen's eyes grew wide as Rose continued.

"He started raping me in the spring."

"Your husband didn't stop him?"

"No, Rory would watch, standing silent, frozen like ice in the doorway while his father debased me."

Aileen wrapped her arms around her friend and held her close.

"I begged him to make the old man leave. He'd say, 'there's not a single thing I can do.'"

"What about your da?"

"When I told him the truth of it, he wailed with tears, but there was nothing to be done. He could not remove me from my rightful husband's home. The law would not allow it. He died soon after my marriage."

"Did you try to escape?"

Running her fingers over the scar on her cheek she replied, "I tried, and then I discovered I was carrying Angus's child."

"It's just horrid, Rose, so horrid."

"Rory took his own life, leapt off a bridge over the River Tay. Angus stole the child, a little boy, and went south. I heard he got the typhoid and died. I searched for years but never found my son."

"After all you have suffered, you found the kindness in your heart to help a girl like me. I've known no one like you, Rose."

Over the next few days, Aileen learned that Rose had endured a decade of cooking, cleaning, and mill work until finally accumulating enough funds to purchase steerage class passage on the Dublin Packet. A cousin who had migrated to Saratoga from Scotland five years before, wrote to her and urged her to join him in America.

Only fifteen years older than Aileen, Rose wore the appearance of an old woman, but her eyes often danced with humor and hope.

At night, alone in her berth, Aileen mulled over Rose's heartbreaking story repeatedly in her mind and appreciated even more the stable life her grandmother had provided for her in Ireland.

One morning, while Aileen's head was pounding a little less, Rose revealed that Jimmy, Aileen's young helper from the docks at Cork, had indeed secretly stowed away on this very same Dublin Packet.

"He's in with the pigs and sheep." Rose explained. "You know how they bleat and moan in a storm? Well, Jimmy plays the mouth harp to keep them calm and it works magic on the beasts! The crew is grateful and treat him like one of their own. I could not let you know about Jimmy at first. Now I know you'd never betray the boy. He's a good one, that Jimmy. I would never have found my way to you were it not for him."

As Rose became more and more essential to Aileen's life on the Dublin Packet, she wondered why Betha had taught her to dismiss Protestants completely. Perhaps her grandmother's parents had passed their bitterness toward Protestants on to her? She vowed never to do the same.

Captain Mick seemed put off by Rose and Aileen's growing friendship. He frequently interrupted their conversations, and often, when he found them taking a meal together in the saloon, directed Rose back to steerage.

On one of their last evenings at sea as Rose left the saloon, he made several loud statements regarding the dangers of the Port of New York for unaccompanied women. Suspicious as ever of his motives and exasperated by his bravado, Aileen played along.

"Given these threats, what should a proper lady do upon arrival, Captain?"

"By all means beware of Greenwich Village," he continued, clearly very happy to have his opinion sought.

"The Catholics have not been welcomed there since the riot of 1824."

Aileen was well aware of this incident that had occurred a decade earlier when the Irish thrashed their enemies after a provocative parade by members of the Orange Order.

The Captain continued, "and if you care for that Catholic throat of yours, you'll stay clear of the thugs and pickpockets of Five Points."

Finally, taking on a superior tone, he added, "I do know a place suitable for ladies further north, just beyond Whitehall Street."

Whitehall Street. The street name rang a familiar and dire note in Aileen's mind. Quickly she recalled where she had once heard this street name and from whom.

"I would be so grateful, Captain. What would the name of that establishment be?"

He smiled broadly at hearing this long-awaited tone of helplessness from her.

"The Bleecker Street Inn, and I know people who can transport you there safely."

"I imagine you do," she said firmly, leaning across the table. The sudden fury in her tone turned every head in the saloon.

"I imagine you will be pleased to have me taken to a place that traffics in young women!"

Now, everyone in the saloon was watching this drama unfold.

"I learned from the innkeeper in Cork not to walk north of Whitehall Street, and I also learned," she stopped speaking, marched down the length of the table and stood directly across from him for emphasis, "that the Bleecker Street Inn is the place where the vilest of transactions take place. They make slaves of young women like myself, fill them with laudanum, and send them west with smugglers."

Captain Mick's face went white, but he controlled himself and kept his voice level. "Whoever said such things must have been well into the drink."

His eyes though, were full of fear as he glared at her. This was the kind of accusation that could ruin the career of a packet ship cap-tain. Aileen knew that ship owners were relying increasingly more on cabin-class passenger fares for profits. Good families would want no part of this business of trading in human lives and would not pur-chase tickets for their family members on ships with captains known for dealing in flesh. Captain Mick's face went red.

"How dare you!"

"Oh, I do dare, Captain Mick. I did not come this far alone to fall prey to your filthy tricks."

She spied Rose's face, wide-eyed and alarmed, peering down from the deck into the saloon. Aileen turned her back to the Captain and rushed up the stairs.

Seated above on deck with Rose, her arms would not stop shak-ing until she squeezed the rosary in her pocket so hard that her hand seared with pain. Her furor with Father Murphy and Rose's father-in-law had all combined to fuel her outburst at the captain. For the first time she sensed that her anger was making her stronger.

"You're quite the bully, darlin," said Rose, admiringly.

"I'm changed, Rose, that's sure. Let's go down to the hold and talk with Jimmy about landing in New York tomorrow."

"Yes, that's the ticket. We'll be safer together, the three of us."

5

THE HARD FLOOR
OF HATE

Sailing into the wide end of New York Harbor on a strong breeze, the occupants of the Dublin Packet seemed universally grateful that no catastrophes had befallen them at sea. Each face was beaming and radiating relief. Within just an hour they would disembark in New York.

"They look like a flock of sparrows ready to take flight," Aileen whispered to Rose, nodding at the line of passengers, chins edged forward in soft, smiling anticipation. Some were absorbed watching the circling, squawking gulls that heralded their arrival. Others pointed to picturesque villages that were barely visible on the coast of New Jersey. Scrubby-looking shrubs covered the rock jetties that thrust out aggressively from the southern reaches of Manhattan Island.

A curious leveling-out of status had occurred from the moment they entered the sheltered American waters. This amused her. Steerage and cabin-class passengers who had acted like total strangers for the previous seven weeks now spoke to one another with familiarity and excitement.

As they came closer to Manhattan, she caught sight of a pier holding a large gang of boys laughing and fishing. In the distance, she spied a perfectly-fenced small farmyard with roosters chasing hens.

It seemed everyone on the Dublin Packet was talking all at once, sharing whatever bits of knowledge they possessed about America from letters, books, or previous visits.

"The city is always hiring more police."

"Dress shops uptown pay a handsome wage if you knows how to make Irish lace."

"Stay away from the Italians."

The one-armed passenger, who weeks before had looked with hunger and envy upon the sailor enjoying a ripe apple, strode up to the railing on her left.

"See that patch of trees behind those docks? My brother, Gill, stays in a fine house there. Fresh linens and pretty gardens all around he says. There's a job for me on those docks."

The Ryan girls, anticipating the sight of their parents and unable to contain their excitement, began a smart step-dance and were soon joined by a dozen others.

"It's impossible not to smile," said Rose, absorbing the optimism all around her.

Then the gangplank was extended and rocked, then steadied the boat as it landed on the pier. The happy chatter ended as the passengers began to disembark. Captain Mick stood where the ship's railing had been removed to allow them to do so.

A tall, strong-looking farmer from Donegal named Tom had heard Aileen's confrontation with Captain Mick the previous evening in the salon and offered to escort their exit.

"I'll help you leave the ship safely, Miss, if you'd like. I have sisters traveling on a packet next month. I'd want someone to help them."

She looked at him, appreciating his strong, broad chest and thick arms. "Yes, please," she replied, feeling relieved and grateful.

Tom took the position nearest the captain and engaged him in conversation as Aileen and Rose slipped quickly by and onto the gangway. They were met by the overwhelming scent of oysters and stunned by the sound of multiple languages being spoken at the same time. At the end of their boat slip stood two beautiful African women wearing yellow turbans and white aprons, peddling roasted corn on the street.

"Slavery was outlawed here in New York three years ago," Rose explained. Then she looked around and declared with some urgency, "We need to listen for Jimmy's ruckus."

Aileen scanned the wharf. Masts stripped of their sails surrounded them making the harbor look like a winter forest rather than a port at the end of spring. Turreted forts with rippling flags could be seen far in the distance, but the immediacy of New York's waterfront was too commanding for Aileen and Rose to focus anywhere else.

The grimy, narrow street just in front of them was crowded with bellowing peddlers and livestock. A man with a decidedly southern accent shouted at the horses pulling his wagon which was loaded with cotton on its way to inland mills. The houses along the street were plain, wooden, and heavily weathered but bordered by a few small red or yellow brick structures.

"I am told those brick buildings are favored by the Dutch," said Rose, peering over Tom's shoulder.

Aileen was caught for a moment by the architecture around her which looked very little like the buildings in Cork or Dublin. The noise and excitement were beyond anything she had experienced in Ireland, and she stared at the scene, wide-eyed and distracted, until Rose yanked at her sleeve.

"We've got to duck in here," she said, pulling Aileen into the deep entryway of a shop. In the window hung the butchered carcasses of what appeared to be lambs and a few geese.

A large rush of pigs, squealing in terrified desperation, charged in their direction, separating pedestrians and upending a cart of ice directly in front of Captain Mick. He swore and kicked at the pigs which brought a *"Hoi, Hoi,* what the hell're you doin'?" from the man driving them.

"This is it," snapped Rose, seizing Aileen's arm.

Aileen turned to her with a confused look. "This is what?"

Rose clapped her hands together and Tom heaved their trunks next to a dozen barrels that were piled in the alley beside the butcher's shop. He tipped his hat, gave the ladies a sly smile and disappeared. Rose swiftly grabbed Aileen's hat off her head and pulled them both down behind the barrels and baggage to hide. Aileen's face and hands went cold. This was her first moment in America—hiding in a butcher's alley?

In a moment, a small boy leaning against the wall of butcher's shop whistled three times. "All clear," he said into the alleyway. "The captain's gone around to the next street."

"Jimmy!" Aileen called in surprise.

Rushing to him, she cupped his dirty face in her hands. Her emotions at the sight of this boy she had known for only a short time surprised her. "What is it about you? You're a child who startles me more than an appearance from the baby Jesus!" She added, smiling, "and 'ya bring me almost as much peace of mind."

"Lovely looking at you, Miss O'Malley," responded Jimmy. His eyes were shiny with delight, but he was desperately filthy, even by the apparently low standards of New York Harbor's denizens.

Aileen pulled a small hankie from her sleeve and held it over her nose.

Jimmy laughed. "I traveled with the swine—what'd 'ya expect?" In a rush, he explained how he had crept back onto the Dublin Packet through a small feed opening on the starboard side of the boat. Amidst the slop, he had made his way to the livestock hold where Irish pigs and goats were kept for passenger meals or for sale to American breeding farms.

Aileen recalled how she and the other passengers were painfully aware of the presence of these animals because their panicked shrieking during storms sounded sharply throughout the ship making sleep impossible.

"How did you survive the stink?—and the noise?"

"I know how to calm them buggers." Jimmy pulled a mouth harp from his pocket and waved it at her and Rose. "A seaman let me stay and brought me food for my trouble." He was beaming, obviously proud of how his wits and ingenuity had gotten him here to the New World.

When they had gathered themselves and their luggage and were sure there was no more sign of Captain Mick, Rose sought transport for the three of them. With coins from Aileen in hand, she waved down a coach moving slowly along the street, its driver scanning side to side clearly looking for a fare.

Once they were comfortably seated, Aileen directed him. "Sir, can 'ya take us to Grand Street?

This was the choice she had made by studying a map graciously given to her by the botanist. This area on the lower east side of Manhattan, she had decided, was a safe distance from the port and not virulently anti-Irish. The Ryan sisters had advised her that Irish Catholics might possibly be accepted as borders there for the two evenings of shelter they required before finding the transport that would take them upstate.

The Offaly girls could offer little additional help, as they were leaving New York with their parents the very day they arrived. "They want us Catholics to move west quickly after we arrive in New York," they told her.

Saloon conversation on the Dublin Packet had also indicated that anti-Catholic sentiments were running high lately in New York. This was ostensibly because Crimmins Construction, the company that won the contract to build the Croton Aqueduct and bring clean water to the rapidly-expanding city, was hiring so many Irish workers at low wages.

"Acts of violence have been escalating," one man had stated, sounding angry. "Irish Catholics from the south are taking jobs that pay less than the wages given to native New Englanders and the Protestant Irish from the north."

Aileen knew her religion placed her in a lower caste in some people's eyes, but she had been fairly insulated from these prejudices at home due to her grandmother's elevated status as a landowner. Also, in the months leading up to her departure, things had begun to improve for Roman Catholics in Ireland. They had recently been allowed to serve in the House of Commons, resulting in the election of Daniel O'Connell. The Roman Catholic Relief Act had also passed, bringing reforms to the landlord-tenant disputes that determined if families would starve or survive.

Glancing quickly at the scarred cheek of her Protestant friend and Jimmy's tattered clothes and thinking of his heavy, tell-tale brogue, she prayed for protection in this strange new city.

When they were many blocks from the port, Aileen took out the three papers that had been shoved at her by a loud representative of the Emigrant Aid Society at the docks. Each paper listed an address where clean housing with running water might be obtained. The sheets included dire warnings about lures and snares to be sure to avoid.

The first address was overcrowded and unable to accommodate them. The second took Jimmy into the kitchen to sleep on the floor, extracting a promise from him that in payment for the accommodation that he would shovel their morning coal. The third seemed hopeful for the tired women until Aileen reached into her pocket to unfold the coins she had placed there, and her rosary spilled out upon the floor.

"Not you," bellowed the man in front of them, looking directly at Aileen. Noting Rose's northern dialect he added, "but she can stay."

Feeling Rose's exhaustion, Aileen calmly responded, "So it will be." Had she let her irritation show, he might have tossed Rose out along with her.

She paid for Rose's lodging for a single night and lugged her companion's trunk from the coach to Rose's feet. Firmly she said to her friend, "I'll be back tomorrow," and left. Rose knew by her expression that it was futile to argue with her.

Outside, the air had become damp, and the wind was rising as she climbed back up to the seat of the coach. The driver looked at her coldly, thrusting out his hand for payment. He demanded his price, which seemed exorbitant considering he put her out at the very next corner.

She pulled her collar close against the wind and dodged her trunk, which the driver had dumped off the carriage. He flicked the horse's reins, and they picked up tempo, disappearing around a corner in just a moment. Now she was alone on a strange street in this unwelcoming world.

All around were half-built or half-ruined structures. In fact, so many buildings were under construction that it was hard for her to discern which structures were taverns, shops or homes for boarders. She procured the services of a boy to lug her trunk, and they perambulated by public exhibitions of drunkenness and people who appeared unassuming and respectable all on the same block.

"Not you!" The man's words erupted over and over in her mind as she now trudged the streets and squares. The man's eyes had become hard and cruel at the very moment he spied her rosary on the floor. She had the sense he would hit her if she objected to being turned away. He seemed to be looking for an excuse to lash out. He might even have been pleased to put a knife to her back when she turned to leave. So much hostility was contained in his expression of those of two simple words.

Her feet and back were getting sore, and she needed to keep herself from faltering. "What," she questioned, "would Grandmother do now, and what would she want me to do?"

She fought down the panic that was tightening her throat and forming a ball in her chest, and then, thinking of her grandmother, she stiffened her back and strode with a more confident, purposeful gait through the rapidly darkening streets. Even false bravado might work in her favor if she had to be out here much longer, and the night people crept out of the alleys and broken buildings of New York.

Circling around, finally she made her way to the back door of the home where Jimmy was asleep in the kitchen. She gave the boy a coin and tapped softly on the window. Jimmy looked up from his bed of burlap bags in front of the hearth and quietly let her slip inside, holding his finger up to his lips as if she needed to be warned to stay silent. All she could do was collapse beside him on the brick floor.

In the dark just before dawn, the coal delivery woke them. Jimmy lit an oil lamp and grasped the shovel needed for his task.

Aileen forced herself to get up from her very uncomfortable place on the floor knowing she had to hurry to make herself as presentable as possible when she returned to retrieve Rose and her baggage. As she straightened her hair, her mind returned, again, to the man who had spewed such hatred toward her, and she realized, once again, that she was still very much in danger. What would happen if she were discovered here? She needed to relieve herself, as well.

The sleep had strengthened her, and she made for the alley in a rush. Could she do what she must, which was to make water, here amid the excrement and trash?

At that very moment, she heard Jimmy talking with a man in the kitchen.

"Oh, I'll get the chute shiny, Sir, you can count on it," Jimmy shouted, in way she knew was intended to be her warning not to return.

With determination she squatted low, vacated her bladder, and lifted her own mind and spirit above her circumstances. She would not judge or condemn the man who reviled her for her faith and turned her away. He was. . .lazy, she decided. It was lazy to let the charge of hate rule your mind and tongue. It was lazy to treat others like cattle. She would leave it at that. Enough. That was yesterday.

Re-entering the street, she purchased a fine large mug of tea from an early morning street vendor. The hot drink further warmed her spirits. She used the hairpins in her carry bag and the window of a feed store to straighten her curls and then returned to Jimmy.

A pale, early sunlight was beginning to seep through the kitchen window. They would need to slip out soon before anyone else rose and discovered she had holed up here. Who knew what consequences that might bring? A summoning of the police? At minimum, her trunk could be thrown into the street or kept in payment.

With a word to Jimmy reminding him of the time of their departure, she stepped back into the street and waited for him to complete his task. It was too early to hail a carriage, so they walked partway to the docks, quickly becoming footsore and shoulders aching from hefting their luggage along.

They hoped to catch a ride the rest of way after gathering up Rose. They would leave this city and steam up the Hudson today, anticipating a more welcoming reception there. Hopefully, she thought, listening to a mourning dove coo from a rooftop, as we move upstate, America will point its hatreds elsewhere.

6

STEWARD
ON THE HUDSON

As she looked upriver, the smell of early summer forests and fresh water blew gently onto her face. She closed her eyes to savor the scent and the moment. She was relieved to be leaving this frightening city and knew the morning mist would soon clear and give her a view of what her father deemed in his letters, "the glorious Hudson." Fatigued by her night on the floor, she leaned against a post and listened patiently to what was turning into a lecture from the man standing next to her in the steamboat ticket line. A handsome gentleman, he punctuated each remark with a long pull on his pipe and the release of a cloud of sweet, scented tobacco.

"The Hudson is packed with boats today and every day, Miss. As you can see, the merchants and hawkers are out in full force."

"Why is that?" she responded politely.

"Bobby Fulton's steamboat and the Erie Canal have made new streams of commerce from this city to and from the south, to Europe, and to enterprising cities upstate possible. This city will soon become the busiest port in the world."

"My father works on the Canal," she offered, hoping to break up his delivery a bit.

"The Canal is a marvel. It has broken open the mysteries and possibilities of the vast plains, Great Lakes, and woodlands of this nation's interior."

His soliloquy began to resemble the conversations she had been subjected to in the saloon on the Dublin Packet. She had learned to dislike American bravado and particularly did not like being preached at.

There it is, that tone, the one that assumes I am blissfully unaware of the world outside my home.

"Yes," she countered, refusing to be bested, "I believe this very port we're standing in is the only one on America's east coast that provides water access to the western side of the Appalachian Mountains and the Great Lakes."

He took another long draw on his pipe and fell silent. Clearly, she had not shown herself to be sufficiently impressed by his show of knowledge.

She continued, "I am told that trade deals in New York City are being negotiated at a lightning pace."

"Ah, yes." The man again fell silent and did not resume his lecture.

Taking stock of her situation, she was now grateful to have made the Atlantic journey. She finally felt permanently out of Joseph Ryan's reach, and it was a great relief not to have him menacingly hovering over her. She recalled spotting an illiterate young man from the village following her and feigning to read a book. This had been the moment she realized that Ryan had employed spies as well. Her grandmother taught her how to give them the slip and tried to explain Ryan's behavior to her.

"Joseph is the kind of man who becomes obsessed with anything he can't have. It's impossible for him to accept that someone he wants does not want him. It's like a sickness of the soul really. He may not even want you, exactly. He just cannot accept the fact that you are saying 'no' to him. It's more about power than love or infatuation."

She was also pleased to be escaping the vile, anti-Catholic atmosphere of New York City. The leering glances of Captain Mick and her new awareness of the trafficking of young women had shaken her badly. Lost children in filthy clothes seemed to appear regularly in the alleys of New York, alarming and haunting her with thoughts of her stepsiblings.

Just then, someone called out the availability of tickets for The Albany, an affordable, three-tiered day-steamer that was scheduled for departure at 7:00 a.m. The clock behind the ticket window said 6:32. Counting out coins for three tickets, Aileen hurried on-board along with Jimmy and Rose.

As the boat eased away from the harbor into the broad river current, rising and falling slowly with the peaks and dips of the waves, she wondered if she would be welcome in Troy and how she would go about finding her da and the children. Turning to look back at the city, she noticed two toddlers crying and holding hands on the rapidly disappearing pier. This image propelled her heart into a rapid, beating panic. This subsided when she spotted a woman in a green cloak bending over to comfort and retrieve the children.

Aileen turned to her companions who were leaning on the rail nearby. Now they were truly entering the American heartland. This was the place that the Irish could not stop talking about. She could see hope physically altering her friends' faces as they absorbed the fresh breeze, rocking boat, and breathtaking scenery.

Aileen knew that in Albany the trio would part ways, and she felt a deep pang of sadness at the thought of it. She would prefer to find her way in America with this spunky lad and kind Protestant woman by her side.

When she joined them at the railing, Jimmy's face beamed. "I'm going to work on the new railroad being built in Schenectady. I'm sure they can use another strong back like mine."

"Just be careful they don't catch you sayin' your prayers," Rose cautioned.

He laughed. "I'll say 'em in private. And after the building is done, I'll get a job with the company. I know there's opportunity here—not like in Ireland."

Aileen could imagine him an engineer before the age of eighteen. His pluck and quick mind would serve him well here in America. She glanced at Rose who was fixed on the view straight north. For the first time since she had looked up into Rose's eyes from her sick bed, Aileen saw a subtle spark of hope and excitement light her face.

"My cousin, saints bless him, has offered me a place to stay and domestic work in Saratoga."

Aileen recalled Rose mentioning Saratoga being somewhere north of Albany. She carried a pamphlet with her at all times on which there was a drawing of two extraordinarily fine ladies entering what appeared to be a Roman temple and with the words "Saratoga's Miracle Baths" scrolled on the front. "Do the waters cure you?" asked Aileen. "The natives think so. The waters are trapped in shale and rich in minerals."

Rose loved the word Saratoga and would say it out loud while staring off into the horizon, letting the vowels roll off her tongue with reverence. "SARA-A-A-T-O-O-O-GA."

"And what of you?" Rose asked.

"I will be staying for a time with the family of a man named Keating Rawson who was married to my grandmother's childhood friend, Annie Eustace. They always said we'd be welcome in their home should we cross the Atlantic. Grandmother sent a letter to Mr. Rawson as soon as we knew I was leaving Ireland."

"Is Mr. Rawson widowed or. . .?" She would not say the word divorced.

"Yes, Annie died, and a sad tale it is."

Aileen knew she was entering a place of treasured memories related to Annie Eustace and smiled broadly as the two women relaxed into a rattan settee on deck.

"Grandmother had a special look, that kind of look that only accompanies happy, uncomplicated love when she spoke of Annie. One day Annie, who was her best mate, disappeared."

"A mystery then?"

"Yes. Annie and her family departed Ireland in a hurry. Grandmother never knew why, and it troubled her greatly."

Clearly enthralled with the story, Rose reached for a woolen blanket and covered their laps while Aileen continued.

"Annie's farewell note appeared in Grandmother's pew at St. Brigid's. No one knew how it got there. The note said Annie had left for America and that she would send Grandmother many prayers and many letters. This, I am glad to tell you, she faithfully did."

"So, their hearts stayed joined."

"I loved the days when a letter from Annie arrived. Grandmother would place it next to an old mustard pot filled with flowers at the center of our grand oak table. It seemed like the letter was winking at us all day long. We'd make the stew and arrange the doilies and silver round it and chat about the paper and the stamps and Annie's fine longhand."

"It sounds lovely."

"Grandmother hummed on the afternoons when Annie's letters arrived. She was never one for singing, said her voice was as scratchy as a crow's, but her humming was lovely. "Aileen's eyes moistened, and she lingered on this thought.

"But the letters were never opened until after dinner when a plate of fine molasses biscuits graced the table with our evening tea. This is how I learned about America—sippin' a cup." Annie died six months ago."

"When did she pass? Was she happy here in America?"

They moved to a small metal table with three chairs, and Aileen positioned herself opposite Rose. Jimmy stayed at the rail, rivetted by the hills and mansions along the Hudson. Aileen was clearly delighted to be recanting one of her well-worn and best-loved stories to Rose.

"Annie met and fell in love with Keating Rawson, an Anglican, after she arrived in Albany." She paused for effect and then added, "but the man had faithful Catholic ancestors. Both of their families opposed the marriage, but in America, it's not the parents nor the priests that have the final say on the bond of marriage."

"I wish that were so in Scotland."

"Mixed marriages here aren't as sour to the taste as they are in my home and yours. So they made a happy union, those two, and a good life in Troy, and they were blessed with two wee ones, Sara and Robert."

"I love this story, Aileen."

"They set about building a fine leather business. Annie joined the Catholics on Sunday and Keating did his duty as a vestryman of Trinity Episcopal Church."

Rose waved to the steward to bring them morning tea as Aileen continued.

"Tragedy came knocking soon enough when their boy, Robert, succumbed to a fever. Annie wrote to grandmother that Keating Rawson moaned for weeks and weeks on end with an agony that could not be quelled with love or whiskey."

"Ahh, the poor man!"

"But listen here, Rose! By witnessing how Annie's devotion had invited Jesus and the Saints to hold her up and carry her through, Mr. Rawson was inspired to return to the faith of his ancestors, and he converted to the Roman Catholic Church."

"I know the terrible pain of losing a child. It turned him Catholic, did it? And what of their girl?"

"Sara married a man named John Tracey," Aileen continued, "and Rawson joined with him in making a malt brewing company. Letters from recent years told a story of loved ones living in peace and the love of God. The Catholics of Troy have no church, so Annie and Keating even made a room in the malt brewery for Mass to be said."

"Love saw them through the darkness."

"You'll come through the darkness too, Rose."

"A friend's eye is a good mirror," Rose replied quietly, and they both fell into thoughtful silence while sipping their tea.

When they decided to stroll the deck, Aileen returned to the story of Annie Eustace and described the exact day when a fateful letter arrived from Troy, New York, with the customary markings but addressed with a bold, right-leaning scrawl that appeared to be the handwriting of a man.

"We were surprised as it was always Annie who penned the letters. I saw Grandmother's jaw turn to stone when she saw that envelope. We picked flowers and pressed the doilies as usual, but she did not hum while pounding the meat and peeling the potatoes, and there were no molasses biscuits that evening. When I saw the tears fall from Grandmother's eyes, I knew her friend was dead. That was only six months ago."

Rose gripped her friend's arm. "Such a fresh loss for the poor man and his family. Well then, may you be a blessing."

Just then, Jimmy called Rose to the railing. As she joined him, Aileen recalled the words of that fateful letter, the one that brought her to this very place where she now stood.

Dearest Betha,

I am secure in knowing that Annie would want me to write to you, her dearest friend for all of these decades past. Betha, our Annie has departed this life. She fell ill and was gone as quickly as a feather in flight. The sacred light of grace surely shone brighter on this earth with Annie in it. I feel certain my burden would be less if I were able to give to you even a small helping of the joy that your friendship gave to her.

The day before she died, she gripped my hand, said your name, and pointed to a small drawer in her jewelry chest. I opened the drawer and retrieved the enclosed medallion. I had never seen it before that afternoon and know not its origin or content. I only know that she wanted this to go to you, and so I am sure of its intent and—if you believe in such things—its spiritual power.

Aileen rubbed the heavy, bronze medallion imprinted with two crisscrossed keys, that hung on a silver chain around her neck. Betha had insisted she wear it on this voyage because she was certain it had been sent along with a powerful blessing. Aileen was unsure but granted her grandmother's wish.

"May you be protected always," Betha had said on that brutally cold and unforgiving day at the cottage.

Aileen had recently begun to question if God did indeed protect anyone, really? Why had he not protected her half-brother and -sister or the Irish girls being sold into slavery?

Aileen knew her faith had been shaken by recent personal events and that it had taken her family's suffering to wake her from the rote beliefs she had learned and accepted as a child. Arriving in America had not strengthened her faith.

Her mission ahead frightened her, and she found herself longing for a safe place to be, in a proper Catholic home, attending Mass on Sunday. . .and getting a good night's sleep.

Jimmy and Rose returned to her. Recognizing the need to lighten the mood, Jimmy offered, "You are as strong as Connemara marble, Aileen O'Malley. Come over here to the railing. You're missing it all."

The view was indeed glorious. Masses of rock were punctuated by springs cascading to the river's edge. The trio stared eagerly at the massive homes that lined the river's banks. At a distance, they could see grounds workers mowing lawns and pruning sculptured boxwood gardens.

"I'll be the King of Schenectady and purchase a great house like one 'o them," Jimmy shouted.

"I'm not caring much for the red roof on that one," Aileen said, pointing out the clay tiles on a sprawling Spanish style estate perched on a hillside.

"Nor do I. Now that!" Rose exclaimed, pointing to their right at a massive, caramel-colored, Gothic Revival mansion under construction. "I wouldn't be off staying there!"

Aileen shook off her heaviness. Leaning on the railing, she allowed the river and the grandeur of the Hudson River Valley to refresh her. Both Annie Eustace and her father had sent words in their letters to Ireland that attempted to describe the beauty of the Hudson. *They failed.*

The beauty unfolded calmly despite the disruption of their noisy, clanging steamer. The river cut cleanly from right to left, east to west, and back again, holding thriving villages and grand estates along the eastern shore. High, deeply-shadowed rock palisades lined the western edge of the river, and clusters of birch trees sparkled pure white when the sun played upon them. The high ridges of the Catskill mountains in the distance seemed to be protecting the bobbing sailboats, wildlife, and pioneers of this valley. She murmured a "Hail Mary" to the Blessed Virgin, pressing the rosary beads in her pocket.

An hour later, they sat together at an inside table with plates of savory mutton stew and corn biscuits. Aileen paused with a forkful halfway to her lips. Jimmy noticed that she was focused on the dignified ship's steward, a free black man whose name, she learned, was Stephen Myers.

"How can a Negro have a proper job here in America that a Catholic would be shunned from in Ireland?" she asked them both.

Jimmy responded quickly.

"It's a fine job he has alright. His name is Myers. He oversees the men, even the white ones, who feed the fire, handle the baggage, and serve us travelers."

"That's an important job," Aileen stated with curiosity.

"The stewards also purchase the food and supplies for the ship." Rose added.

Jimmy, eager to explain with a mouthful of biscuit blurted, "I was havin' a good jawbone with the captain, and he said the owner of this ship is worried about losing Myers. This black-skinned man is courted by the merchants and farmers he deals with in all the towns along the river because he has quite the head for business and a way of charming people."

"There are plenty of free Blacks in the northern places of America," Rose added. "They aren't all the sorry lot that Captain Mick describes with chains on their wrists and weak in the head." She mimicked the captain's dramatic flourishes.

Aileen could see that Stephen Myers was an impressive man. His neat, white shirt with up-turned collar was fastened with a thin, black satin tie. His eyes had a wise and canny look, and his cheekbones were high. When in conversation, he rested the second knuckle of his right index finger into the sharp indentation in his chin. This gave him the appearance of being in deep consideration, something likely required of the steward of a Hudson steamer.

"In Ireland, it's the north that's unfriendly to papists like me," Aileen mused out loud. "Here, it's the south where Negroes have their necks put beneath the foot just for being who we are. I wonder why where you are placed on this earth has anything at all to do with how you are treated?"

"It's always been that way in Ireland," said Jimmy, shaking his head, "but here in America things change fast. Trains are being made that can race faster than the finest horses. There's plenty of work to be done and lots of land for everyone. I'm thinking they won't keep the Irish or the Negros here in America down for very long."

Rose intervened.

"Everything's not coming up roses here now, Jimmy. You'd best keep your eyes open once you don't have the likes of me to steer you right."

"What shall I ever do without ye, Rose?" Jimmy planted a kiss on her cheek.

Unable to suppress a smile, Rose turned to Aileen.

"There's more than geography that burns this hateful fire, both here and in Ireland. My cousin tells me there's plenty of trouble for Negroes in the north of America as well as the south. He knows of a boy who was hung by his neck on an elm tree in Saratoga for smiling at a white woman."

Myers happened by their table, and Jimmy took advantage of his proximity to ask, "Can you tell us how you learned stewarding, Sir? How is it you keep the steam in the hole from blowin' this crate into a million pieces?"

Myers paused in his mission to ensure that all of the luggage was properly tied in the hole.

"I had the great good fortune to marry Harriet Johnson of Troy. Her family operated a cargo sloop on the Hudson for many, many years, and they taught me all they know."

"And the fire?" repeated Jimmy.

"That is easy. To keep the flames from overheating, only two ingredients are truly necessary." Jimmy waited eagerly, and Myers looked from face to face before responding. "Patience and fortitude," he smiled, "needed for so many things in this world."

Aileen said, finally, "Mr. Myers, you have wisdom. Can a Black man really allow his wisdom to show here in America?"

Surprised by her candor, Myers responded with a question of his own. "Can an Irishman have the best seat at the races?"

"Not with a British boot on his throat."

"I imagine both must show mountains of patience."

"And the will to keep trying."

"And the discipline not to knock one another down," added Jimmy.

They smiled warmly at one another, and Myers left the table.

"There is opportunity here—yes Jimmy, and Mr. Myers is proof of it."

Aileen looked straight into Jimmy's face, "But there is hate here, too. There's hate a plenty. I think of the man at the inn who turned me away. When he saw my rosary he said, 'Not you.' You saw him, Rose, his face was viscous as a wolf."

"And?" Jimmy responded.

"Maybe you should be just a little less certain about America wrapping her arms around you. How can this be the 'land of the free' when children and young girls and Negros are bought and sold like cattle?"

"Well, they can try to hate the Catholics and Negros all they like," Jimmy shot back. "But with work to be done and men like Stephen Myers and hard workers. . ."

"Like yourself?" said Rose.

"Like myself, yes. The sleevans won't win in the end. Didja' hear how those business owners taught Myers everything? That's grand. You'll see, things are different here in America."

Rose crossed her arms over her chest but said nothing.

As dusk settled over the river, a ring of gaslights became visible in the distance. The lights shimmered on Albany Pond, where all of the boats ascending the Hudson had gathered. Aileen, Rose, and Jimmy returned to the upper deck to watch and feel the wonder of their journey's end.

"This was a whale of a time, Miss," said Jimmy. His hands, still coated in coal dust from his morning job in New York, covered Aileen's delicate fingers on the railing.

"Yes, it was," interjected Rose, adding her hand to theirs. "Now I am going to SARAAA- TOOOGA."

They laughed loudly together. It was apparent each of them would miss the special mates that accompanied them to this jumping-off point where they would begin their new lives.

Grateful for the moment and these companions, Aileen touched the rosary beads in her pocket again. *Lord, be with them wherever they go,* she prayed silently.

Appearing stoic on the surface, inwardly Aileen was terrified to be on her own with such an important mission to accomplish in this strange, new land. In fact, she had slipped her hand out from under Jimmy's, not so much because his was gritty with coal dust but because hers was trembling slightly. *How will I find them?*

Her self-doubt was appearing again as she ended this river journey. She knew it was Jimmy and Rose's friendship that had helped her to push forward and drive her fears away. *Soon my good mates will be gone. Please God, do not let go of me.*

In a little while, she made her way to the ship's railing without her companions and found Stephen Myers standing there looking thoughtfully at the Hudson's deep flowing current.

"I assume," he said, without looking at Aileen, "that you have come here to America seeking a better life and greater freedom than where you've come from." She wasn't in the mood to divulge her mission and simply nodded.

"So many dreams of freedom coming up this river," said Myers. "So many, many dreams."

7

———

THE BLUE SHAWL

The remnants of grief in the widower's gait were apparent by his slow, slightly heavy step along the pier. As she prepared to disembark from the steamer, Aileen knew this man was Keating Rawson. He was exactly as described in Annie's letters: a robust man in his mid-sixties, with a salt-and-pepper beard, striking gray eyes, and red hair mixed with silver that curled around his ears. Behind him in the distance she could see the busy streets of Albany rising in a staggered line of crisp, red brick and gray, granite buildings above the river. Beyond lay glorious miles of green forests. There was a rolling beauty to the land around Albany.

Recognizing Aileen, Rawson called out, "Miss O'Malley, you're every bit the striking young lady your grandmother described. And—," he glanced at his pocket watch, "—your vessel is exactly on time." He nodded to the captain who tipped his hat.

Aileen acknowledged him with an enthusiastic wave, and he motioned to his driver to retrieve her locker from the dock where a ship's man had placed it and load it onto the back of the black carriage with its handsome chestnut horse.

Glancing around, she noticed a man in a battered hat watching her from a distance—staring actually. Was he one of Captain Mick's men? She had not been secretive about her plans to come upriver to Troy, and at this moment she was very grateful that Rawson was punctual in meeting the steamer.

Though she had looked forward to meeting the Rawson family for months, she felt a bit off balance. She knew of these people by letters. *What would they be like in person?*

Nonetheless, she beamed. "I couldn't be happier at this very moment, Mr. Rawson. Am I seeing you with my own eyes, Sir?" Her mind cast up a dozen scenes of this man that had been described in Annie's letters: holding a new-born, lifting barrels of oil along with trimmed and salted hides for his tanning business, holding his wife's hand as they selected the land upon which to build their home. She imagined him as a twenty-five-year-old, besting the storeroom worker who tried to steal his tools. All of these stories and images she had absorbed over tea and molasses biscuits at her grandmother's table. Annie Eustace had used her pen to create vivid impressions of her American life, including her husband, church, and the gardens where she relaxed on Saturday afternoons to knot lace.

Aileen now recognized that she had absorbed an idealized view and had brushed aside some of the more difficult details, some of which rushed to mind now.

"How do you find America?" asked an elderly woman standing next to her. She wore mourning black and the deep lines in her face were offset by sparkling blue eyes.

"I find it a beautiful but frightening place, Ma'am. Perhaps a bit too anxious to expel Catholics from its shores and slaves from its conscience."

The woman smiled again, enjoying Aileen's candor. "You're young and beautiful. America might bring you what you seek."

"Will it be possible for a woman to get a university education here?"

"The change will be too slow to benefit these old bones of mine, but you, young lady, might just be able to make a life here that is of your own choosing."

Encouraged by this exchange, Aileen thanked the woman and helped her onto the ramp to depart the ship. She glanced to the harbor deck again, and the man with the slouched hat was still watching her, though now it was obvious she was under Rawson's care. *Am I even safe here? I do not feel safe.*

Turning to say goodbye to Rose and Jimmy, Aileen saw they were each engaged in conversations with fellow travelers. "I'll be just a moment, Sir," she shouted to Rawson. Despite her immediate thoughts about America's rough reality, her voice remained bright with excitement for meeting this man of family legend.

Jimmy was cheerfully quizzing a dapper gentleman with a red tie about transportation to Schenectady while helping him to lug several huge bolts of fabric down the gangplank. "I'm headed for the Mohawk and Hudson, Sir, planning to give that new steam engine some strap rails to ride on." *He's perfect for America,* she thought. *Will this place reward his spirit, though?*

"Goodbye!" she called, waving. Jimmy dropped his end of the bolt and ran to her side. Out of breath, he nodded at the man he was just helping. "He'll be making collars, that gentleman. And he said I can help in his factory." Grinning and looking up at Aileen he added, "If you were any longer, you'd be late!"

She felt a mix of joy and sadness. That phrase had endeared him to her in Cork. Now, said in parting, it caused a pang of sadness in her chest. "Make yourself a grand future, Jimmy." Her lip quivered as she pressed a small bag of coins into his palm. "Thank you for sneaking aboard the packet, and for playing your mouth harp for the animals, and for sending me Rose when I was ill, and—well—thank you for everything." In this instant his eyes moistened and he could not respond.

"Now, you'll remember your promise to me, won't you?" She asked this, although she knew with certainty that he would keep his word. He had proven himself to be pure gold.

Nodding vigorously, he pointed to Keating Rawson on shore. "That's him I take it. The man you're to meet. You can know for certain, should I ever hear rhyme or rumor of your da and the wee ones, I will make haste to contact that man, Mr. Rawson, straight away." Impulsively, he threw his arms around her waist and gave her an awkward embrace.

Gratefully she pressed his face to her bodice, still puzzled by how she found such a comforting sense of safety in the company of this skinny boy. *Will I find this sense of security among the Rawsons?*

Rose walked across the deck to join them. "Goodbye, Jimmy," she said, tousling his hair fondly. "You're as good a lad as I have ever known." With a warm smile for both women, Jimmy raced back to his task leaving Rose and Aileen to confront their own difficult farewell.

"I have never known one like you, Rose," said Aileen, tenderly cupping one hand around her friend's scarred face. She closed her eyes for a moment in silent prayer. *Keep her safe, dear Jesus, for this*

Protestant woman lives your commandments more faithfully than any Catholic I have ever known.

"It's all from the top of the mountain now!" Rose responded, looking away, pointing her arms north, and holding back tears. "I asked an old gent on the packet the meaning of your name, Aileen. In the Gaelic it means 'bright shining light and the giving of little dignities'. That's what they'll say about you as time goes on. I'll be hearing tales of a tall, dark, Irish lass with a strong mind and stronger back. They'll tell of the little dignities you carried from Ireland to America and how you made this a better place."

Hearing Mr. Rawson giving instructions to his driver, Aileen grasped Rose's hands and stared intently into her eyes. "I didn't know there were people like you, Rose. You wiped my brow and became my teacher. Thank you." Turning to leave, she thought of the horrors her friend had endured at the hands of her father-in-law in Ireland and considered the shabbiness of Rose's coat. Reaching into her carry bag, she pulled out her mother's lovely, blue shawl, then turned, swung it into the sky and wrapped it gracefully over Rose's shoulders. Finally, she said, "America is privileged to receive the likes of you." They embraced for what was likely the last time and parted.

8

CONFESSION IN TROY

As their carriage rattled noisily over the bumpy road to the Rawson home, Aileen's thoughts rested on Rose and Jimmy. Other than saying goodbye to her grandmother, she had never experienced a farewell that pulled so deeply and so hard on her heart as did parting with the two of them. *In Ireland, I would have shirked off a Protestant and a grimy lad, and I would have been so much the poorer for it.*

Rawson caught her thoughtful expression, offered a warm smile, and placed a green blanket over her legs to fight the chilled late afternoon air. "It's all different here," he said and tucked the cover protectively into the rich leather bench. "It will take time to get used to America."

With this small, caring gesture, Aileen felt a bond forming with this man. The trust that had connected Betha and Annie across the sea for over five decades began to settle upon the two of them as they traveled amiably from the docks at Albany to the City of Troy.

When the carriage climbed up the muddy hillside road, Aileen tried to imagine Rawson's home which Betha had described to her in great detail. *She called it Greek Revival architecture.*

"I can see why Annie loved it here." She pointed to a hillside covered in tall grass, hollyhocks, and wildflowers. The calming voice of a small stream reached them as they crossed over a narrow, wooden bridge.

"She always claimed Saint Lucy wanted us right up there," he responded with a smile, nodding up at the pillared home painted bright white that came into view at the top of the hill. His smile revealed the slightest gap between his front teeth and the bright, beaming spirit of the man. "Annie believed that St. Lucy, being the patron Saint of the eye and all, would forever remind us to reflect the light of Christ in how we lived upon this hill."

"And so, you do, Mr. Rawson," Aileen replied. She was aware of his conversion from Episcopalian to Catholic following their son Robert's death ten years before.

"According to Grandmother, the news of your conversion to the true faith was the most exciting letter that ever traveled from America to Cork." His smile remained as she continued. "She told me Annie's letter was proof that when the world places the heaviest pain upon you, God sends his strongest angels to raise you up." "It surely took the strength of an angel to knock sense into this hard Irish skull."

"I can recall Annie's actual words from the famous letter. Would you like to hear them?"

"Indeed, I would."

"There was a touch of the poet in her lines." With a flush rising on her face Aileen carefully recited her favorite phrases. "'Keating saw the comfort I received from our faith when we were made to say farewell to our dearest boy. He came to me in the garden and asked me to kneel down with him on the moss and pray. That very moment, with my heart full of the most terrible pain, I cried the happiest tears I've ever known. The Holy Spirit gathered and took me on the wind, and I traveled from my deepest sorrow to my most precious dream—to share my faith with the man I love.'"

For a long time, the only sound was the steady clop-clop of the horse's hooves. "Thank you, Aileen," Rawson said finally, his voice cracking a little. Then he added, "Please call me Keating." A contented quiet fell between them for the remainder of the journey.

As they entered the stately Rawson home, the smell of lye rose from the freshly-cleaned pine floors and reminded her of her grandmother's insatiable drive that their cottage in Ireland be kept immaculately clean. Freshly-laundered white curtains blew in the frames of the glass doors that opened onto the pillared veranda overlooking the river. When Aileen and Keating stepped through the open doors onto the porch, Keating's daughter, Sara, and her husband, John Tracey, were holding hands while seated in adjoining wicker chairs. They quickly rose and extended their hands in greeting. Sara was petite with dark-brown eyes, her father's red hair and a gracious, warm manner.

"Welcome to our home!" she said, her voice was happy and excited. "I feel as though I've known you always."

Until that moment, it had not occurred to Aileen that this family likely knew as much about her life as she did theirs. It made her uneasy imagining a lifetime of letters from her grandmother to Annie stashed somewhere nearby. Her grandmother had secrets. Had she shared all of them with Annie Eustace? Fleetingly, Aileen wondered if the letters explained why Grandmother leaned on the low stone wall and cried so often before making her way up to the cottage door.

Forcing herself away from this line of thought, she engaged in polite banter with her hosts, though she was feeling the weight of her travels. "Would you think me terribly rude," she asked in a half-hour, "if I asked to go to my room and have a bit of time to freshen up after my journey?"

"Not at all," Sara replied. "It's a lovely ride up the river but certainly a tiring one." She nodded to her husband. "John will carry your locker to your room, and we can talk about, uh, things over dinner." John stood to get her bags, and as he moved, Aileen could see his form was robust and his features plain and agreeable. He lifted her bags as though they were packed with straw and ascended the stairs.

She followed him wondering—had she picked up a slight tension in Sara's words? *What are the things she wants to discuss?*

Alone in the Rawson's guest room, she relaxed. The room was painted a lovely blue and smelled of rose hips. She fell asleep almost immediately, fully dressed, on the bed with a carved wooden headboard that covered most of the eastern wall. *You're really here, just a bird call's distance to the Erie Canal*, she mused as her mind drifted off. *Now what?*

Her plan had been to get here and escape Joseph Ryan's clutches. Nothing beyond that was clear to her.

When she awoke, she was startled to find herself looking directly into the eyes of a small, plaster-cast statue of the Virgin Mary standing on the table beside her bed. She gazed quizzically at the scarred face as she floated in the confusing space between sleep and wakefulness. Had it been there before she fell asleep? She couldn't recall. The thought that someone might have slipped into the room while she was sleeping, even for the good cause of placing a statue of the Virgin there, for her was mildly unsettling.

She studied the austere figure with its graceful expression, which was chipped badly in several places. The statue did not seem to belong with the gilt hairbrush, beveled mirrors, and other fine amenities in the room. A missing triangle of paint created a white scar across the left side of the Virgin's face. *Just like Rose's scar.* Aileen imagined her friend happily arriving in Saratoga and began to relax.

A dull thump startled her and she sat up, recognizing the sound. A bird had flown into the window. Rising, she went to look and peered out at the sky which was seeping deep shades of pink and orange dramatically over the distant hills. She stared at the small feathers and tiny drop of blood that clung to the outside glass and felt sadness arising. *She flew the wrong way. Poor bird. Lost her path, that's all. I must stay strong and focused on my path. I must find Father, and Molly and Michael. This is just a respite.*

Her thoughts shifted again. *What was on Sara's mind?* Quickly, she washed and changed into her favorite dark green floral dress and went downstairs in search of her hosts. Passing through the parlor, she was relieved to feel wrapped in familiar comforts. She could hear an Irish lilt in the voices of those in the dining room. The embroidered doilies and lamps, though more elaborate than her grandmother's, showed the same practical taste and love of cleanliness she had known all her life. On one wall was an engraving of the Madonna and Child nestled cozily within a thick, oval cherry frame. This was indeed a Catholic home and there would be no mistaking it as such. The loudly-ticking mantel clock read 7:32, and only now did she real-ize how long she had slept. "I'm so sorry if I've delayed your dinner," she apologized, stepping into the dining room.

"Not to concern yourself," Keating replied. "The cook is moving a little slow this evening, so no one's in a hurry."

The scent of cod simmering in sage and butter and corn porridge came from the kitchen, and Aileen nodded to Sara and John who had just entered the room. Keating was seated at the head of the long, exquisitely laid dining table and poured her a glass of sherry while nodding to the empty place next to him. She made her way next to him, and Sara and John took their seats as well.

"I wish my Annie were here to see what a fine and brave lady Betha's granddaughter has become. It was December when she left us. She died on her knees, saying her prayers in the middle of the night you know." The tone of his voice and the look on his face made it clear that Keating was adrift since Annie had contracted tuberculosis and died just six months before. Aileen's grandmother had explained the depth of their feelings for one another but witnessing his pain made it even plainer. She had never seen a man mourn the loss of a woman this way. "Her health and vigor just left her," he concluded quietly, "like water off a drainboard." The room was still for a moment, with a deep silence.

"Yes, Grandmother told me," Aileen ventured. "It happened just before Christmas, did it? Where is she laid? I have bog rosemary seeds and strict instructions for the prayers I am to plant on her grave."

Sara responded to Aileen's question. "I am sorry to say, vandals defiled Mother's grave." She looked anxiously at her father. "Father has purchased a plot of land to create a Catholic Cemetery, and both my mother's and my brother Robbie's remains will be laid there together in the future, side by side."

Noticing the startled expression on Aileen's face, Keating

stepped in. "I know what you're thinking. Tampering with the resting place of the dead is unheard of in Ireland. It's heinous. I've published a reward for anyone with information to convict the scoundrels who did this thing." Then, more quietly, he added, "I alienated my kinsman when I converted to the old religion."

Another man burst through the swinging door from the kitchen, followed by the cook, and yet another servant carrying platters and serving bowls full of steaming food. "Allow me to introduce my brother, Jedidiah," said John, smiling.

She smiled and stretched out her hand to a handsome man who was as striking in appearance as his brother was plain.

"I overheard what Keating here was saying. You will find, Miss O'Malley, that religion sets souls on fire here in upstate New York, particularly in summer when the revival gatherings are as glorious as our weather." He accepted her hand and graced it with a kiss, and she studied him quickly. In fact, she could not help herself. His gray eyes and ruddy complexion complemented his full head of fair hair. His dark-blond eyebrows were pronounced, making him appear extremely thoughtful.

"We have all been awaiting your arrival," he said, letting go of her hand. His voice, like his appearance, had a deep, magnetic quality. Aileen hoped she was not blushing, which would make the dinner awkward. She found it impossible to look away when he spoke.

"Let's have our meal," Sara interrupted, nodding at the empty place set for Jedidiah.

Aileen turned her eyes back to the table with its crystal stemware, lace tablecloth and fine Irish porcelain. A dozen tapers cast a glow over all of them. Keating bowed his head, and realizing what he was about to do, so did everyone at table. Aileen folded her hands in her lap. "Bless us, oh, Father," Keating prayed, "for these, Thy gifts, which we are about to receive from Thy bounty, through Christ, Our Lord."

"May I add something?" Aileen said tentatively, the moment he finished. Keating raised his eyebrows in question but nodded. "And thank you, dearest Lord, for your wisdom in bringing me to a table where your presence is so surely known and deeply felt. Amen."

She could now feel Jedidiah's eyes on her, but she kept hers fixed on her serving of cod.

"Tell cook we'll have the port now," Keating said to the servant who was clearing the plates when dinner was over. Then he turned to Aileen. "I'm eager to know about the changes in Ireland following emancipation. What can you tell us of Daniel O'Connell?"

Delighted to be asked her opinion on a political matter, she replied, "O'Connell's our champion in every way. He'll not abide the mob. He's seated in the House of Commons now, working night and day for separation. He is the first Catholic there since 1688 and his rallies draw near a hundred thousand citizens. Grandmother said King Georgie calls him the 'King of Ireland!'"

"And what of the Protestants in the north?" asked Jedidiah. "If O'Connell succeeds with separation, what will become of them?" "Ireland is a Catholic nation," she replied flatly. "The Protestants have had all the advantages till now. They will just have to get on with it." There was silence.

Knowing that her answer was insufficient, she adroitly posed her own question. "Why are Catholics so unwelcome here?"

"On what basis are you saying this?" asked Keating.

She briefly described her experience in New York.

"Americans resist rules," Keating replied lightly. "They fear the Pope himself will boat over and start telling them how to live—it's enough to send all of them running to the tavern."

"They're right to have concern," injected Jedidiah. "We Americans should question all faiths and work to find our own salvation in this land and nothing else."

The young man who had come in and was pouring the port in their glasses hesitated, and Aileen felt the ease she had experienced upon her arrival in this good, Catholic home slipping away. *What was Jedidiah suggesting—that people forsake the Church? the Faith? the Sacraments and saints? These are the guideposts of my life. Work to "find" religion? What in the world does that mean?*

Sara broke the silence. "Aileen, you weren't wrong in your observations in New York City. So many harsh feelings are concentrated there where so many begin their American journey. A cruel man can be anonymous in a crowd. What Jedidiah refers to is the flowering of new religions occurring here, Aileen, all along the Erie Canal. One of the evangelists, Charles Finney, calls this the 'burned over district' so alive it is with religious fire. The Millerites' believe the end is coming. Revivals last for weeks, and camp meetings are drawing thousands. Whole new sects are being formed, and there are even appeals to the supernatural. If this turn toward religion, any religion, results in less anger toward the Catholics, I am glad for it."

"But we belong to the only true Faith," said Aileen. Jedidiah choked a little on his port.

John said patiently, "This is not Ireland, Aileen. There's more than Catholic and Protestant here. The Canal has opened the continent, carrying in people, good and bad, from lands with different customs and cultures all around the world. Daunting it is, making a future in this place when starting without a shilling. These new religionists are choosing the faith that drives them forward and brings them succor. We have Quakers, Methodists, and Unitarians. Religions are being created so quickly it extends the power of perception. The pioneers who come here are brave, and they refuse to accept that their fate is determined by God."

"Then why is there such hatred here in this land of so many religions toward our Faith?" she pressed.

Keating answered, "I believe the anti-Catholics are more anti-immigrant than anti-Catholic. The Irish arriving now are poorer, less skilled, and hungrier than the Brits and Scots who came before them. They are willing to work for just a penny a day. It's less the taking of Sacraments than the taking of jobs that Americans object to." Aileen nodded.

Sara added, "It is perplexing, as so much here is. The natives and the Negroes have it worse than the Irish. There's always someone on the lowest step getting the boot while others climb the stairs."

"That is exactly like Ireland!" said Aileen. "There, it's always the Orange climbing up the stairs."

"So, it is" Jedidiah agreed. "The Calvinists and the Catholics believe we were born in sin and must keep our heads low to atone for it. Here, the new religionists believe we are born with free will and can make the life we choose. This helps Americans find God's grace." He looked around the table. "Some men believe salvation is open and available to all and—"

Keating interrupted him. "Jedidiah, I will thank you to refrain from offering a sermon at my table." His admonition was delivered with such a warm tone that it relaxed the moment, and Keating quickly changed the subject. "Let us toast America's first

Irish President. To Jackson!" he declared, raising his glass. "A leader for the common man!"

"Not a chance" Sara declared, not raising her glass. "Removing native tribes from their sacred lands and keeping slavery alive, is this the Irish leader America's common man desires? We should all seek forgiveness for the cruelty shown the Negroes by the likes of Jackson."

Though Aileen had raised her glass out of respect for Keating, the others had not, and the toast fell flat. Stunned, Aileen decided that the thing she liked most about this household, and possibly all of America—time would tell—was that a woman had a right to speak her mind. Had she countered, say, an Irish uncle over dinner the way Sara had just upbraided her father, her face might have been made red from a backhand slap.

"We received a letter," Sara said when they moved to the parlor and the awkwardness had passed, "from a man named Joseph Ryan." The cook followed them into the parlor, offering small bowls of stewed apples and cream.

"Not welcome news?" said Jedidiah, looking at Aileen's horrified expression. "He's not. . .a friend," she replied, and it occurred to her *so this is what Sara wanted to discuss.*

"He told Father you might not welcome his correspondence, so he directed it to him," Sara continued.

"He claims to know the whereabouts of your da."

Her face reddened a little. How much had Grandmother told them? Aileen set her dessert aside on the small, maple side table next to her. "May I see the letter, please?"

Keating stood and opened the rosewood music box sitting on a shelf beside the fireplace. The sad notes of "The Boys of Wexford" sounded from it as he removed an envelope and handed it to her. The dark, early summer night had finally enveloped the household, and this tune seemed to cast about seeking refuge in the quiet assembly.

"I know this music," she said quietly, trying to conceal the mild panic she felt rising in her chest. "It commemorates the rebellion of 1798. The man who wrote this song was betrayed by Joseph Ryan's father. Grandmother said he foiled the fight by telling the Brits where the weapons were hidden." She felt the confused eyes of her hosts upon her as she unfolded the parchment and read its contents silently.

To the Honorable Keating Rawson, Troy, New York

Father Nathan Murphy of St. Brigid's Parish, Kildare, advised me that Miss Aileen O'Malley will be enjoying your hospitality when first she arrives in this country. Miss O'Malley has declined my affections and proposals of marriage and thus, in all likelihood, will not be pleased to receive my correspondence. Therefore, I entreat you to pass to her this information which has come to my attention and relates to her mission in America.

Aileen paused, feeling a slight shock. How did Joseph Ryan know of her mission here? Who had told him, and how had news arrived ahead of her? Had Father Murphy sent word? She felt as she had felt when a man at the landing in Troy was staring at her—watched.

A businessman from Waterford, Mr. Samuel McVicar, has advised me that he hired a former canal

laborer, a Mr. Dennis O'Malley, in April of this year to transport a printing press ordered by Mr. Joseph Smith of Palmyra, New York. O'Malley is Aileen's father.
Thank you for providing her with this information.
Mr. Joseph Ryan, Kildare, Ireland

When she lifted her eyes from the letter, the others were watching her. "I'll tell you the story," she said, nervously winding the parchment letter into a cylinder on her lap. Every eye was on her now.

"My father indentured himself to the Canal in order to come here and find his children, Molly and Michael. They were born to the Protestant woman he married after my mum passed." Before unveiling the next, more difficult part of the story, she searched for an understanding pair of eyes and found them on Sara's face. "His wee ones were stolen by a kidnapper and sold to a ship's captain bound for New York." She looked around the room at the faces staring at her. "They sell poor Irish orphans on the docks in New York. Did you know that? They sell them like the slaves off a ship from Africa. It's not just orphans they sell, it's children been stolen from the ports of Ireland. Did Grandmother explain?"

Keating had come up beside her and laid a gentle hand on her forearm. "Yes, dear girl, she did."

"Go on, Aileen," said Sara. "What is your plan for finding your father and the children?"

Sara's question was so simple and innocently posed that it brought Aileen to a complete standstill. She had enough money from her grandmother to stay in America for only two months. She had no way of actually contacting her father as he was traveling himself, looking for the children. From his letter, she was aware of his one solid lead on Michael's whereabouts. He had likely taken the job of delivering the printing press to Palmyra in order to get closer to the Batavia farm where Michael might be laboring. Little Molly's location was a complete unknown. Had she even survived the passage? Aileen thought of her twirling a curl around her index finger and rubbing black pudding on her smock and began to cry.

"I don't know how to find them. All I know is that I must and—," she looked at the apparently faithless Jedidiah, "—that God will help me." Joseph Ryan's letter fell from her lap, and she unconsciously lifted the medallion from behind the collar of her dress and began rubbing it with her fingers while fighting to compose herself.

Sara's eyes went to the medallion. She glanced at her husband, and an understanding registered on their faces.

Aileen could not continue. She wouldn't tell them that that the children had been stolen because they foiled Ryan's plans for her. She owned the children's pain for this and many other reasons. Their fright and whatever unspeakable harm was being done to them lived inside her day and night. Her heart pounded and she broke into a sweat.

Sara stood, came and knelt beside her, and slid an arm around her shoulder. She moved Aileen's trembling fingers off the medallion and held it in her own. "This medallion engraved with crossed keys, it was my mother's. It was important to her, but I do not know why. She wore it each Saturday when she went to say her confession to Father Thomas. Keys, you know, are the symbol for Penance."

Aileen looked up at her, wide-eyed with confusion and despair.

"My mother asked father to send this to your grandmother just before she passed."

Aileen's tears had stopped, and she stared at Sara quizzically. "Grandmother gave this to me to wear on this journey. I do not know why."

"You will find the children, Aileen," said Sarah.

There were nods all around, except for Jedidiah. From his look, his thoughts seemed to be far away.

That night, lying in her bed, Aileen looked across the room at the statue of Mary. "Guide me, oh Mother of Mercy," she prayed, falling into a deep, exhausted sleep.

"We'll help you as best we can," John said to Aileen three weeks later. On this late June morning, the family was sitting on the veranda overlooking the Hudson River and the Erie Canal. From this perch, one could take in the full glory of upstate New York's landscape.

"This is like Ireland in so many ways" said Aileen brightly. "But here there are lakes, rather than seas I am told."

"Our lakes are the size of seas, Aileen," John responded proudly.

White cumulus clouds appeared to be at eye-level and moved across the sky as calmly as a fleet of schooners in Limerick Bay. Aileen glanced to the north, thought of Rose, and sent a morning prayer toward the soft, blue-gray outline of the Adirondak mountains in the distance.

Keating nodded. "I've given your journey careful thought. Our malt business has made a good profit since the opening of the Canal, and we have business agents all along the route. Jedidiah organizes those agents to write orders in all of the towns from here to Buffalo. I think you should summer here with us, Aileen. You'll miss the fever season and can head west in early autumn to find your father. We'll apprise our men to look for your father and siblings in advance of your trip. I'll write to your grandmother for permission."

"I believe we'll find your family," said Jedidiah. "I do a lot of traveling, purchasing barley from farmers and selling malt to the brewers. I know my way all about the Canal and frontier."

Aileen wished she had not cried in front of them on her first evening in Troy. Her voice was barely above a whisper, though she sounded a little defensive. "I. . .thought I would go myself. I am not a weak person."

Jedidiah smiled. "I strongly suspect you are not, or you wouldn't have made the journey here to begin with. But the fact is, your mission, well it's a tall mountain to climb, and you will need help."

"Are you sure you're the one to help her?" Keating asked point blank. "After the disaster you created in Little Falls?" Sara and John turned to look at Jedidiah.

He stooped until he was eye-to-eye with Aileen. Rather than answer the remark he said directly to her, "Everyone fails. I have suffered my defeats, and they have made me wiser. I'll go to Palmyra with you. We'll follow that printing press in the fall." His firm response seemed to settle the matter, and Aileen thought better of objecting again.

Several weeks later, Aileen and Sara were surveying the bending daisies and blue delphinium bursting from the garden. They were alone in the cool of the early morning and had wrapped themselves in light shawls. "Come walk with me," said Sara. On her arm was a small basket containing needlework.

Stepping into the grass that was still moist with dew, they strode along slowly, enjoying the birds calling loudly from the boxwood and yew hedges. In a moment, they reached a mossy stone bench far out on the east lawn and sat looking west from their vantage point on this promontory above Troy. Thick pine and maple forest created a lush and fragrant backdrop for their conversation and added a touch of natural mystery to their surroundings. Just below was the shining swath of water that was the Hudson.

Even from this distance, the fast pace of commerce and immigration moving west could be seen. Miniature, bright-colored boats could be seen climbing the lochs above Cohoes Falls and plowing onto the Erie. For the first time in months, Aileen felt there might be a way forward knowing the Rawson and Tracey families were behind her difficult venture. "I don't mourn for the rain, but I do miss the purple heather that covers the Irish hills in June," she murmured.

Sara, who was expertly handling the needlepoint antimacassar on her lap, smiled. "Father recalls that heather fondly. All the same, he never regrets leaving Ireland. He insists that nothing ever changes there. He loves this country and is glad for the chance he's had to put his back to work and see something come of it."

"You've the luck, Sara. I don't know what my father loves."

"I'm sure your da is a good man, and-" she hesitated, "-I'm sure you'll make him a better one."

"He wanted me to come here, and of course I wanted to help." A wave of anxiety rose again as she thought of what she had not divulged.

Sara stopped her needle work.

"What is it, Aileen? What is this burden you carry? I have seen it in your eyes, sometimes you're sad even when you're smiling."

Aileen studied the gentle, compassionate look on Sara's face and struggled for a long time before finally speaking. In the distance, a train whistle echoed mournfully among the hills.

"It's a memory that haunts me, Sara. You'll think me shameful."

"I'm thinking the priest has loaded you down with the guilt of original sin, darlin. I am no one's judge. You can tell me, and whatever you have to say is safe, tucked in my very soul." Sara reached out and placed her hands on Aileen's. "I have felt such a great weight hovering about you since you arrived."

Aileen touched her shirtfront, feeling the medallion beneath. "The wee ones wouldn't have been stolen were it not for me."

"Oh, no, Aileen."

"'Tis true. My pride led me to flirt with Joseph Ryan, though I never wanted him at all. This made him want me all the more, and he wanted my da gone so he could have me without the scandal of him and his children nearby."

"But surely you couldn't control that bad man."

"No, I couldn't control him, but I actually helped the devil with his evil plans."

"Helped him? How in God's grace did you help him?"

"By seeking God's grace in the Sacrament of Confession. I had lied to Grandmother and was seeing the children in secret. I went to confess my sin, but Father Murphy, he cared less about sin than he did about lining his private collection basket with Joseph Ryan's money."

"I don't understand."

"He asked me everything, Father Murphy did, where the children walked and when, where they snacked and played. He was gathering it all up, all the hints that would help Ryan's kidnappers to find them, and he got it all from me."

"The sin is Father Murphy's, Aileen, not your own. You mustn't carry it any longer or it will be the death of you."

"Maybe it should be the death of me, Sara, you don't understand!"

"What don't I understand? A cunning priest partnering with an evil man? There's plenty of that lot in this sad world."

"But I wanted them gone." Aileen shouted. With this last protestation the birds stopped chirping and the wind slowed to a whisper. Aileen bent over suddenly, feeling stabs of pain. With her arms crossed in front of her, she began rocking and continued in a monotone voice. "I was jealous and angry about Father never coming around. I hated how he was always giving his time and his laughter to those little ones and having none for me. I visited them alright, but I found myself scowling at them when they ran down the alley into his arms when he returned from the docks. He never hoisted me on his shoulders as he did them."

"You were never allowed to be a child?"

"No."

"And your granny, she did her best, but I recall from her letters to Ma that she disliked him so."

"Yes, she disliked him, but she never spoke ill of him when she had the strength to refrain."

After a few quiet moments of reflection, the worry lines seemed to evaporate from Aileen's face, and she stood to face Sara. "I walked head-first into their scheme, but it wasn't mine of the making was it, Sara?"

"No, my darling, no it was not. But you've taken on a heavy penance for what was in your heart. Now listen to me." Sara rose and planted her hands on Aileen's shoulders. "No one who feels the anguish of conscience as you do is beyond mercy, and I think more of you for having the courage to tell me your sorrow." Sara turned to leave. "Take all the time you need out here," she said, her voice calm and gentle. "This is the place where my mother brought her pain when Robbie died. The Lord sees your good soul, Aileen, and He will come to you and let you know of His forgiveness. I'm sure of it. What you need is time by yourself now. I will have supper brought to your room."

Alone that evening, her supper tray untouched, Aileen felt a hint of an autumn breeze coming in through the open bedroom window, stirring the curtains. It carried the scent of freshly-mown hay fields and the sound of a nightbird singing softly. Lying on her back, staring at the dark ceiling, Aileen realized the heaviness she had carried in her for months was lifting. She felt lighter and knew that this was largely due to the grace shown to her by Sara. Perhaps she was not beyond redemption. What was left now was the work of finding her father and siblings.

Dressing for breakfast the next morning with a firmer sense of resolve, she glanced at the scarred statue peering at her from the table beside her Jenny Lind bed. *Thank you, Blessed Virgin, for bringing me to Sara. She is both the mother and the sister I never had. Grandmother said facing the devil is better than letting the evil creature have the run of you. Right she was, and blessed are you for helping me drive the devil away.*

Thoughts of demons brought Joseph Ryan to mind. She was grateful for his letter identifying her father's destination but was entirely suspicious of his reason for doing so. *I thought by leaving I'd be done with him.* Holding the marred image of Mother Mary on her lap, she prayed again. *Help me, Mary, to find the children. Help me to overcome the anti-Catholic bigots in my path. Help me to restore my honor and gain God's forgiveness through your intercession and love. I will honor your martyrs and stay true to your holiness until the end of my days.*

When she looked up, Sara was peering into the room from the hallway. In her hands, she held a small nosegay of white daisies and blue cornflowers. "I'm sorry. I didn't want to knock and interrupt your prayers. You should take the figure with you when you leave in a few weeks."

"It has been something of a mystery. I didn't see it when I first set foot in this room."

"I placed it on your table on the afternoon you arrived and took a nap. It belonged to my mother. Something told me to put it there."

"Thank you, Sara. A very big part of me wants nothing more than to stay here with you."

"You can always return here late in the late fall, if. . .," she stopped.

"If I haven't located my father?"

"Or even if you have. Especially if you have. You can both come. We'll have the winter together. It's lovely here in the frost and snow. The holiday decorations of Troy will cheer you, and we will celebrate the birth of Christ together. How my mother would have loved that. There will be long, dark days and less of this sparkling light we're enjoying today, but we'll enjoy many an hour before the fire. Your first winter in America should be here with us."

Aileen forced a faint smile. "Even if I do find my father, he won't be able to come with me here. He's still indentured. He is a slave but thank you." Eyeing the flowers, she added, "And thank you for the lovely bouquet. I'll put them in water."

Sara smiled. "They're not from me. Jedidiah came by specially to bring these, and I told him you were resting. He asked that I bring them up to you."

THE SHAKERS IN NISKAYUNA.— RELIGIOUS EXERCISES.

1834-1835

"Nothing tends more to cement the hearts
of Christians than praying together.
Never do they love one another so well as
when they witness the outpouring of each
other's hearts in prayer."

Charles Grandison Finney

9

THE SHAKER DANCE

The oak stairs tapped as she skipped down them, anxious to join the Rawsons for breakfast on this glorious late August morning. Laughter could be heard coming from the dining room and the smell of baked ham and biscuits seeped into the hallway from the sideboard. With the parlor windows open she could feel a cool breeze and hear the crinkle of paper-thin leaves pushing against the home's foundation. The beebalm and daisies had fallen and the field grasses were beginning to turn golden brown.

Grandmother would have loved it here.

Hesitating at the bottom of the stairs to breathe in her happiness, she was greeted by John holding a copy of the Troy Sentinel.

"Good morning, Aileen. I trust the night was good to you?"

"Oh yes, slept soundly I did, John, thank you."

She reflected on the quiet kindness, stimulating conversations, sumptuous meals, and privilege of uninterrupted sleep she had enjoyed all summer long in the Rawson home.

"Keating has amassed every support for your journey to Palmyra. He's found you a fine packet, too."

"I am forever in his debt."

As John made his way out of the front door he grinned at her. "My brother has the list of contacts and letters of introduction. I have every confidence that your travels will be productive."

She found the company of John's brother, Jedidiah, intriguing but somewhat disquieting. What was his reason for so eagerly inserting himself into her life?

Passing through to the dining room, she hesitated a moment as a flood of thoughts came. *Jedidiah's enthusiastic attention was flattering, but despite their hours of conversation, she still felt she barely knew him. His bravado made it seem that he was holding something back.*

It was exciting to know a man who seemed to genuinely respect her thoughts. For her birthday in late July he had given her a packet of essays on slavery, abolition and temperance, and when he arrived following business trips west, he generally held newspapers beneath his arm and left them for her to read.

Does a few-days' journey on a slow vessel, gliding on a man-made river—even one passing through the wilderness—really require his protection or guidance?

She thought it unwise to encourage any romantic notions he might hold for her and did not allow herself to consider any she might harbor for him. She had a mission and would not be distracted.

As she entered the dining room Jedidiah stood directly before her, chatting and smiling with Sara and Keating. She held back an embarrassing gasp. His charm, deep voice and striking looks had startled her once again.

"Such a lovely morning" she murmured, turning toward the buffet.

Sara had told her that when Jedidiah strode down the jostling streets of Troy and visited the pubs, he drew admiring glances from ladies and gentleman alike. There was something in his demeanor that drew attention and often made her touch her rosary when he came into view. She reached for it now.

"Jedidiah's back from Syracuse, raving about the salt ponds," said Sara brightly.

"We love your charging enthusiasm for all things American, Jedidiah," added Keating, "religious experiments and all."

Jedidiah held back a chair for Aileen politely. She wondered as she took her seat, *What does he believe?*

Only the echo of her grandmother's strict admonition that she express gratitude for every kind gesture shown to her by her hosts forced her to accept this upcoming travel arrangement, even though it left her unsettled.

I will accommodate his presence while keeping a watchful eye and distance.

When she realized she had been staring at herself in the mirror above the buffet for too long, she felt irritated with herself.

Why, do I wonder what he thinks of me so often and whether he likes my looks? This is nonsense. Stop it.

Bright sunlight streamed into the room and bounced off the cut crystal Waterford goblets. The cook bustled around, refilling the serving platters and topping off pots of hot beverages.

"Do you all know of Mother Anne Lee?" Jedidiah asked, taking his seat at the table.

"Yes," answered Keating. "I am told she is a remarkable woman."

"How about you, Aileen, ever heard of her?"

Aileen felt tested and it irritated her.

"Despite my knowledge of the native Confederacy, the Hudson

River paintings of Thomas Cole and Asher Durand, the burgeoning villages of Utica and Syracuse, and the Falls of Niagara, I am forced to admit, I do not know of Mother Ann Lee. Is this another new religion you are going to tell us about?"

Ignoring her sarcasm he continued. "She worked in an English factory and lost all four of her children to sickness. When she came to America, she found the fire of faith right here, just across the river from us, in Watervliet. 'Hands to work, hearts to God,' is the motto of the religious colonies she's formed."

Curious now, Aileen put down the toast she was about to bite into. "Religious communities started by a woman?"

"Yes, and now there are six thousand Shakers, as they're known, in sixteen communities as far as Kentucky and Ohio."

Aileen became quiet. She was aware of holy nuns starting religious communities, but those were sanctioned and overseen by bishops.

This woman started religious communities all on her own?

"It's unusual, I know, and could not happen in Ireland. Shaker women and men actually share leadership, spiritually and in all aspects of community life." He sipped, set the cup down, and continued. "Everyone is celibate. They share all of their possessions and devote their energy to creating a life on earth that God would be proud of."

"Does America need these new spiritual outlets?" she questioned. "With the growing tension over slavery, Ralph Waldo Emerson's teachings and Jacksonian Democracy, I wonder if it is all a mass of confusion that needs sorting."

"The confusion in Ireland needs sorting, as well," added Sara softly, trying to break the tension at the table, "as does our dear mother church. I doubt God is proud of the poverty and hunger among the Catholics there."

"One also doubts He can be happy with the priests who tell the impoverished to accept their lot because a 'better world' awaits," added Keating.

"Americans don't want to wait, for anything, and there's something to be admired about that," pronounced Jedidiah.

He noticed Aileen's reflective gaze and shot her a satisfied grin. He was enjoying provoking her and making her mind churn. He continued, "The Shakers share their property, take in orphans, and give themselves over to God in all they do. As a result, their farms, architecture, and furniture are exquisitely well made, all crafted carefully, with God's grace in their hearts and minds. They invent things, too. They turned the round broom into a flat one and created a cloth that sheds water."

Aileen smiled. "You made up that last bit, didn't you? About the cloth."

"I did not," Jedidiah feigned injury. "It's all there to experience, as I said, just across the river. Would you like to go and see?"

Sara wiped her lips delicately with her napkin. "Perhaps a day out in the fresh air would do you good?" Sara suggested innocently, and Aileen took her deeper meaning.

"What did you call them—Shakers?"

"You'll understand the name when you see them dance." Jedidiah winked. "I'll let that be a surprise."

One thing Aileen unquestionably enjoyed about Jedidiah was the way he invited her, even pushed her, to think in new ways. He had also mentioned orphans. Molly and Michael were never far from her mind.

Could the Shakers have taken them in?

At that moment she pushed away her apprehensions about Jedidiah, rose from the table, and went to fetch her bonnet from the mirrored stand in the entryway. The road would be dusty, and she needed to tuck her hair up carefully. Sara was encouraging her because time alone with Jedidiah today would tell her what she was in for during the days ahead. A day in full sunlight would also help to lift and fortify her spirit, and she knew she needed strength for the journey that lay before her.

"Pull his reins harder," Jedidiah urged, as they yanked their horses onto the ferry and tied them to a railing in preparation for a rough ride across the spring currents of the Hudson.

From the middle of the broad river, Aileen could see the shadowy Adirondak mountains and she wondered why Rose had not responded to her letters. Then she surprised herself by turning away from her worries and looking at Jedidiah instead of the scenery.

"Mostly wilderness up there," Jedidiah said touching her arm to steady her, "and a lot of lawless men."

When they had crossed the Hudson, they were greeted by the tidy, bucolic village of West Troy.

A boy in a bloody apron was driving three pigs in from the country toward a butcher who shouted at the boy from his shop, "Hurry up. You were to be here two hours ago. I gots to slaughter these and hang them up to bleed."

"This is the eastern terminus of the great Erie Canal," Jedidiah said.

"I've read about the ascending and intersecting locks. They are impressive."

"You read like a hungry bear, don't you? I'm fortunate to benefit from your curiosity."

"These locks are renowned in Europe. They have boosted Americans' reputation for ingenuity."

They tied up their horses and briefly strode along the Canal's towpath, staying out of the way of mules and drivers loading packet boats with crates, lumber and animals.

"Look at how this works, Jedidiah!"

Aileen was amazed watching the boats be lifted and dropped to various levels of the waterway. Once at the appropriate level, the colorful vessels were guided by young men and boys in tattered clothing who drove teams of mules and horses along the towpath. Some of the animals looked half-starved and others were adorned in full regalia with brass fittings on their saddles and feathered bonnets on their heads. The sky was constantly changing, beaming sunlight at one moment and shedding soft gray rain the next.

She noticed a quiet smile on Jedidiah's face. He was clearly enjoying her company. "There's eighty of these locks now?" she questioned.

He came alive and answered with his typical pride. "Yes, all made of stone cut from wilderness quarries."

"I wonder what my father's work on the Canal has been."

"It's backbreaking work, widening and repairing these walls. New York keeps expanding it, creating new reservoirs, and shoring up the places that collapse in bad weather."

"He's given three years to this."

"Bless him! 'Clinton's Ditch' has already reduced the cost of shipping goods by ninety percent. Your dad is helping to make New York City the busiest port on the continent."

She graced him with a radiant smile, and they stepped up their pace, trying to avoid a terrible stench that wafted toward them unexpectedly.

He saw her studying the stonework. "The engineering is first rate, isn't it?"

Suddenly she felt relief, certain they would be able to carry on pleasant, informed conversations on their journey.

"It looks like a staircase to the clouds," she remarked, feeling enthusiastic about the trip for the first time in days. Rumors of mosquito borne diseases, sury packet boat captains, and minimal accommodations for cleanliness had made her concerned about traveling on the Canal.

"Do you think we'll find them, my father and the children?"

"Yes" he responded with his usual confidence.

She began worrying once more. *If they found her father, would he be free from drink and able to join forces to accomplish their mission?*

"I don't have experience with him in situations like this."

"What do you mean?"

"Well, situations that require reliability and seriousness of purpose. Uh, Grandmother said more than once that my father lacks these traits."

"His children are missing. He crossed the Atlantic to find them. He'll rise to it."

As they finished their walk and mounted their horses, the sounds of the chattering people clustered in small groups along the pier faded.

"They're pacifists," Jedidiah called to her from his horse as the Canal's vivid activity faded from sight. "In this tiny settlement of

Watervliet, the Shakers made a community. They say, 'they're called to love.'"

Was that a sense of proprietary pride in his voice? She wondered, *Could he be a member of this unusual and devout group?*

As they rounded a bend in the road, Aileen saw a group of gleaming, white buildings and carefully painted red barns in the distance. The structures appeared idyllic in form as did the striking row of Lombardy poplars lining the entrance road. Riding into the settlement, she experienced the deep stillness of a what should be a busy place for this time of day, but one that was devoid of people. The quietude was comfortable, and the sunlight emerged, yet again, from behind the clouds.

Along the well-kept lane on which they traveled, every plant was carefully trimmed. Handsome white buildings held beautifully-framed, two-story, oak windows. Circular stairwells with delicately carved railings were visible through them. Each structure achieved visual harmony with the gates, herb gardens, and pathways surrounding it.

Every structure except one.

Aileen turned to ask Jedidiah about the silence when loud music began to pour from a circular stone structure at the far end of the settlement.

"They are worshipping. No telling how long they have been in there." Jedidiah's face flushed with excitement, and he urged his horse to pick up the pace. "Come."

When they entered the large, barn-like structure, Aileen was overwhelmed by swelling, harmonious singing. Almost immediately, a wild shriek pierced the air followed by the pounding and clatter of several hundred feet.

A bit stunned, she pressed herself against the rear wall of the circular hall to watch the spectacle. From this position she stared in disbelief as Jedidiah threw off his jacket and joined a roiling mass of joyful dancers in the center of the room. At least fifty women wearing white silk bonnets and long gray dresses with triangular white bibs stamped their feet and moved joyously in a circle. In the opposite direction danced a circle of men. Hands upturned, feet pounding, the congregation kept circling one another and singing songs that reverberated from every wall and rafter.

She closed her eyes and listened to the ecstatic sound, trying to summon the courage to stay. This was beyond the range of anything she had ever experienced at St. Brigid's. Once the initial shock wore off, she felt strangely at ease. A raucous ballad like this would never be sung in Catholic Ireland. Only Latin and somber faces and moods were allowed there. This was stunning.

These joyful people followed a woman in trying to bring the life of God to this earth. No marriage, no property, no war—and they take in orphans.

This last thought caused her eyes to snap open, and a new question to form in the back of her mind.

Where are the children? Hadn't Jedidiah mentioned something about a small schoolhouse for teaching the orphans? What if not all of the children here are orphans?

The music faded as she stepped out of the door to investigate the grounds. She was aware of a lingering sense of joy and calm. It occurred to her, *Jedidiah is not irreligious. He is simply open to God in many ways. Surely there is nothing wrong with that!*

Grandmother had taught her to be suspicious of overly-pious

priests and those who wore their scapulars conspicuously at St. Brigid's.

This Shaker worship clings to the air. God must be pleased with it.

Reflexively she reached for the rosary in her pocket, to pray in her own way, when she heard the laughter of children.

Following the sound across the green, she was drawn to an open window on the side wall of a small, red-roofed cottage. Peeking in, she saw twenty youngsters. Their ages appeared to be from six to twelve years old. They were all clean, properly dressed, and sitting attentively in a circle on the floor. Her heart skipped as she studied their faces.

The children were listening to an elderly woman in the front of the room who wore a kind expression and spoke melodically with words that seemed to come directly from her heart.

"Clean your room well, for good spirits will not live where there is dirt. There is no dirt in heaven, my darlings."

They recited in unison "Yes, Sister."

"Do your work as though you had a thousand years to live and as if you were going to die tomorrow."

"Yes, Sister."

"Take good care of what you have. Provide places for your belongings so that you may know where to find them at any time, day or night."

"Yes, Sister."

It occurred to her that these were the same lessons her grandmother had taught her in Ireland. Although when she received them there, they were delivered in a considerably sterner voice, with an overlying threat of damnation should she fail to absorb and act upon the rules provided.

The faces of the children commanded her attention. Despite her small wisp of hope—silly, of course—none resembled Michael or Molly.

The search begins tomorrow.

Someone gently touched her shoulder, and she startled. Jedidiah was standing close behind her, gazing at her with curiosity.

"I saw you leave and followed. I'm sorry I startled you. Are they here?"

"No, it was a foolish thought."

"Not foolish, eager," he said. His demeanor had changed, and he looked at her with true tenderness in his eyes. Gone was the swagger.

A thought occurred to her, so she asked him, "Is this why you brought me here, so I could see whether or not Michael and Molly had somehow been brought to the Shakers?"

"The thought crossed my mind, yes, but I didn't want to get your hopes up. I thought, well, if they are here, it will be a wonderful surprise."

She felt an urge to kiss him for his thoughtfulness and for engineering this wonderful trip today, but pushed away the impulse, and became wistful.

"Listening to the children's teacher made me think of home."

"Did you feel this kind of peace at home?"

"With grandmother I felt peace. But she didn't sing as well as these people! Are you finished dancing? I believe I overheard you promise Sara we would be home for dinner, and there is tomorrow's departure to think about."

He smiled broadly and went to fetch their horses. She smiled after him. *He will be an excellent traveling companion after all.*

Before dawn the next morning, Keating drove the steeds,

carefully avoiding the large muddy channels created by the previous evening's rain. Around her finger, Aileen continuously wound the twine that held the bundle of Sara's biscuits on her lap. She no longer imagined herself the heroine explorer, and with the loss of that naïve, but affirming self-image, her faith, innate practicality, and sharp intellect came to the fore.

"We'll travel eighty miles a day, is that correct, Jedidiah?"

Aileen had been studying him closely since their conversation at the Shaker community when her opinion of him had shifted. He had been so considerate to take her there hoping she might find Michael and Molly. Instead of the distance she had felt between them, she was warming to him.

Jedidiah had pulled his hat down over his eyes to catch a last bit of sleep, but he raised it to answer.

"Oh, now that's a generality Aileen. More often than not the schedule falls away—washouts, sick mules, abandoned barges—any number of things can cause delays. But we'll still make it in lightning speed, four to seven days' time, by floating on the Erie. If we were riding on roads like these, it would take more than a month to reach Palmyra."

The wagon hit a rut, jarring the carriage, making his point and causing the three of them to erupt in laughter.

The note from Sara that came with the bundle of biscuits read,

> *Dearest Aileen,*
> *Despite the fact that you were with us but one season,*
> *you have become like a sister to me. I will pray for you*
> *daily. Return to us safely from your heroic efforts.*
> *Much love, Sara*

At the landing alongside the Canal in Troy, Keating became serious.

"Aileen, I'm not much of a praying man anymore, but I will think of you and hope for good success."

His lip had trembled slightly then, and he quickly turned away, saying over his shoulder, "I wish you Godspeed." Then their luggage was loaded by porters, and the packet boat captain shouted for them to board.

With her locker tucked neatly in the hold, she returned to the deck, and, unlike Jedidiah and the other passengers, she moved to the rear of the boat to gaze at the ribbon of brown water they were leaving behind.

With a sense of wonder, Aileen grasped the rosary in her pocket and held it to her breast. She closed her eyes and prayed.

This journey is a precious gift God's given me. I'll become strong like Betha. I'll learn. I'll live the life I choose.

10

HEARTS AND SOULS ON FIRE

As they boarded the Agenoria that morning, she caught Keating's eye and shouted, "I have her with me, Annie's Madonna with the broken cheek." Their understanding of one another was curious and profound. She knew this was exactly what he needed to hear.

Keating smiled at her knowingly, then gave Jedidiah a look of such intensity there could be no mistaking his instructions. Care for Aileen with your life.

Calico curtains and grey velvet settees made the bright green and yellow Agenoria one of the finest packet boats in view. She was grateful that Keating had made such fine arrangements for them.

After experiencing the luxuries of the Rawson home, she felt a twinge of discomfort when she spotted a bright-blue tin ladle chained to the deck above a barrel of fresh water. It was positioned next to a tin basin and a mirror hanging by a rope.

Is this how we'll bathe?

The enthusiasm that accompanies the beginning of all journeys could be heard in the conversations of their fellow passengers. A crowd of suppliers were shouting orders, and the anxious mules, horses, and barking dogs made her ready to get underway.

The Captain announced from his position at the tiller that twenty more passengers would join them in Little Falls. He seemed a friendly man and admonished everyone to enjoy their spacious accommodations until that time. His tall brown hat and a tailcoat with badges and symbols on the lapels gave him an air of refinement that Aileen found reassuring.

"The hoggees have rough lives," said Jedidiah when she returned to sit across from him in the cabin. He pointed to the ten- to twelve-year-old boys who drove the mules and horses along the towpath. "Many are orphans. Others try to support families where the farms have failed. They work so hard they sometimes fall asleep astride the animals at night. The beasts show them more mercy than some of the boat captains."

At that moment, sounds of violence interrupted the scene and made everyone stir and crane their necks seeking the source of the interruption. To her horror, Aileen saw a large, disheveled man shouting wildly at a hoggee and beating him mercilessly with a belt. The man was swinging it so hard that the buckle was cutting the flesh on the small boy's arms and face.

"You lazy filth. Do what 'yer told."

"No!" Aileen shouted, standing up to charge from the packet and stop this horror. Jedidiah grabbed at her. She imagined Molly or Michael the target of this vicious beating and strained forcefully against his restraining arms.

"No, you cannot!" he said, pulling her back down next to him. "It isn't done. If you interfere with a captain's running of his barge, not a one will let you board their own."

"But the child—this is merciless, wrong, savage! How can it be allowed? Is a canal boat captain a king in America?"

"Are you telling me poor boys don't get beatings in Ireland? Are you saying the magistrates and priests always come to their aid?"

This silenced her while the boy's moans and cries echoed even louder across the dock. She stared out the window with tears in her eyes, watching people turn away or look down in uncomfortable silence. A few moments ago, she had viewed these fellow passengers with pleasant curiosity. Now she seethed with contempt at their cowardice.

Staring into Jedidiah's face belligerently, she stood once more. This time he did not hold her back.

His voice was serious but not angry. "Yes, it's wrong. So much is wrong. Yet, Aileen, if you accost that drunken lout, what will happen to your urgent quest to find your little brother and sister? He could get us thrown off this boat if we interfere. Look, it has ended."

She reluctantly accepted that he was right. She also knew that the vulnerability of a child being beaten struck directly at her personal terror and unraveled the carefully woven façade that cloaked her guilt and self-blame for Molly and Michael's disappearance. She sat down just in time to see their own captain gather up the injured boy and carry him to their boat for bandaging. The beater strode away mumbling about a mule that hadn't been fed.

After an hour had passed, the boy's beating still angered her, and she had to force her thoughts in a different direction. She turned to Jedidiah.

"I want to go to Ossersnenon. I know it's along the route, but I have no idea where."

"The place of the French Jesuit's martyrdom?" he responded. "I heard about that from the farmers in the Mohawk Valley. You want to pay your respects?"

"I do."

"Alright. I'll ask the Captain about visiting there."

It took hours for a sense of normalcy to return to the vessel. Aileen left the cabin to sit on the roof and absorb the late morning sun. Other passengers talked quietly amongst themselves. She found herself enjoying the gentle ride, including the frequent necessity to bend down when floating beneath bridges that posed a serious threat to tall or distracted passengers. She was intrigued with the many types of boats and people traversing the waterway, particularly those vessels serving as both livelihood and home to families. She could see mothers attending the cook stoves, fathers at the tiller, children walking the towpath, and smaller ones, to her amazement, literally tied to the railings with rope. Jedidiah had stayed in the main cabin, reading a book entitled "The Book of Mormon" by Joseph Smith.

After several hours, he joined her on the roof.

"If Ryan's information can be trusted, the presses your father delivered to Palmyra were used to create this volume. I received it from a customer of the malting house from Rochester. Smith claims this is God's record of dealing with the ancient inhabitants of this land, and that a prophet named Moroni appeared and revealed this to him."

She sighed. She could feel the faith of the singing and dancing Shakers, but not this.

"Would the Native Confederacy verify his claim? How would

Smith know what came before here.”

"He claims he found golden tablets."

"Another American prophet?" she questioned, skeptically.

"America is a remarkable place, Aileen." He was really trying to reach her now, sensing that her cynicism would close their communication. He stared at the passing landscape of fields and rolling hills and spoke carefully.

"Everything is not as it should be here," he said quietly.

"I thought America would be different than Ireland,." she replied. "Treating people like property is as common here as at home."

"It takes time to change people."

"Then time needs to go faster."

"At least we've made a new start here, and that's something."

"What do you mean?" She wanted to shed her suspicions of him and understand his unbridled love of this land.

"This is a place where the revolution taught common people that their thoughts and beliefs are theirs alone; to be cultivated or not, by their own decision; a place where the seeds of spirituality are planted along with the corn and wheat, where the need to pull a stump from the ground begets a man who creates an invention never before seen in Europe or anywhere else on the earth! This canal we are floating on is drawing people to it from around the world, and these people can change the world."

She had no response to Jedidiah's speech other than to think about it. She looked over at the towpath and watched the lone, obviously weary hoggee, drive the horses forward. She noted the expert attention required to ensure that the pull-rope connecting them to the boat did not snag a shoreline branch or stump that would halt their progress.

A few moments later, a canal line-boat filled with lumber heading east faced them and temporarily disengaged from the towpath. Several native men sat erect astride the lumber. Aileen noted they avoided eye contact with the passengers on her boat and recalled what Sara said in her outburst regarding native Americans at her first dinner with the Rawson family.

"How much of a new start has really been made here?" she asked Jedidiah.

"Which of America's flaws are you referring to?"

"I've read about Andrew Jackson. He's Irish, southern, and driving the natives from their lands." She lowered her voice as they ascended the stairs. "He's as bad as the African colonizers. Is it civilized or Christian to steal the natives' land and force them to leave? Is it right to send free Negroes back to Africa?"

"No, it is not right."

"I hear all the languages being spoken here. I see all of the religions being born here, yet I wonder."

"What ?"

"If America's promise is to look across difference, to make a nation that is better and freer than those that came before it. If America proclaims its citizen's right to worship as they choose, then why train hearts to hate? Why condone slavery and servitude?"

"The anti-removalists and abolitionists will join forces to fight these evils. You'll see if you stay here. This nation will be the light of the world."

"I hope you are right. I see too much planting of hate. It's like putting poison in the furrow next to the seed."

He nodded quietly. "Resistance to Jackson's Indian Removal Policy is growing. The abolitionist movement will give all fair-minded people hope for our future."

"I hope you are right, Jedidiah." She felt her cheeks become warm.

"It can take a long time for people to change. I, for one, am willing to strive for change, believing it will come if we work for it."

She looked again at the hoggee and his mule and hoped that change would not come at the plodding pace of that poor, burdened creature.

He smiled at her and returned to the Book of Mormon. She touched his arm to regain his attention and make one more point.

"It's just like Ireland, Jedidiah, the treatment of the natives here. Years of rent paid, and plows pushed, and then the sod is stolen right out from under them. "

"Just like Ireland? I think not." He placed the book down on the table between them. "This very waterway we are gliding upon is a contradiction. It has pushed native people off their land, but it is also making a path for millions from many nations to follow. They will help to create a better world."

She was beginning to enjoy his optimism. When he returned to his book, she walked down the stairs to the main cabin where stuffed chairs, oriental rugs, and various newspapers sat until the space would be transformed for the noon meal.

Glancing at an edition of the Rochester Journal and Post Express, she read the headline "Finney Lights Revival Fire". Raising the paper to her face, she was confronted by a sketch of Charles Grandison Finney. The man stared directly at her with piercing, defiant, eyes. Only by looking away and then returning her gaze to the image did she notice the pronounced, bald forehead, stately cheekbones, furry brows, beard, and hair that surrounded those penetrating eyes.

The article explained that over one hundred thousand people had found their way to Rochester to hear Finney extoll personal redemption and urge the rejection of sin and pride. Conversion of prominent Rochester citizens to Christ was apparently happening throughout the bustling and notoriously ungodly city. This quote from one of Finney's sermons caught her eye: "Christians seem to act as if they thought God did not see what they do in politics. But I tell you, He does see it—and He will bless or curse this nation according to the course the Christians take in politics."

Issues of race, religion and politics are boiling over the top of the kettle everywhere along this Canal.

She then went to find the captain and inquire about Ossernenon. The priests at home often spoke of the Jesuit martyrs in the new world, and she wanted to know more about this place.

The Captain had a kind face and seemed startled by her inquiry.

"Excuse me for a moment, Miss," he said, pulling the tiller hard to the right to avoid crossing the Mohawk River too close to the whirl-pool that skirted the southern shore. "The leaves and sticks circle around the eddy here. I have to avoid the deeper current of the river."

They were about forty miles west of Troy at midday. As he completed his expert steerage of the packet, he returned his attention to her.

"There is no good reason to stop in Ossernenon, pardon me saying so. The French burned it to the ground years ago in retribution for the death of their missionaries. I know you wish to pay your respects, but it isn't feasible. How did you come to know of the place, Miss?"

"We aren't complete strangers to the Jesuits in Ireland, Sir," Aileen responded, "although those in power have tried mightily to keep them from our island."

"Not for the Jesuits, are they?"

"The very prospect of Irish Catholics having access to abundant and excellent education, the kind of education the Jesuits bring, well, it strikes fear in the heart of many a British landlord."

"So, you think well of them, the Jesuits?" He was intrigued by her curiosity and obviously sharp intellect.

"Father Murphy from my parish calls them the 'Soldiers of Christ'. He said that with the blessing of the Pope, they do Christ's work and educate the masses from as far away as China to Canada just north of here."

She stared intently at the wooded shoreline, preparing herself to brave whatever information he had been choking down since she began asking about the remote village. She decided to address the question directly.

"Are the Jesuits honored as martyrs here, Captain?"

He cleared his throat before answering. "Some natives considered the Jesuits sorcerers, what with their strange practices and mumbo-jumbo religion," he replied, his tone growing caustic. Clearly, he had some disdain for Catholics.

"My father knew the Mohawks," he went on, his tone changing. "He traded with them and respected their ways. The last Mohawk who lived in Ossernenon was his friend, a holy man who returned over and over to this very forest. He sang in these woods at night and went by the name of Aurie. The name means 'golden one.' He was by all accounts a fair and good man, 'a light in the wilderness', many said of him. He was so respected that a village, Auriesville, was named after him about eight miles north of here."

"Good and decent?" she pondered out loud. "Why then are the natives who killed the Jesuits called savages?"

He made a disgusted sound and raised his voice. "Nothing is more savage than what the French and English did to the natives here and what the Spanish Conquistadors did to them down south."

"Why were the Jesuits tortured and killed?"

"The natives did not understand the missionaries any more than the missionaries understood them. Sickness and crop failure followed the French. Had the French joined with the natives and prayed for their crops, they might have been seen as people to respect. Some were. But the Jesuits too often called the natives demon worshippers and scorned their ways."

Aileen started to object but stopped herself and listened closely. The captain kept on.

"Would you trust someone who told you that your religion was that of the devil?"

"Many have. Of course not."

"The Catholic Brothers never sought permission to teach native children their faith. They made the children kneel under the symbol of a dying man on a cross. Would you want your child forced to worship a strange God?"

"No, of course not," Aileen mused.

Even the subject of martyrdom is complicated here. One person's martyr is another's devil.

She thanked the captain and returned to Jedidiah, who, still reading, was now inside the cabin avoiding a sudden downpour.

"We shan't be going to Ossernenon," she told him." It no longer exists."

"Alright" he responded flatly.

Later that evening, resting on a sleeping board hung from chains in the women's quarters, she felt even more confused by this alien-feeling land—America—than when she had first landed in New York Harbor.

Now I am questioning my faith?

She clasped her rosary to her chest and started weeping involuntarily. She had not anticipated this. Her faith had kept her steady all of her life. Catholicism bound her to her grandmother and Ireland. She determined to keep her new doubts from Jedidiah, lest he believe that he had single-handedly pried open her Catholic convictions. It was not just Jedidiah but this journey, this new nation, this corridor of canal towns so full of strange people and new experiments that were making her search for new answers.

How would a break with the old faith help? It's as much a part of me as my eyes and heart.

She recalled Sara confirming rumors she had heard that some of the Jesuits were brutal.

"Jesus walked among the people with love. He didn't trample over them with fear," she had said.

Aileen was not ready to disregard or disrespect men whose mission was sanctioned by the Pope himself. But now she had less certainty about their methods and other of her core beliefs.

11

LIBERTY AND JUSTICE FOR ALL

Aileen awoke to the unpleasant scent of sewage buckets on the open deck. The young girl in the bunk below her began coughing and the child's mother rushed to her with opium syrup. Aileen covered her face with the linen handkerchief bordered in pink roses that Sara had embroidered for her and slipped away to join the quiet line of people waiting to use the washing basin.

The wilderness bordering the Erie was green and still in the morning sunlight. Panthers and bears were known to prowl these woods but today the pervasive calm of the forest seemed to wrap their boat and its passengers in perfect silence.

My first morning on the Erie. Where shall I say my morning prayers?

"Little Falls is where we next disembark," said the captain making his morning rounds.

Jedidiah approached her as she sat alone on the front deck with her rosary in hand. She saw his face cloud over. *He clearly has trouble with the Catholic in me, but I think it's our visit to Little Falls that is blackening his mood.*

She noticed a large red hive appear just above his collar.

"We'll be in Little Falls soon," she offered, along with a morning smile.

He sat next to her, somber and sad. She leaned forward.

"Will you tell me what happened to you there? I need to know before we arrive, don't you think?"

"It won't be a comfort to you."

He appeared vulnerable for a moment, and she hurried to soothe him.

"It could be more comfort than you think. I know of mistakes made and unresolved."

"Perhaps we'll discuss it later," he dodged. "At present, I'm intent on understanding the Angel Moroni." He was still carrying The Book of Mormon.

"Why do you give credence to all of these outrageous new religions? I asked the captain about Joseph Smith's claims, and he said the Iroquois speak of no such ancient angel. Surely, they would know."

"Perhaps Mormonism is simply another way to help pioneers break with the old world. I just want to understand it. We are headed to Palmyra after all. Your Joseph Ryan pointed us there."

"He isn't 'mine', and I don't understand why he has been following my father's travels."

He turned to face her and blocked the sun with his full crown of auburn hair. "Ryan's letter said you spurned his proposals. Why?"

"I'll tell you about Ryan when you tell me about Little Falls."

"Is he obsessed with you?"

She forced herself to turn away. "Apparently so."

"I will get back to my reading."

Irritated, she circled the deck, descended the stairs, and came face-to-face with an elaborately dressed woman who was a member of the Messrs. Gilbert and Trowbridge Traveling Theatre Company. She had learned from a fellow passenger of the troupe's intention to stage a Shakespearean production in the assembly room of St. John's Hotel in Palmyra. Jedidiah had suggested they attend the production when they reached their destination, but she had dismissed the idea, considering it an unnecessary distraction from finding her family.

She was intrigued with the actors, though, and very happy for this opportunity for conversation with a woman of the world.

Extending her hand to Aileen, the woman said, "I am Miss Catherine Durling from New York City. How lovely to meet you."

"I am Aileen O'Malley from Kildare, Ireland."

That seemed to please Catherine, and in the moment's hesitation before their next words, Aileen quickly took in her features which would have attracted the attention of any man. Catherine had cascading blond curls framed by a blue, wide-brimmed hat. The scent of primrose added to her near perfect presentation, which included an exquisite figure—narrow at the waist and full at the hips and bust.

"Are you an actress?"

"Yes. Does that surprise you?"

"I've never met one is all."

"Walk with me. I love your Irish accent and need to memorize its sounds and cadence for a part I want to play in an upcoming production. Tell me all about yourself, Aileen."

The two women walked arm in arm about the deck and spoke companionably for more than an hour. They compared observations and reactions to the menagerie of boats, people, and goods being shipped east as they made their way west to Palmyra.

Every man they passed stared at Catherine. The fact that they fixed their eyes on the actress and not on Aileen bothered her not at all. Men were a distraction to her at best.

"Do you like acting?"

"Oh, I do. For now."

"For now?"

"I mean to find something else to do with myself before they have me playing one of the old crones in Macbeth."

To Aileen's delight, Catherine seemed eager to divest herself of all pretenses. When her hat flew off in the breeze and revealed that her hair was thinning at the crown she remarked, "It's what hair pieces are for," and they fell into peals of laughter.

As they passed a settlement under construction, Aileen remarked, "My goal is to find my family. I don't know if I will stay here when I do. I'm startled by all of the different church steeples in every town and uncomfortable with the sprouting up of new religions here."

"All different. All sure theirs is the right religion, and all of them on their guard against the likes of me."

Aileen suspected what she meant before Catherine said it.

"Actors are considered to have the lowest of morals; and actresses?—surely, we're all loose women."

Aileen's eyes widened.

"Well, they're on guard to keep us out of their churches, but as far as many of the men are concerned—including the clergy—it's fine if we consent to take them to our beds."

Aileen felt a shock of surprise, and at the same time, she could not put Catherine together with the image she had just painted.

Catherine patted her arm. "Don't worry. I'm not so inclined." Then she added, "I learned my lessons a long time ago where men are concerned—religious or otherwise."

"I pine for a proper education," offered Aileen to change the subject. "It's not to be had for me in Ireland. Is it possible here do you think?"

Suddenly a strong breeze blew up the channel. Aileen pointed and exclaimed. "Look there!"

She and Catherine watched as a red and purple canal packet approached, pulled by four plumed horses and driven by a hoggee with unusually fine, tailored clothes, and well-shined, black leather boots. As the ship neared, they could see a properly-dressed Captain and his family playing jacks on the deck, and through an open door, they spied a cookstove within the cabin that would have been suitable for a very fine home.

As the boats came abreast of one another, Aileen noticed a girl sitting apart from the distinguished-looking family. As they came closer, passing in the opposite direction, Aileen was horrified to see that the disheveled girl was tied to a boat stave like an animal. She appeared about eight years old. Her shoulders were rounded and her blond head drooped forward, propped up by two dirty hands.

Aileen gasped, then shouted, "Molly? Molly is it you?"

Catherine stared, too, mouth agape at the pitiful sight.

Turning, Aileen made a dash to find the Captain and begged him to stop the boat, all the while shouting, "Molly, it's Aileen, Molly. Raise your head, dear. Let me see your face."

Jedidiah heard the shouting and rushed to her side.

"Is it her, Aileen? Your sister? How do you know?"

"I don't know for certain, but it looks like her, and I just feel it. It must be her!"

The boats had almost passed each other, one heading west, one east. At the last moment, the girl slowly raised her head from her hands and stared piercingly at Aileen and Jedidiah as they leaned over the railing.

The songbirds and the soft, lapping clicks of water on limestone fell silent as the crafts moved away from one other in different directions. The young girl stood and seemed as if she were trying to say something or send a signal with her hands. . .and the ships kept moving.

Aileen felt sick and the whole scene spun into darkness.

She glimpsed the profile of a woman with a dark braid draping down her left shoulder. "Mother?" she murmured into the dark room. Then light stung her eyes.

"Aileen, you're here with me, Jedidiah. We're at the Fairfield Medical College in Little Falls. You've had a spell, some sort of spell, and the doctors are going to help you."

Raising herself up on her elbows she took in her surroundings, the distinct knit in Jedidiah's brows and the young, serious looking physician standing next to him. She could see by the slanted rain lashing at the windows that an early summer storm was in full sway.

"I'm fine. I've never fainted in my life. I failed to eat this morning and then I was startled by–" She sat up quickly.

"Jedidiah, who owned that boat? Did it stop here? Was it Molly, I wonder? Why was the girl filthy and tied that way?"

"They passed by so quickly, Aileen. I don't know the boat and neither did Miss Durling or our Captain. You thoroughly collapsed.

The Captain was good to bring us here. Dr. Sweeney thinks you may have hysteria."

"Nonsense." She looked defiantly at the doctor. "You will not be touching me, Sir." He stepped back.

She had learned from her grandmother to beware how the doctors in Ireland sometimes treated women for hysteria—by massaging the pelvis until something called paroxysm was achieved. No, the gawking young doctor standing next to Jedidiah was not going to reach beneath her skirt. She quickly slid off the table, brushed sweaty curls from her forehead, and in a dignified fashion, walked out the door.

Jedidiah followed in swift pursuit.

Once out of the Academy of Medicine, they stood in the columned entry being pelted by the driving rain. He opened an umbrella to shelter her, and she took in the Village of Little Falls.

How long was I unconscious?

As the storm abated, she stepped onto the street and was momentarily stunned by the light shining on a breathtaking gorge just ahead of where they stood.

"It's so beautiful here."

Cascading rapids, gristmills, an octagon-shaped church, and a graceful stone aqueduct framed this place, which was also dotted with neat houses and tree-lined streets.

"We need to return to the ship," said Jedidiah. They passed a sign with the words LABORERS WANTED and caught a whiff of a pungent odor as they made their way past a row of milk wagons rolling into the wide-open, barn-like doors of a large, brick building.

"It's the cheese you smell. They export hundreds of pounds of it to New York."

Why was he talking about cheese instead of the child on the boat or his history here? Keating wouldn't have remarked upon it if it were not important.

She knew if she allowed his lecture to go on their conversation would never arrive at whatever events Jedidiah had precipitated in this place. Determined to excavate the story—finally—she turned to face him, blocking his path.

"Tell me now, this minute, not later and not tomorrow," she demanded. "What are you keeping from me?"

His head dropped and shoulders slumped, as he led her to a covered bench next to a feed store.

The rain finally stopped. Pointing to the sharp inclines of the surrounding ravine, he began, haltingly. "This is the only cut in the Appalachian Mountain range north of Alabama."

"No geography lesson Jedidiah, please."

"This fact matters. You see the Western Inland Canal in this village had already been built when first I came here." He pointed to a canal basin on the north side of the Mohawk River.

"I knew the Erie would soon be here as well. I was young, foolish, and so eager to make my fortune that I failed to protect my reputation and that of my family."

"What brought you to this place?"

"Charles Grandison Finney was conducting a revival here."

She recalled the dramatic face she had seen in yesterday's papers.

"He is magnificent, spellbinding actually, and full of new ideas about bringing people to God. He converted many before my eyes."

"Go on, please."

"I came to know many people here during the revival, which

lasted for several weeks, including a man named Alexander Elliott. I thought he was a man of God."

"I was also fooled by a man of God," she offered.

"I had funds from selling malt and a sum I'd inherited from our father. I used the funds to purchase land from Elliot on both sides of the river. I told the people here that I would sell them plots and help them to build this village and eventually obtain a charter. I wanted to do my part to help build this new nation."

His eyes reddened. Aileen felt empathy for her usually over-confident companion.

"Elliott, who owned everything here, saw a young fool in me. People began developing plans for mills and factories and when they came to me, I sold them property. Only then did I discover that the contract I had entered into with Elliott allowed him to continue controlling the waterpower of the falls. Despite the transfer of land, he refused water to every project that failed to suit his own goals and ambitions. Even the charter failed to protect the local citizens' rights. They thought I was in on the scheme. I lost my money and my reputation. With Keating's help I eventually returned their funds but could not return their dreams."

"I am so sorry," she said, reaching over to touch his arm.

They sat together in silence for a few moments, then stood, and began walking back to the basin where their packet boat was docked. To her surprise, she found they were holding hands. The touch was unconscious, as though their fingers were meant to lace together.

As they walked along, Aileen realized his story did not bother her in the least. His mistake was one of gullibility not avarice or neglect, and he did his best to make restitution to those he had harmed.

Before her eyes, Jedidiah had fully transformed from a thoughtful but often brash, self-assured idealist to a chastened man who understood hard realities and made his own mistakes.

She could breathe easier in his presence now and wished she could find some way to make restitution for her own mistakes. She began to consider the possibility that Jedidiah could actually help her to do this.

It took more than a full day for her to recover physically from her collapse. The image of the small girl tied to the eastbound packet was never far from her mind. She now fixed her thoughts on the mission of finding her father. Hopefully, he would put her on the right track to finding Molly and Michael.

As they moved past Little Falls, the weather turned balmy. Warm air moved above the narrow, murky waterway, stirring the branches of the overhanging trees. To distract herself, she began asking Jedidiah, who was now so changed in her eyes, questions about the various scenes playing out before them.

She was fascinated by the energy of the people and the explosion of commerce they saw at every turn. She was struck, however, by the contradictions between what she saw and what she understood to be in the American Constitution.

"Americans seem to believe they can cast off old religions, begin new ones, be converted and start anew; but if you mention ending slavery, they say it's impossible. If individuals can convert to new religions, then tell me, why is it that this nation cannot convert from slavery?"

"We live in a slave economy, north and south. Did you have sugar in your tea this morning? Are some of your clothes made of cotton? But to answer your question, I believe this nation can and will change," he responded.

"Your Declaration of Independence speaks of the tyranny of Britain. I'm Irish. I know that tyranny. Why inflict it on the natives and debtors and poor people here? Is this really and truly a new world, Jedidiah?"

"Yes, it is. Not perfect but new and full of promise." He smiled at her with admiration. "So many questions."

"Grandmother taught me to question everyone," she told him grinning, "except Mother Mary and Jesus, of course."

"Of course," he retorted, flashing a smile.

"You always take off your hat when we talk, Jedidiah. It makes me think that you just might be enjoying learning what's on my mind."

When she said that, he looked down at the cap in his lap. "Answering your good questions is making me a smarter and better man. And you, you're forcing me to think before I speak."

"Was that not the case before?" she asked.

He looked up at her, soberly. "The Rawson family would say it was not. Now may be different. What would you say?"

She left him hanging for a long moment. "I would say that you have so much going on in that head of yours, that much of what you say just spills out—and all the better that it does." With that compliment hanging in the air, she felt herself flush.

The next evening, as the sun slipped behind the clouds on the western horizon, Jedidiah held her chair as they joined Catherine Durling for dinner in the cabin. Glancing out the window, they floated past a lock tender's shanty and an impressive, limestone manor home that was under construction came into view. The large structure with four massive chimneys was covered with busy workers on ladders and charged by the clang of hammers and the chipping sound of stone masons' tools.

Catherine set down the water glass she had just raised to her lips and addressed Jedidiah. "How many times have you traveled this way?"

"I've canaled, oh, twenty times or more since it opened in '25. Each trip brings its own revelations and surprises. Something's always new. I've had smooth steady days like the one we enjoyed today but plenty of washouts and dam breaks, as well. I've waited days at the end of a long string of packets with the insects biting and captains cursing."

"All the languages," Aileen mused. "When I was on deck today, I heard Nordic speakers on the packet behind us. Danes, I think. Can one nation contain all these different people?"

"The lure of making your life your own," Jedidiah declared, "of casting away the shackles of class and rejecting religions that insist God wrote your story even before the day you were born—that's the quest that will make old languages and customs fall away. Citizens guided by reason and enlightened by education will guide the future here."

"He's an optimist this friend of yours," Catherine said to Aileen approvingly.

"That he is. I'm more unsure. Daniel O'Connell thinks slavery will soon get the boot in Britain and even in stodgy, old Catholic Ireland long before it happens here."

Catherine replied quietly. "I've met outstanding people along the Canal. This boat may be gliding on a vein of freedom. There are Quakers, free Negroes, temperance activists, so many for whom the abolition of slavery is their life's work. They stow runaways in their attics and barns and help them make their way to Canada. They publish newspapers and use their fortunes to make the case for freedom.

Some theatre troupes even help. "

"My friend, Gerrit Smith, is such a man," Jedidiah added. He was thoroughly enjoying the conversation but careful to speak in a hushed tone.

"Several years ago, I purchased some land in Fayetteville from Smith. He's started a school where former slaves learn trades alongside white people in his village of Peterboro. We're about to float past the Oneida Institute which admits Negro men to college."

"So, the roots of abolition are watered by this Canal?" asked Aileen.

"Yes," replied Catherine and Jedidiah in unison.

"Are there colleges here that admit women?"

Jedidiah replied, "There will be. That change is coming. There is talk of an academy for women in Troy."

Seeing her excitement he added, "Charles Grandison Finney allows women to pray aloud at his revivals. You never saw that in Ireland. We can advance social reform here and make this new nation grand. Finney's voice and this Canal, most of all, will make that possible."

"How will the Canal help?" asked Catherine.

"The slave states won't win the west now that this ditch is here. Instead of slavery being carried up the Mississippi, our ideas will follow this path of trade and commerce and flow into the West."

As dinner concluded, Catherine retired to the women's sleeping quarters and Aileen's mind returned, as it had almost every hour, to the image of the girl she'd thought was Molly, tied to the packet boat like an animal, her piercing blue eyes glaring, imploring, between the fingers of soiled hands.

"Why would they be taking that girl east, do you think? I wonder if she was Molly."

"I wish we had answers for you. We'll be in Palmyra in a few days. If your friend, Ryan, has spoken the truth, we're likely to find your father and some answers about your family there."

"Joseph Ryan is not a friend," she responded in a clipped manner. "He got it in his mind that he needed to own me. It's somehow related to our family's history. I never understood it. I'd hoped he'd given up on me when I left for America."

"I can understand his persistence," he smiled warmly at her. "But," he added, not smiling, "I deplore that he makes you so uneasy. He'd be wise not to show himself while I'm with you."

In the days that followed, their boat passed the small, growing city of Rome where the dig had started, and near perfect weather greeted them on the flatlands south of Oneida Lake. There they caught a glimpse of native boys running in the tall golden grasses on shore. They were holding long sticks and passing something through the air. The trees swayed to the rhythmic sound of water-filled drums. Leaves began to yellow. Close to the edge of the Canal, a beautiful Oneida child leaned against an upright man who was fishing.

"Look, she has fallen asleep on his arm," remarked Aileen with admiration. "It's nothing like I was told, is it?"

"Those are the Oneida. They're hardly 'savages,' if that's what you were told." He continued, "I learned about them from the son of a Presbyterian minister named Samuel Kirkland. We wouldn't have a nation if not for the honor of those people."

"What do you mean?"

"The Oneida were Washington's scouts, soldiers, officers, and spies during the revolution. They fought alongside the patriots rather than the Brits. More important, they took food to Valley Forge when the Continental Army was starving."

"I've never read of this."

"You won't. Despite Washington's efforts to recognize and repay them, the Oneidas have been treated as badly as all of the other native tribes. Their villages were burned, their culture attacked, and their traditional lands, promised to them by treaty, were stolen by the State of New York. Many have already left for a reservation in Wisconsin and more depart every year."

"Have you spoken with members of this tribe?"

"Yes, at Gerrit Smith's home. He welcomes them in Peterboro.

"What else have you learned?"

"You will be interested to know that unlike in Europe, inheritances pass through the women of their clans."

"The women?" Aileen expressed shock.

"Women choose the leaders as well. Our debt to the Oneida nation is immense."

"Their lives seem familiar to me," Aileen responded wistfully, "except the part about the women, of course. We Irish were also considered savages. We were labeled 'wild beasts' butchered, starved, and slaughtered. Our clans, well, they were tribes really, weren't they?" Her sense of conviction and tone of voice grew firmer with every realization. "The circle around our cross is the sun. Our lands were stolen. Our language was outlawed."

He interjected, "And it is story-telling and strong women who keep the Irish culture alive, is it not?"

She stared at him, surprised. "Yes, strong women like Grandmother, and Annie Eustace, and Sara."

"And you?"

She could not hold his gaze. "I want to be strong."

"You crossed an ocean alone. You were going to undertake this search alone. Do you not see how strong you are?"

I only see how frightened I am inside.

After a long pause, he said, "In the morning we can take a walk on the towpath if you like. We'll pass Canastota near Gerrit Smith's farm and see the salt boiling houses of Syracuse."

She let herself return to the conversation. "Yes, that would be lovely."

He could see she was only minimally paying attention to his plans for the next day.

A Negro man and woman carrying a toddler boy boarded their packet boat in Syracuse and were greeted politely by the Captain. This family was anxious and she overheard the man ask the Captain where they could sit out of sight..

"Why out of sight?" Aileen asked the Captain that afternoon. "Isn't slavey abolished here in New York?"

"Slave patrollers," he responded. "They take free Negroes and sell them into the deep south."

In conclusion he added cryptically, " My grandfather fought for liberty and justice for all."

12

PORT BYRON

That evening as the air grew humid and thick, the captain's wife took her guitar from beneath a bench in the cabin and built a smoky fire on deck to repel mosquitos. After removing her grease-stained apron, she sat on a stool and strummed until a few passengers created a huddle around her. Aileen and Jedidiah joined them and began swaying and tapping their fingers on their chairs. An elderly gentleman in fine clothing pulled a harmonica from his pocket and accentuated her melodies by sending plaintiff refrains into the dusky sky.

This was the kind of music that allowed everyone to fall into their own minds and reflect upon their experiences that day travelling the Canal. Busy, exciting places like the city of Syracuse had been punctuated by long stretches of open lands and green serenity. Soon, the red velvet curtain would be drawn across the cabin below, separating the men's and women's sleeping quarters, and they would climb onto their sleeping bunks, which, when lowered, fell into the creaking melody of swinging metal chains.

Later, Aileen fell asleep to the sweet sounds of the Negro woman's lullaby to her child, the hum of insects, and the hoggee's gentle encouragement for the mules to press on through the dark.

The next morning, it was cool when they arrived at Port Byron, a busy mill town where, according to Jedidiah, notable figures from the city of Auburn, like William Seward, a prominent anti-Mason and member of the New York State Senate, often boarded packets heading east to Albany. A breeze pushed them by the new Baptist Presbyterian Church as they slid into port, and the smell of grain and peppermint from a nearby extract factory filled the air. Aileen and Jedidiah had risen early to avail themselves of the wash bucket and mirror and were anxious to step off the boat and stretch their limbs in a morning stroll through the town.

As the passengers stood to disembark, two very rough-looking men on horseback and carrying rifles forced their way through the small crowd of residents at the water's edge. Aileen and Jedidiah instinctively turned to the Negro man on their packet and saw him take a knife from his belt. The woman beside him, who was carrying a small child, looked terrified.

For an instant, they thought the man would fight off the two who had jumped down from their horses and were charging toward the packet, but they saw his mouth and hands start to tremble, and then, methodically, as if he were slaughtering a sheep, he pressed the knife to his neck and sliced across the front of his throat.

There were screams and shouts as the man fell on the deck in a spreading pool of blood. The Negro woman hoisted the child in her arms and shouted a prayer into the wind. Stepping to the edge of the packet boat, she jumped off into the dark, dismal water of the Canal.

Aileen, horrified and in shock, was at the same time distracted by a Quaker man sitting in a wagon on shore. The tall man stood, threw his black hat into the back of the wagon and dove into the muddy water where the woman and her child had fallen. For long moments, the surface of the water remained smooth. Then he emerged, sputtering, and holding just the child. He searched the faces of those on the packet, which was now tied to the dock, until he saw Aileen and his gaze rested on her.

He handed the choking, gasping child to a woman on the Canal bank, then returned to the water again, diving under and coming up empty-handed. Again and again, he went under and rose up without her.

Finally, exhausted and out of breath, he left the Canal and a moment later, the woman's limp body emerged far downriver, face down and unmoving, obviously dead.

Jolted into action now, Aileen ran from the boat to assist the woman who was holding the small child. The boy was trying to escape from her, arms outstretched, crying desperately for his mother. She took him in her arms and turned to see the men on horseback spur their horses and gallop away.

"Who are they?" she pleaded to Jedidiah. "What just happened?" She remained stunned as she watched Jedidiah provide the Quaker man with a cloth to dry himself. "My God, he saved the child but now the boy's an orphan."

The Captain had told her about such men, but she'd had a hard time believing anyone could be so evil and determined as to ride hundreds of miles into free territory to catch human beings who only wanted to live in peace and not be worked to death.

"Slave catchers," remarked Jedidiah, who came to her side and caressed the toddler's cheek. "I've seen many notices as of late with bounties offered for finding and returning escapees. The Negroes would rather die than return to the whip, it's clear."

The child was quieter now, thanks to Aileen's soothing hand rubbing his back. They approached the Quaker gentleman who was sadly replacing his hat and untying his horses.

"My Lord, man, you do yourself and this village proud with your actions. I am Jedidiah Tracey, from Troy, and I'm honored to make your acquaintance."

"Hello brother. I'm John Germain. I wish I could have saved her." He stared, forlorn, down the Canal where several townspeople were retrieving the corpse of the child's mother.

The three of them shifted their attention to the small boy in Aileen's arms. The child was beautiful, healthy, and now totally silent, resting his head against Aileen's lace shirtfront. She reached for her necklace engraved with keys and the child rubbed it with his chubby hands.

"This wee one's in need of ministrations," said a black-haired woman crossing the street toward them. Her skirt was torn at the hem in several places and Aileen flinched when she noticed how dirty the woman's hands were as she lifted the boy from her arms and placed him on her hip.

"I will take him to Pastor Smith and his wife." She pronounced, "They help orphans, and I am sure they will find a good, safe place for the child."

Aileen nodded, feeling unsure but exhausted and compliant. Jedidiah also hesitated but went along with the woman's plan.

"We will be here for a bit. Let's go for breakfast at the Boatman's Tavern over there."

"Why, yes," Aileen replied. She remained dazed from the suicides she had just witnessed.

As they walked to the tavern, they noticed the Captain and his wife scrubbing blood from the deck of the packet.

"Much of what I thought I knew before boarding the Dublin Packet has been wrong."

"The land of freedom is often portrayed as heaven itself in Ireland?"

"Yes. I never believed the myth, but I could not have imagined the horror."

"I've just witnessed a man–," she choked on the words, "–cut his own throat to keep from being dragged back into slavery and a woman jump to her death with her child in her arms. This is a free state. I don't know how to make sense of things here."

He repeated what he had said before. "You're right to question everything that others tell you to believe as fact."

"Even what you tell me?"

"Oh, most certainly question anything I tell you," he said with just a flicker of a smile. It was clear the terrible events of the morning still weighed heavily.

As they waited at their table, Aileen found her way to the washroom behind the tavern and poured fresh water from the porcelain pitcher into the bowl to splash on her face and neck. The days were much warmer now than when they left Troy. Her clothing felt heavy, and she was somber and didn't feel like eating.

Then she heard voices in the back alley.

"How much you want for the pickaninny?" said an unfamiliar voice.

"Ten dollars from the Bank of Auburn."

Recognizing the second voice as belonging to the woman who had taken the child from her arms, her hands flew up to cover her mouth, and she moved toward the small window above the washroom pump. Out behind the building, she witnessed the woman with black hair thrusting the Negro child into the arms of tall man in a long gray coat and accepting a bill, which she quickly shoved into a pocket.

Aileen felt a fury she had never known, like fire racing through her body. Dashing out of the tavern's back door, she saw the man who had purchased the child mount his horse, quickly spur the creature hard in the flanks, and start to gallop away down the back street.

"Stop him!" she screamed so loudly it strained her throat. She charged after the man, running through dust left in his wake, and stumbled over uneven cobbles in the street, falling hard and sobbing. The woman saw her fall and ran away.

Now she fully understood. That woman needed money. That sweet child would be auctioned, made to pick the worms off plants for hours in the hot sun, even made to eat the worms if he misbehaved. This was the fate of the youngest slaves sold south.

She stood and began furiously brushing the dust off her clothes.

Maybe it's more than finding Da and the little ones that brought me here. I feel moved to join this fight.

Jedidiah had come running as soon as someone inside had shouted about the commotion on the road. She let herself lean against him but remained silent, deep in thought. Then she stepped back and touched the place on her breast where the child's small hand had so desperately gripped her.

Why was I so stupid?" she finally asked him. "Why did I trust that woman? Grandmother said only years of living would teach me to recognize and step away from those who care only for themselves."

"A wise woman, your grandmother."

"That woman traffics in people, just like the slavers, Captain Mick and the crone who stole my sister and brother."

Jedidiah held her hand on their walk back to the dock. "The woman who took the child sold the child?"

"Yes" she replied, as they walked onto the boat, "to a slave catcher."

That evening as she tried to say her prayers, she found herself unable to recite the mantras she had held in her heart since childhood. She rose, went into the galley, and pulled a stool up to the smoldering fire in the stove.

Why, if you are an all-powerful and good God, do you allow such savagery to happen?

The Captain's wife saw her distress and wiped her brow gently with rose-hips tea.

"Yes, this world can be a terrible place," she said, shaking her head with a disgusted look, "and also a grand one. Best to seek out the roses, darlin'."

"But the thorns last when the petals fall," Aileen responded.

"Ah, yes," she added with a slight smile. "But the beauty of the blooms—so grand it is." And she walked Aileen back to her bunk and gently rubbed her back until she fell asleep.

13

PALMYRA

The Montezuma swamp leading to Palmyra was as dismal as Aileen's mood. Catherine Durling stood next to her as they floated through the tall reeds and large birds and held her close with a shawl pulled tightly about her shoulders.

"It's been a horror these past two days. You've seen the worst of this wilderness, Aileen."

"Selling children? Yes, nothing worse."

The suicides and sale of the Negro boy burrowed under her skin. They reemerged each time she swatted a mosquito with deadly vengeance.

"This trip to Palmyra may be a trap of sorts."

"That Ryan fellow, he's the one who pointed you here?"

"Yes, in a letter. Said my Da was headed to Palmyra with a printing press. He knew I would follow. More of his schemes may await me."

"Men don't like to be humiliated. Those accustomed to getting their way, even less." Catherine spoke as someone with deep experience dealing with the hubris of men.

Jedidiah, absorbing her tension, had wisely moved to the rear of the ship and become engaged in conversation with the captain's wife and their daughter, Polly. Aileen watched the child place her corn husk doll in front of her face and mimic conversation. The girl reminded her of Molly.

"Eyes haunt me, Catherine; the sad, vacant stare of the filthy girl we saw tied to the boat; the grief on the face of the Negro man just before he slit his own throat; the terrified eyes of the mother as she jumped into the Canal."

"I understand."

"My prayers, they fail to ease this."

"I abandoned prayer altogether once, but now the peace that comes from asking for help is coming back to me."

Looking up at the general store, painted a brilliant red, she added, "I'll be headed for the St. John's when we tie up."

Embracing Aileen, she added, "Don't give up, Aileen."

A cobblestone structure overlooked the water just before their packet docked on Canal Street.

Jedidiah took her arm as they disembarked. He asked her to wait at the embankment while he conversed with some local tradesmen.

He returned, speaking in an excited voice. "I learned that Smith's been run out. It seems they don't like the Masons or the Mormons hereabouts. A lady named Lucy Harris filed charges against Smith for fraud. Apparently, he failed to pay to print the Book of Mormon. It was a local publisher named Grandin that did the printing, on a press brought here—hear this, Aileen—by an Irishman on the Canal."

"So, Joseph Ryan's story is true? How did he know this, I wonder."

"Let's find out."

They made their way to the brick building that housed a bookstore below Grandin's printing shop. Copies of The Book of Mormon were prominently displayed for sale in the Main Street window. Entering, they were greeted by bell, the glow of sunlight on oak floors, tall shelves and the wonderful scent of books.

A gentleman with thick, white hair, wearing a ragged leather vest limped jerkily down the narrow stairwell, clutching the rail to keep from falling.

"Can I be of assistance?"

Aileen spoke right away. "I am seeking the man who delivered your press from Troy, Sir."

"Ahh, the Irishman who climbed out of the deep." He smiled warmly and invited them to sit at a table at the back of the store.

"His line boat sank right here in the harbor as he arrived with my press. I'm grateful they saved it."

"Who saved it? Did they save the man, as well?"

"The men who believe in golden tablets hauled my press and the bloke who brought it here from the drink, the Irishman, a good fellow, stayed in town for the winter. Once he found his boy, he became a follower of Joseph Smith."

"He found his boy? What was the boy's name? What does he look like? Are they here now? Both of them? Where can I find them?"

Her questions came with an urgency that compelled the man to take her hand.

"Now, Miss," he began sadly.

She interrupted. "You see, I believe it's my father who brought you your press, and it may be my brother, Michael, that he found. Michael's been lost, kidnappers you see, and Da came here to find him. Is there a girl with them, as well?"

The man looked at her and Jedidiah with heaviness in his face before answering. "I'm sorry to tell you, the man who brought my press here to Palmyra and stayed the winter—the man Thomas—he left and never returned."

"When? Why?"

He took the job of delivering my press without the permission of his foreman. Said he needed the money. Digging ditches pays a poor wage. A man could starve. Strange, come to think of it, I've had no word about him for months."

Jedidiah inserted himself in the conversation. "And the boy that was with this man?"

"After his father left, the boy showed up here with Smith. He was baptized a Mormon and went with the rest of them, Smith's followers, to Colesville."

"Where is Colesville?"

"Not far west of here, but there's no sense in going. Smith was run out by a mob. It was the exorcisms and all. People didn't take to it."

"Where could they be now?"

"I'm told they went to Harmony, Pennsylvania, and then west. The boy was a good lad. I hired him to sweep and stock for me. Brown hair and a chipper way about him."

"What was the man Thomas's last name?"

"O'Malley, Thomas O'Malley. And the boy, his name was Michael."

They thanked the gentleman and walked in a daze about the village for almost an hour before taking tea under a brightly colored canvas awning near the dock. Aileen was despondent but could not weep.

Images of her father in Ireland—walking up the path to Grandmother's home, laughing with the blacksmith and carrying Molly on his shoulders—returned to her mind.

He urged me to come here to help him find them. Now he's gone. I know not where, and Michael's headed west with a religious sect?

When she found her voice she asked Jedidiah, "What has become of Molly do you think? Why didn't he seek her out before heading to this strange place with golden tablets and angels?"

"I don't know, Love." Realizing what he had said, Jedidiah looked away.

Even in her misery, his last word made an impression. She turned in her chair to hide her reddening face and stared off in the distance, fighting despondency but feeling herself drowning in it.

Soon she spied a tall gray stone steeple standing between two huge, old trees. She rose, straightened her skirt, and headed toward it.

"I'll be back shortly," she murmured, as she took to the street.

The center aisle of the long, narrow room cut through rows of dark wooden pews. Stained-glass images of men wearing bright robes and women wearing veils and waist length braids marked this as a Catholic church, but this failed to comfort her.

She slid into a walnut pew and reached for her rosary. Tears began to fall and her prayers, once again, failed to comfort her. She was aware that she was fighting to hold onto her faith.

Something drew me here.

Startled by a slight rustling noise to her right, she turned and found herself sitting diagonally from an ancient nun. The woman's blue eyes reflected the only sparks of life in her waxy visage, but Aileen felt a warmth and kindness emanating from her.

"You are. . .," the nun hesitated. "You are Aileen O'Malley?"

"Sister, how could you possibly know that?"

"An agent from the Rawson malthouse came here last week asking after Thomas O'Malley. He said O'Malley's daughter was coming to Palmyra to seek him out. He described your tall, straight back, dark curls, and the birthmark on your cheek."

"I am she."

"He said you were tall and fiery. I've been praying that I would live long enough to give you what Mr. O'Malley—your father, I assume—left for you."

This is likely the only Catholic church in Palmyra, but still, this seems too miraculous to be true.

"This is impossible," Aileen breathed.

"With God very little is impossible."

"O'Malley is my father. Did the man say where he is? I must find him."

The old woman bowed her head and with her long, wrinkled fingers slowly made the Sign of the Cross.

"He and some others were sent to dig drainage ditches near a swampy area of the Canal as a kind of punishment. They tried to object, knowing that such places bring on the deadly fever, but they were told the word would go out that they went against their employer, and they would never find work anywhere ever again."

She stopped and looked at Aileen with deep sorrow in her eyes.

"The fever. . . dear God, no!" Aileen crossed herself. "He's dead. My father is dead. Is that what you're saying?"

"He is, child."

A blade went through her heart.

"He is buried I know not where. It should have been here in the yard of this church, where he often came for Mass."

He had returned to the Catholic Church?

"He sent this letter for you from the camp, after he became ill. It was delivered here by a man who runs packages." She reached into the pocket of her black habit and retrieved an envelope. "Mr. O'Malley believed that somehow we would find you or you would find us. He told the man to tell me to look for you, and that you are a good Catholic girl."

Aileen fought against images of her father's remains cast by an uncaring employer into a lonely, nameless grave and accepted the envelope with her name, in her father's hand, scrawled across the front.

"Thank you, Sister," Aileen replied. She felt the need for air.

"Find peace, my child," the woman said as Aileen rose to leave the chapel. "He was nothing if not a good man, your Da. The man who brought the letter said you and your sister, Molly, were on his mind at last breath."

"Thank you, Sister" she said again, rushing out to a small garden next to the chapel where she sat beneath an arbor of sagging, salmon-colored roses. Not too distantly, lightning cracked amid dark thunderheads, birds complained in chorus and the wind began to rise as she tore open the letter.

My darling daughter,

 Sister Agnes is kind woman. She will accept the task of staying alert for your lovely presence in Palmyra, so that she may deliver these, my last scribblings on earth, to you.

 It's a bet you know I found our dear Michael. He was toiling hard with a good farmer near Batavia, just as I had been told. Within a fortnight after we found one another, he became his joyful self again. The only exception is the tears he sheds when his sister Molly's name is spoken.

He cared well for his little sister on the boat crossing the ocean, but when they arrived in New York, she was taken from him by a man who sells children. Nightmares of her cries when she was torn from his arms linger still. I fear, they may haunt him all his days.

Michael will fare well with the Mormons. He took their beliefs into his heart and they soothed his remorse for Molly being taken. It's a pity to see him carrying pain for not fulfilling a duty he never should have owned.

I still don't know why or how the children were stolen, but the loss of Molly scars my soul. I was told by a railroad man that a minister named Noyes from Vermont, and his son, John, have freed some children, including some young girls that were sold to slavery on the docks of New York. Noyes believes that the Second Coming of Christ has already taken place and is said to be planning a new community near the Mohawk River.

That is all the information I have to give you from these months and years of searching in America. Find Molly, Aileen. Michael has found peace and Molly's the one who needs you. You always were the strongest of us all.

Know that I go to my grave thanking God for your mother, and for Molly and Michael's, as well.

Better women never graced Ireland's shores and sweeter children were never born than to those two good women—one Catholic and one Protestant, it never mattered to me. I go to my Maker praying for forgiveness for bringing scandal upon you and Betha and for failing to protect Molly, as was my obligation. Thank you, Daughter, for coming to America to help me. Please find your sister and pray for my soul. Da

By the time she finished reading the letter, the clouds were starting to deliver rain. She returned to Jedidiah, disheveled, damp, and crestfallen, but also feeling a strange anger that was simmering close to the surface.

"He's dead, Jedidiah. My father is dead. Joseph Ryan somehow knew this. It's why he sent us here. He'll have me or ruin my life. Let's leave this place."

Jedidiah nodded and stretched his arm over her shoulder as they headed down the canal road, back to the packet to return east.

"Never have I been so alone," she stated flatly.

He pulled her under the leafy canopy of a huge maple tree to protect them from the rain.

"No. You never have to be alone," he replied seriously. He lifted his thumb and traced her jaw with it, slowly and carefully.

Glancing up at him, she saw—clearly, for the first time—the love that he had for her, and she turned away.

How bitter, she thought, to see that he truly cares for me just when I want nothing more than to be left alone with this terrible grief.

"We'll find your brother and sister. We will."

"How?"

"We'll get the counsel of Gerrit Smith. There isn't a gentleman in this land with better connections or a kinder heart. He values freedom. He'll help us."

She was inconsolable. "Help how? Can he stop Joseph Ryan from making me suffer?" She looked around feverishly. "Is he here now, watching me fall apart, spying from behind some building or tree?"

Jedidiah was silent, with a look that said he wanted to answer but could not.

The pain of such a great loss, of having come so far and learning that her father was in his grave, stung. She wondered, *"How did Rose do it? Suffer the way she did and keep a heart full of love in her chest?"*

By closing her eyes and thinking more of Rose and Jimmy and how they had given to her so selflessly and risked harm to themselves to protect her, she soothed her pain.

She looked up at Jedidiah with a sense of resolve. "I will find Molly and Michael without my father. I will think more about the children and less about Joseph Ryan and myself. "

"Of course you will," he replied.

Their packet departure was delayed because the Captain had failed to locate some needed supplies. Sun was replacing the rain clouds, and she felt her determination begin to grow in the full sunlight.

They walked from beneath the tree to a bench where the town's buildings began, and she closed her eyes and envisioned her mother's face in the tiger oak frame. Then she recalled her father shouting to her, "It could be a whole new start," before descending into the bowels of the ship that brought him to this land where he would meet his end. An image of Betha, bargaining with a tradesman, hands on her hips and fury in her eyes, also played before her and gave her strength.

Jedidiah's hand reached out, and, with a white handkerchief, he wiped the tears that were slipping down her face.

"We'll not give up, Aileen," he said, repeated with strength of conviction.

Then he raised her hands to his mouth and kissed them.

"We'll not give up ever. If it takes our whole lives."

Our lives? What is he saying?

"You. . .understand, don't you?" she implored, "that I can't give up this search?"

This good and handsome young American, with his open heart, close, loving family, and head full of dreams, actually understands my plight. I can see it in his eyes.

"Grandmother is all I have left, Jedidiah, and she's across the sea. I'm alone. I've not a single notion how to find Molly and Michael. I'm in this country that I don't understand, and if I can't find the children, there will be no peace for me here or anywhere."

Jedidiah pressed her hands together between his larger ones. She leaned against him and felt his warmth and racing pulse.

Holding her close, he lifted her chin and gently touched his forehead to hers. When he spoke, she could feel his warm breath on her face.

"You are not lost. You are not alone. As long as I draw breath, you'll not be alone. You are the bravest, smartest. . . ." He stopped, and swallowed hard before he could go on. "I never dreamt that someone as fine as you, with your caring heart and hate for injustice, someone as brave and lovely as you—I never dreamt a woman as fine and good as Aileen O'Malley would come into my life." He touched the birthmark on her left cheek. "Even this, is perfect."

She stared at him, feeling her heart begin to race. *Where is he going with this?*

"Aileen, you question with the clearest of hearts. You probe the truth and search for faith. You teach me to see a larger world, the bitter and the sweet. I love discovering what is right and what is wrong through your eyes, and knowing we agree."

He held his breath for a moment, then looked into her eyes. "Marry me, Aileen. Will you, please, marry me?"

If he wants me to be his wife when I am so sad and in despair, well then, this is the man I should spend my life with, the man I've been trying not to fall in love with all this time.

"My first impressions of you were that you were brash and full of yourself, drawn to strange religions and far too bold. I was wrong. So wrong. You are the very best of men, Jedidiah Tracey, and yes, I will marry you."

He slid one hand behind her neck and drew her face close so he could kiss her. With the other hand, he stroked her dark curls, neck, and face. She closed her eyes, drank in his affection, and recalled him striding into the dining room at the Rawson's with the sun on his face and a copy of the Troy Journal meant for her beneath his arm.

How great the chasm she had crossed, from that place in Troy where she'd felt she could hardly tolerate him, to this moment, when she was sure she wanted only him, forever.

They kissed again just as a couple marched past them toward the Canal. The woman coughed loudly to signal her disapproval of their public show of affection.

"And to think you dance with the Shakers," Aileen said, ignoring the woman and musing. Grandmother would certainly not approve.

But then, she's over there in Ireland, isn't she? And we're here. I will write her right away."

In a little while, they rose and walked, hand-in-hand, back to the packet heading east, where they would go back to the Rawsons' and tell them of their plans.

Just before they boarded their boat, Aileen's thoughts wandered over the events of the last few days. *So much darkness and so much light. Father is gone, yet I have a growing love in my heart. Molly is lost but I am exactly where I belong. This is what the Captain's wife meant about choosing the roses, thorns and all.*

That afternoon, she reached for her rosary and found herself able to pray for the first time in days.

Thank you, Lord. Loving and trusting Jedidiah feels as natural as a morning walk. Nothing I've ever felt has resided within my soul with such certainty, so softly and true. Help me to find Molly, Lord.

As they descended the stairs from the roof of the packet that evening, Jedidiah slipped ahead of her. At the bottom, he turned, reached up and gripped her waist with his large hands, lifting her down until she was standing directly in front of him. He did not take his hands off her waist.

At this close range, she sensed something different in his demeanor and felt a sudden rash of heat on her neck.

"I enjoy holding you."

His hands moved up her body a little, and his thumbs gently pressed against her ribs. When she didn't pull away, he said, "I could do this over and over—for years."

Tongue-tied and unable to respond, she stepped around him, hurried down half the length of the packet, and entered the ladies' sleeping quarters which were concealed behind a thick red drape.

Shaking a little, she removed some clothing and lay down on her bunk, pulling the quilt up around her chin. Her body was on fire and her mind raced at the excitement of his touch. She admitted to herself it was the same thrill she had experienced the first time he walked into Keating Rawson's home.

Now, she imagined Jedidiah across from her and imagined his head full of wavy hair and his strong body resting next to her own. As a good, young, Catholic woman, she had forbidden these thoughts when they had tried to arise before. She did no longer, and what felt like a fire below her waist kept her awake for hours.

14

COMMITMENT

"How will this country ever survive with a stain this dark growing at its heart?" she posed to Jedidiah the next morning while holding a poster with a drawing of a runaway slave and an offer of one hundred dollars for her return. It read,

$100 REWARD—Mulatto Woman, Maria

30 to 35 years of age and stout.

Ran away or decoyed from the subscriber living near Beltsville, Prince George's County, Maryland.

Aileen carefully looked around, then crumpled the paper into a ball and stuffed it in her bag. "There will be fewer eyes on this drawing going east," she said with satisfaction. Then her expression changed. She was excited.

"The drawings, they must work or they wouldn't pay to have them made. Perhaps I could have some drawings made and printed of Molly and Michael!"

Her green eyes sparkled as she looked at Jedidiah, proud of her idea and thrilled at the prospect of finding a new way to search for the two young ones.

Jedidiah's face lit up. "Brilliant, Aileen. I'll add a reward and we'll have them distributed by our agents all up and down the length of the Canal. Can you recall the children's faces well enough for an artist to make their likeness?"

Of course, she could recall them, their smiling faces haunted her. "Yes, I can," she answered quietly.

Jedidiah's tender attention, and a long winter's rest after the arduous trip west, restored Aileen's spirit. Staying with the Rawsons was like settling into the heart of a family, hers now. The snow-covered streets of Troy had a fairytale quality. She and Jedidiah often raced through them on a horse drawn sleigh, their legs huddled beneath goat-fur blankets.

"I won't be going back to Ireland. I sensed it at the docks in Cork, but now I am certain," she said to him in front of the fire one evening.

"You'll miss her, your Betha, and the hills of Kildare," he replied. "But we'll make a grand life here, I promise you that."

"I am posting her letter tomorrow." Aileen pressed the red sealing wax onto her most recent letter to Betha and placed it in a basket by the door.

She had related her father's death, despite knowing this news would not pain the old woman then told of her decision to marry Jedidiah.

He is as good and strong a man as you've ever known, Grandmother. He has made it possible for me to imagine a future filled with good work, kindness, and love. When I stepped on the ship in Cork, I never imagined this. I hated leaving you. You know that. Thank you for helping me escape Joseph Ryan. A life with him would have taken me to an early grave. I don't understand why his eyes stay trained on the likes of me. He says it's to do with our "family history" and we have none that I'm aware of. I thought he'd be married and have sired his first-born by now.

Don't you find it grand that Jedidiah and I found one another in the home of your dearest friend? You and Annie would be pleased to see me take the sacrament of matrimony with someone who shares so many of the principles I learned from you. You can believe it, Grandmother. We will work hard and build a life that will make you proud.

The slavery and injustice are rising here like yeast in the soil. But there's also a hopefulness here that's not to be found in Kildare or Killarney. It is an "experiment" in self-governance, they say. As you know, the Irish love an experiment, and I'm no exception.

You took risks for the good of our homeland during the uprising. I sense I may need to do the same for this, my adopted land.

We've hatched a new plan for finding the wee ones. We'll have an artist draw their dear faces with pen and ink. Then we'll print them up, offer a reward, and spread the flyers up and down the Erie. Say a prayer at St. Brigid's on Sunday that we succeed. Perhaps the children will have a chance to finish a life well that started so

*poorly. Pray, too, that I can put this pain that weighs
so heavily on my soul behind me. I fear it may consume
me if I cannot.*

Your loving and devoted granddaughter,
Aileen

The following spring they married with Keating, Sara, and John looking on as the beaming couple, caught up in one other, declared their vows beneath an arbor covered in Annie's sunflowers.

Clearing his throat several times and blinking hard against rising tears, Jedidiah repeated after the priest, "I take you, Aileen, to be my wife, for better or worse, in sickness and health, as long as we both shall live."

Remembering a passage from the Old Testament book of Ruth, she whispered to Jedidiah, "Wherever you go, I will go. . . ."

The following week, while walking with Sara in Annie's garden, Sara said to her, "You're so in love with Jedidiah. It's lovely and plain to see. I only hope you can keep him safe." Aileen startled. "Safe? What would threaten him?"

"Those who hate abolitionists."

The moment the words came out it was obvious Sara regretted them. "Oh, I should never have said such a thing. I am so sorry. Here's you, newly wedded to the man you love, and here I am saying dark things. Forgive me and forget my foolish words. Please."

"There is nothing to forgive." Aileen laughed and her voice became quiet and conspiratorial. "But do wish me luck in keeping up with him. He is passionate, and that's all I'll say. You'll not hear another sentence from me about that."

Sara looked at her with a curious smile.

"Well," Aileen added, with a devilish look, "not unless you ask."

That spring, a copy of The Liberator, published by William Lloyd Garrison of Boston, was included in the pile of newspapers and pamphlets thrown on the Rawson breakfast table. Jedidiah picked it up.

"I find him admirable, this man, Garrison."

"Yes," Aileen agreed "He's got it right. Half-measures are folly. The slave owners are as bad as the thieves who stole my siblings."

"The impulse for freedom is like hunger," said Sara. "It can be delayed but not denied."

"The escapees show such bravery,." said Aileen. "They steal away in the night, often with no shoes or food, only to be chased by dogs, beaten, and sent further south with irons round their necks if they're caught. Those who make it to freedom, usually young men, only do so with the expert help of free Negroes and a few Quakers. Those who succeed have still lost their families."

"Garrison attacks the colonization movement, too," Jedidiah added, looking at an article on the bottom of the page. "Even some Quakers think it's right to send Negroes to Liberia. Even my friend Gerrit Smith once supported those efforts, but no more."

Keating entered the room and stopped for a moment to take it in. "Annie would have wanted this," he said, pleased. "She would have wanted this as well."

He placed two piles of posters on the table before them.

The first carried an image of Michael. Aileen had painstakingly guided the artist and enlisted the help of those in Palmyra who saw him before he left for the west. She had enjoyed describing every curve and mark on her brother's face and was pleased with the result. The poster read,

$100 REWARD

For information leading to the location of the boy Michael O'Malley. Stolen by kidnappers from his family in Kildare, Ireland, along with his sister, Molly, in 1831. Approximately 13 years old, freckles, brown hair, approximately 5'8" tall, sturdy build. Last seen traveling west from Palmyra, New York. May be in the company of the Mormon followers of Joseph Smith. His loving sister, Aileen, wishes to be contacted with any information regarding his whereabouts via Gerrit Smith of Peterboro, New York.

Jedidiah had received Smith's permission to use his name. It would lend the reward credence because Smith was well-known as a businessman and man of character throughout the territory.

Molly's rendering was also quite skillfully done, but it made Aileen sad to see her image, which was a combination of the happy, curly haired child she was in Ireland and the sad, unkept girl tied to the packet boat in Little Falls. The poster read,

$100 REWARD

For information leading to the location of Molly O'Malley Stolen from her family in Kildare, Ireland, and shipped to America. Separated from her brother, Michael, and last seen on the docks of New York City in 1831. Now approximately 11 years old, reddish, blond curly hair, green eyes. Her loving sister, Aileen, wishes to be contacted with any information concerning her whereabouts via Gerrit Smith, Peterboro, New York.

"We'll place fifty in the penny presses across the Canal and have fifty posted near the ports by Jedidiah's agents," said Keating.

Again, he used the term "agents". This time it stuck in her mind. She knew he transacted with farmers on the grain needed to make malt and brewers on the dried finished product, but why were they called "agents"?

Soon a letter arrived indicating that a false lead had been given to Gerrit Smith. Jedidiah seemed to be in more frequent contact with him now, though he spoke very little about it.

Dearest Aileen and Jedidiah,

I received a visitor yesterday, a young vagrant holding the poster with Michael's face. He claimed to have seen Michael in Buffalo, but upon interrogation could not recite a single detail. My sources tell me this fellow is a wayward drunk, notoriously untrustworthy and looking for cash. I gave the poor fellow the warmth of a hot bath and a good meal and sent him on his way. I regret that Ann and I were unable to travel to Troy for your nuptials. I had committed to speaking at the Hamilton College graduation in Clinton, New York, that week and Ann was in Philadelphia with our daughter. You know we wish you both every happiness the Lord can bring.

Yours very truly.
Gerrit Smith

Gerrit Smith had taken the trouble to write to them, wishing them well. This mystified and pleased her.

To keep her spirits up, Jedidiah took her for walks along the Hudson, sometimes going to the docks to see the vessels arriving with immigrants from many lands.

On one such walk, Jedidiah saw an old friend. They had just stopped to talk when she recognized the finely-dressed steward from her steamer trip up the Hudson. "Mr. Myers," she exclaimed, moving alone toward him.

Stephen Myers seemed startled by her greeting and studiously ignored her. Quickly, he finished directing two young men who were moving a large, wooden barrel off the steamer and onto a wagon pulled by two strong draft horses. When the men nearly dropped the barrel, Myers barked at them. "Be careful with that." His agitation confirmed what she suspected, the "goods" inside were precious, indeed.

Abolitionists had told her and Jedidiah about the work of Stephen and Harriett Myers of Albany. They were known for publishing reform newspapers for free Negroes and having, according to New York City Abolitionist leader David Ruggles, "the best organized section of the Underground Railroad in New York State."

Part of their organization involved shipping escaping slaves up the Hudson River to Troy in wooden barrels. From there, the "cargo" was driven north to the border and across the St. Lawrence by fishing vessel to Canada. Sometimes, however, the north was rife with slave hunters, eager to slip chains around the terrified escapees and even take off a part of their foot as punishment for fleeing. These hunters were making the northern Hudson to St. Lawrence River route a particularly treacherous one as of late.

Casually, she approached Myers and stuck out her hand. Clearly, he did not remember her or at least he acted as if he didn't.

In a very quiet voice she said, "Sir, I am a friend of Mr. Gerrit Smith. He knows captains in Oswego who carry cargo on western routes to Canada if need be. I've heard it's difficult crossing north of here at this time."

A light breeze coming up the river ruffled the hem of Myers' waistcoat and he studied her for a long moment before responding.

Well, Miss," he said, tipping his hat, "it can be a great challenge shipping salted fish to Canada at any time." His face remained expressionless.

She nodded and kept her voice low. "I'm quite sure the captains I know can help. In fact, they are most eager to."

Slowly, as if he were searching for something inside the wagon, he scanned the docks and surrounding warehouses. No one seemed to be watching them, though Aileen knew they could not be certain. "Contact me in Albany," he said quickly in a whisper. "I cannot do business with you here."

He produced a scrap of paper and a pencil from his waistcoat and hastily wrote down an address—194 Livingston Avenue. Then, looking around again, he slipped it into her hand and, giving the reins a shake, drove his wagon quickly away from the docks.

Watching him leave with his "cargo", it suddenly made complete sense to her why the Hudson would be an important path for slaves seeking freedom. Stewards like Myers and other free Negroes worked on the steamboats that plied its waters. Of course they were a driving force behind successful escapes.

She also knew it was possible to disguise escapees as free Negroes in New York State where gradual emancipation had been passed as a law in 1817. The law was flawed in that it required slaves to remain in bondage until they reached twenty-one years of age, but it had freed many people. False papers identifying slaves as free Negroes were starting to be created at print shops along the Canal.

"William Still of Philadelphia and David Ruggles of New York are the primary strategists for escapees in the northeast," Jedidiah explained when they were back at the Rawsons. "Some Quakers like John Germain, the man we met who rescued the toddler in Port Byron, have been helpful, as well."

Can I be a part of this, helping runaways reach lives of freedom? I was a runaway. People helped me.

She had asked herself this question many times in recent months. Now, her unexpected encounter with Myers told her she should try.

"Don't be angry with me," Jedidiah said, taking both Aileen's hands in his. "I have involved us—involved myself, rather—in work you may not want me to take on."

"You mean in the work of abolition? Why would I not want you to do this?"

She lifted his hand to her lips and kissed it. "Dear husband, do you think I know so little about you? I sensed your growing anger during our travels—the girl tied to a boat rail, the Negro child sold, even the news about my father stuck in forced labor. I felt your anger. I am angry as well."

"Why do so many do nothing?"

She leaned close and took his face in her hands. "I don't know, but I do know that is not how you are made. I have sensed your abolitionist work, your contact with Gerrit Smith, plus the fact that you have 'agents' up and down the Canal."

"I knew you were still in grief at the loss of your father and didn't want to add to your concerns."

She kissed his hands.

He smiled and explained his plans. "Through contacts arranged by Gerrit Smith, I plan to become adept at negotiating transport for escapees from Mr. Stephen Myers' home in Albany to Gerrit's home in Peterboro, then on to Oswego and to Canada and freedom.

"Yes. I feel it in my heart as well. I spoke with Stephen Myers about this today."

Jedidiah stared at her, stunned.

"I also must move further west to continue my search for Molly and Michael. The posters have brought in so few leads."

Later that evening, thinking once again of her stolen siblings and the rushed escape that she, Rose, and Jimmy had taken north, she recalled something Myers said standing beside her on the deck of the packet boat from New York City. He'd looked at the waves and said, "You can almost feel um. . . .so many dreams of freedom coming up this river."

PART THREE

1835-1840

---

*"Even murder is less a crime
than slavery."*

**In a letter from Gerrit Smith to his cousin,
Elizabeth Cady Stanton**

15

GENTLEMEN
OF WEALTH AND
STANDING

"Please be cautious. You know you'll be in constant danger, don't you?" said Sara, her look dark with concern. "Anti-abolitionist sentiments are running so high."

"I have my statue of Mary with me" Aileen responded brightly. She reached into her bag to prove her point and took note, once again of the statue's deeply scarred cheek. "If you hear anything from Rose, please let me know right away."

"You know I will. Curious that no one knows her whereabouts." Sara embraced Aileen and hurried back inside her home to conceal the sadness she was feeling at her departure.

Aileen loaded the last of her cases into the wagon and hoisted herself up onto the seat, to wait for Jedidiah to finish saying his good-byes to Keating. She was pleased with the plans they had made to own and live above a mercantile store along the new feeder canal in the Village of Fayetteville. This decision promised a decent living and placed them in a strategic location, east of Syracuse for their secret dealings between Peterboro and Oswego.

Soon after settling into their new home, they traveled to Utica for a gathering of abolitionists. It was October and six hundred people were expected to convene for the purpose of forming the New York Anti-Slavery Society. They found a pew near the back and watched the seats fill rapidly.

"So glad to see you here," said a Negro man in a gray, gabardine vest and jacket. He pumped Jedidiah's hand and tipped his hat to Aileen. "You two are a force we very much need."

"Was that Douglass?" she asked.

"Indeed, it is" replied Jedidiah, flushed with excitement at the size of the gathering.

"We sent some 'packages' his way, did we not?"

"Yes, when Gerrit's man in Oswego was under surveillance, we arranged a transport to Rochester and Douglass."

"Captain Dodge is here and the Murphys from Pompey Hill," she noted.

"He was an Irish peddler, that Murphy. Now he's getting Irish immigrants to trudge up Pompey Hill, making the place Catholic and Abolitionist, as well."

She saw the familiar face of the Quaker, John Germain from Port Byron, and waved to him across the room.

Soon Alvan Stewart, the brilliant lawyer from Cherry Valley, took the podium to open the proceedings. "Slavery desecrates our nation, saps our strength, and makes a mockery of our American Constitution," he bellowed to loud applause.

"There are troublemakers outside," Jedidiah whispered to Aileen. "So-called gentlemen of wealth and standing who persuaded the City Council to rescind their permission for us to meet at the Utica Academy. That is why we are cramped into this space."

"They see slavery as an economic necessity. We see it as a path to ruin." She responded. "Some of the fellows lingering are full with liquor."

The sanctuary was filled to standing room only now, and Gerrit Smith crowded into the pew where they were sitting.

This was Aileen's first chance to study the man who her husband admired above everyone else. Smith was the beneficiary of a fortune made by his father who worked in the fur trade and real estate with John Jacob Astor. Jedidiah had partnered with him on a small land deal in Eagle Village and found his attitude toward the Oneida nation surprising and enlightened. Everyone there was aware of Gerrit Smith's presence. His immense wealth and reputation for fairness and generosity were renowned and he struck a tall imposing figure.

He nodded in greeting to Aileen. "You are as lovely as your husband described you. Come soon to our home in Peterboro and meet my dear wife, Ann."

To Jedidiah he said, "I will be a spectator here this morning, nothing more. Glad you invited me. I want to learn."

"There will be no disagreement on the resolution," Jedidiah responded." Would you like to meet Reverend Beriah Green while you're here? He runs the Oneida Institute of Whitesboro."

"Yes, I would like that very much."

Aileen stayed in the pew, feeling happy about the large number of people who had traveled long distances to join forces for abolition on this striking autumn day.

Is this how Grandmother felt during meetings of the United Uprising?

Sunlight dove through the stained-glass windows and seemed to light the floor beneath their feet. As Jedidiah had predicted, the meeting was proceeding congenially.

Just as those in attendance prepared to vote on the resolution creating the New York Anti-Slavery Society, a low rumbling sound crept into the room. Confused and curious looks passed all around, and the noise grew to a roar of angry male voices. Suddenly a mob banged open the doors and pushed inside the church.

"Oh, dear Lord," Aileen said, stricken with horror.

A large group of anti-abolitionists came storming down the center aisle, pushing people down and shouting "traitors."

One of the intruders, stumbling and obviously drunk, ran to the altar waving an American flag. He shouted, "Leave, you troublemakers. You'll not shame us by meeting here! This is our country and our city."

Others began hurling brass candle sticks and hymnals and swinging wooden canes at the abolitionists in their pews. Smith's brow furrowed. He stood and loudly exclaimed, "How dare thee?" to the man stepping into the pulpit.

"Congressman Sam Beardsley of Utica," Smith bellowed, "how dare you stand in the spot where the gospel of our Lord is preached and deny these Americans their right to assemble?"

"I demand that this anti-slavery meeting be disbanded!" Beardsley shouted over the uproar. Smith leapt to his feet and strode directly toward him, eyes flashing.

"We are Americans, Sir!" Smith bellowed, glaring. "It is our right to assemble and to speak our minds."

The room fell silent. Turning his back to Beardsley as though dismissing an errant school boy, Smith smiled at the shaken crowd and it quieted the room.

"I invite all of you to Peterboro," he explained. "I can guarantee you will have a peaceful meeting there." I know you have already traveled far, but trust me when I say, the people of Peterboro will make you welcome."

He took a deep breath and scowled at Beardsley and his mob before continuing. "In Peterboro, citizens experience human kindness and American civility. There you can complete the work you started here today."

The abolitionists began talking among themselves and shaking their heads in affirmation.

"I'll hire a Canal captain and barge to bring those of you without horse and wagon to Canastota. Then we will enlist help to get you up the hill to Peterboro.

Stepping toward Aileen, Smith took her arm. "Perhaps you will get to meet my Ann much sooner than we expected."

Leaving the church with Aileen on his right arm and Jedidiah walking on his left, Smith was about to shout to the crowd again when he was hit in the forehead by an egg and then with a lump of mud. With careful dignity, he reached for his ascot, stared across the church at the enraged mob, and wiped his large head clean.

At that moment, a large piece of angle iron flew past Jedidiah's head, just missing him. The hunk of metal lying on the ground was large enough to have smashed in his skull.

From the group of six hundred abolitionists who had convened in Utica for the first meeting of the New York State Anti-Slavery Society, four hundred were soon traveling by horse, wagon, and canal barge over twenty-seven, rain-sodden miles to Peterboro.

Aileen and Jedidiah rode the lumber barge having given their horse and wagon to a lame man from Buffalo. The Canal ride was damp and cold, and they huddled closely listening to a young Quaker woman sing hymns. They were touched by one in particular:

My life goes on in endless song above earth's
lamentation,

I hear the real though far-off hymn that hails a new
creation!

No storm can shake my inmost calm, while to that
Rock I'm clinging,

Since Love is Lord of Heaven and Earth—how can I
keep from singing?

The words penetrated Aileen's fear and gave her comfort. *Maybe God's love will rule after all.*

In the bliss of that belief, she managed to get several hours of sleep resting in Jedidiah's arms as the barge moved down the night Canal.

Jedidiah was thrilled by the spectacle of one hundred four abolitionists disembarking the lumber barge on the banks of the Erie Canal in Canastota and marching up the steep nine-mile hill to Peterboro, The exhausted travelers did not wait for wagons. They sang freedom songs as they made the trek and shouted to farmers along the way.

"Has war begun?" A farmer yelled from his barn.

"The war on slavery," a walker responded. "Come to Peterboro, and join the fight."

"I failed to understand," said Jedidiah to Alvan Stewart as they finished the climb. "Our movement has stirred the passions of so many."

The white clocktower of the Presbyterian Church came into view. Smith's columned mansion was on their left as they walked toward it. "Gerrit is so outraged by Beardsley and the mob," added Stewart, "he has embraced immediatism."

"With Gerrit Smith behind our cause," responded Jedidiah, "we will prevail."

Although she shared his optimism, the violent attack in Utica and near deadly assault on Jedidiah had shaken Aileen.

Soon however, the friendliness of their fellow citizens in Fayetteville and Manlius helped to cheer her. Their neighbors carried home anti-slavery bulletins from the store along with the flour and nails they purchased there. Asked by Dr. Hezekiah Joslyn and his wife, Helen, to speak about slavery at community gatherings, they did so, often recanting the horrible suicide they had witnessed in Port Byron.

When a packet boat captain strode into their dry goods store and stared at the posters of Molly and Michael hanging on the wall above the counter, she felt suspicious of his intent.

"It's Gerrit Smith that's looking for these children, is it?" he asked Jedidiah, who was filling a barrel of flour from three huge burlap sacks just retrieved from the mill.

"Yes. Do you know something of the children?"

"Smith's trouble, he is. Helping them runaways. What's he doing looking for these children? They ain't colored."

Jedidiah held his tongue and repeated, "Do you have information about these children?"

"Maybe I do. What's your interest?" the man replied.

Jedidiah shot back, "They are my wife's brother and sister who were kidnapped and sold."

The Captain seemed to be calculating the connection between Jedidiah and Gerrit Smith for a moment but replied, "Negroes is one thing. The Bible says they are the sons and daughters of Ham, cursed with the yoke of slavery. But white children, that's another matter. I saw that boy at a farm in Batavia some while ago. He looked, oh, thirteen or fourteen years old."

"The likeness is similar?"

"A friendly and decent young chap, as I recall."

"We learned he had been helping on a farm in Batavia. He was allowed by his employer to go to his father who had traveled to Palmyra in search of him. But the boy's dad is dead, and the lad is no longer there. He went west, they say, with the Mormons. Ever see him again, after Batavia?"

"No, can't say that I have, and it's a pity. My boat needs repairs. Could've used the reward."

"Should you ever come upon him again, would you let us know, Sir?"

"I will."

Jedidiah retrieved a bag of carrots from behind the counter and handed them to the man.

"So, your only business with Smith, that troublemaker, is having him search for your wife's lost kin?"

Jedidiah handed him his carrots and did not reply.

"I hope for your sake you're not in cahoots with Smith," he called on his way out the door."

The posters of the children caught many eyes. One morning as Aileen dusted and straightened the front of the store, she stopped and stared longingly at them. So much more time had passed, she questioned whether the drawings still bore any likeness to Molly and

Michael and prayed they did.

They continued their work as anti-abolitionist riots broke out in Central New York, Boston and Philadelphia. The U.S. Congress issued a gag order, forbidding representatives to introduce official anti-slavery legislation. Jedidiah had almost been seized by two men from the south searching for runaways who had stormed a small meeting at one of Gerrit Smith's properties close to the Canadian border

"That boy is lifting canal gates in Lockport."

She turned to see a gray-haired, bearded man with a deep voice squint at the posters as soon as he entered the store.

"Welcome to Fayetteville. What makes you believe so, Sir?"

"Well, he's a bit under six feet now. Tall, like yourself. The freckles and the grin look right. Resembles a lad of Irish stock. They call him Mickey, they do."

Afraid to become hopeful, she thought of the hundreds of fifteen-year-old Irish boys with freckles who could be found working on the Canal.

"And he was always whistling that one, whistling a jig." He nodded at her respectfully. "My name's Abner Wood."

Then he began whistling "The Wind that Shakes the Barley", a tune Thomas O'Malley had sung all his life.

Aileen felt a jolt of longing and excitement as she envisioned her father, strolling up the old church road singing, with Molly on his shoulders and Michael whistling that tune at his side.

"Mr. Wood, can you possibly travel with my husband to Peterboro? It isn't far from here. I want Gerrit Smith to hear what you have to say."

The man agreed. When they returned the next day, he happily held part of the reward in his saddlebag with a promise from Smith for more if he were to travel west and return with Michael.

Lockport was the first legitimate sounding lead they had garnered since the posters were printed. Feeling hopeful, she reached her arms around Jedidiah's neck and rested her face on his chest.

"It's so good to feel a bit of sunshine isn't it darlin? I can feel our baby growin too, healthy and strong, and maybe, just maybe, Michael's coming home. The rest is all so sad. The violence and people not listening to one another. They say the north and south could even go to war."

"Old men standing around a dry goods store say things like that. It's just talk. Americans will never take up arms against other Americans."

That evening she said the rosary for the first time in months. Kneeling in their upstairs bedroom before the statue of the Blessed Mother with the chip in her cheek, she reached for her jade beads with the silver crucifix and placed them back in her apron pocket.

The next morning, as they sipped coffee and ate corn biscuits, Jedidiah gave Aileen a wink and stood to leave the room. She knew the signal. He was helping a freedom seeker who was arriving from Peterboro on the underground railroad. They were becoming known for providing comfort and assistance to "packages of hardware"—men—and "dry goods"—women—seeking freedom.

She remained painfully aware that Smith, a powerful and wealthy landowner, was more insulated from harm than her husband, the owner of a modest store along Fayetteville's feeder canal.

Before Jedidiah departed, she went to him and said, "I'm finding it hard to sleep. I fear for you all of the time now. I know our work is needed and I share your glee when we succeed in delivering another 'package' to John Edwards in Oswego." She stopped and cried for a moment before continuing. "I just regret that we live in a place and at a time when people are persecuted for doing what's right."

Jedidiah returned her embrace and solemnly went downstairs to the warehouse.

To calm her nerves she moved to the harpsicord in their front parlor and began playing a waltz. When she heard music, for some reason, she thought of Rose.

Why no replies to all those letters?

She had even paid a man to go to Saratoga in search of her, to no avail.

Rose would understand my fear. How I miss her.

Then she played Sinngedichte, by a young Viennese composer named Johann Strauss. Grandmother told her in a letter that when he first played it some months ago for an audience in Vienna, he had to play it again, and again—nineteen times.

I know our cause is right.

She thought of the couple that passed through their store a fortnight ago. The man was scarred from his waistbands to his neck and his wife had lost four children from abuse in the fields. The scars of their abuse made them even more determined to risk all and find freedom.

If our fortune and friendships, even our lives, are the cost of helping these brave people to begin anew, so be it.

She felt the exhilaration of helping that couple reach Canada. Yet something troubled her—the feeling that a noose of violence was tightening around all their necks. Later that evening, without thinking, she unhooked Annie Eustice's necklace engraved with keys from around her neck. She had worn it almost every day since her grandmother placed it around her neck. Just then, the center medallion slipped from the chain, fell into her lap, then slid off her skirt onto the floor. Carefully, she picked it up and studied it.

My grandmother was sent this by her dearest friend who hastily left Ireland to come to America. Why? And why did Annie send this back to Betha? Why did Grandmother give it to me?

She looked at the medallion longer, studying its intricate design carefully.

Keys speak of the power to both open things and close them.

Impulsively, she went to the hallway and slid the medallion into the inside pocket of Jedidiah's coat.

Then, loud voices outdoors startled her. Jedidiah was conferring with some men on horseback. She watched them from the porch then made her way down the stairwell just in time to see Jedidiah putting on his coat.

"What's happening?"

"Gentlemen of wealth and standing are burning Alvin Stewart and Beriah Greene," he replied sarcastically.

"Dear God. Burning?"

"No, burning them in effigy. This is happening in Boston and South Carolina as well. Wealthy men in top hats are creating anti-abolition riots to keep cheap cotton coming into their mills. I must check on Alvan with the others."

Wrapping his arms around her, Jedidiah pulled her to his chest. Outside, maple trees were losing the last of their fall color, dropping and turning gray. He studied her face, and kissed her softly on her lips. "Please get some rest, and don't worry. I'll ride with Gerrit and the others to ensure Stewart's safety."

"Jedidiah, please be alert for treachery. I feel a shift in my bones. These thugs are everywhere. They've been paid by the merchants and politicians to attack us. Violence against effigies will not satisfy the mob."

He drew her close again and breathed deeply. She felt the rhythm of his heart and his warmth.

"We belong here, Aileen, doing this work, loving this land, making America a place for our children."

She placed her hand lightly on her stomach. Feeling her gesture, he eased her away from his body, and his eyes sparkled. "We'd best be thinking of names soon."

Her own mother's death in childbirth haunted her, but this moment, with danger all around them, love and hope overcame her fear.

He whispered in her ear. "Thank you."

"Ride carefully," she whispered back. Her mind raced with images of the riot in Utica weeks before.

Jedidiah stepped away and mounted his horse, joining a group of men in carriages and on horseback. Amid anxious conversations and the sound of horses being aligned, they set out on the muddy path that led east.

As he left, Jedidiah called back to her. "I will see you back here tomorrow."

She felt a rush of deepest love followed by a rush of apprehension but would not let herself give in to fear.

He's travelling in a group. He'll be safe. He has to be safe.

By day's end, Aileen took comfort in the fact that she had firmly placed the keys medallion inside Jedidiah's coat next to his heart.

Pulling up their horses at a hotel in the small village of Vernon, Gerrit and Jedidiah's troupe halted, in need of water, feed and rooms for the night. A messenger from Utica had arrived and told them that

Stewart was safe. It was well past midnight, and they were exhausted. They fell asleep four men to a room.

Jedidiah was startled awake in the dark by the sound of shattering glass. He leapt from his bedroll and plunged down the stairs followed by several other men. In the entryway of the hotel they discovered, to their disgust, a bloody calf's head wrapped in rags on the floor. Cold November air came through the broken glass of the front window, and men's voices could be heard outside—a dozen or more by the sound of it—from the direction of the carriages, hollering and laughing.

Charging out onto the porch, Jedidiah ducked a blazing torch that narrowly missed his head and sailed inside the hotel. From behind, he could hear the other men shouting and stomping out the fire. From the darkness, more torches were thrown, smashing in more windows, and in only moments, black smoke and yellow flames ran up the draperies, rapidly catching the furniture and wooden walls on fire.

There was chaos and shouting from inside and outside the hotel as Jedidiah dashed back inside, at first joining the bucket brigade and then abandoning it as the old building roared into conflagration. They had to charge outside quickly or be burned alive.

Several hours later, with help from villagers, the fire was extinguished and the hotel residents, all of whom survived the catastrophe, were wrapped in blankets and taken to the general store to recover. Gerrit Smith was simmering in silent fury as he located his horse, then searched for Jedidiah, who was nowhere to be seen. His inquiries led nowhere. Few of the men who had followed Jedidiah down the stairs remembered when they had lost sight of him.

"There were more horses arriving," said one man, "I think he stepped around back to see if the attackers were regrouping."

No one recalled seeing him return to the General Store. Smith contemplated: Maybe he had ridden ahead? But would he have abandoned his mates in a crisis? Jedidiah? Never!

Frustrated and as angry as he had ever been, Smith formed a resolution in his heart and spoke it to those gathered in the store.

"I will give escapees all that I can, money, and the land they must own to have the right to vote. I will never again be so deeply ashamed of my nation, as I am tonight."

He took one last ride around the village looking for signs of Jedidiah. Finding none, he rode on as rays of red sunlight streaked above the horizon of the Mohawk Valley.

16

RYAN'S RETURN

Aileen stared out the window, as she had done throughout the winter months, while she lived with the mystery and misery of Jedidiah's disappearance. Spring had come, and the closer she moved toward her time of delivery, the greater was her grief. The roads east and west of the store in Fayetteville remained empty of him and there was no word.

She reached for her grandmother's letter, the one that had arrived last month, and sat at the breakfast table to read it once again.

Dearest Aileen;

The news that you are with child made me dance a jig with Polly Brady on the sidewalk outside St. Brigid's last Sunday morning. I admit, I'm hoping for a girl with the same green eyes and black curls as you and your Mumm. 'Dark Irish' they called the both of you, saying the Spaniards dallied with our ancestors long ago.

Dark or light I care not a wit, you were each the loveliest lass in Kildare when you graced this land.

I'm sad to have some distressing news to report. Our plan for that scoundrel, Joseph Ryan, has failed. He never fell in for our scheme to rid you of him. He discovered, down at the wharfs in Cork, that you'd gone to America and was enraged. Apparently, he set about finding you like a hungry dog in a famine. The eejit charmed Mary McDermott at the post office and the silly girl alerts him when letters arrive from you. This is how he found your location and I know not what he'll do now that he has. Ryan's perfectly mortified that he wanted you and you crossed the sea to avoid him. There's something more with his obsession for you that I still fail to understand. I've not seen or heard a lick about him for weeks so he may have made a crossing to find you on his own.

Father Murphy turned red about the neck when I questioned him on this. That's a sign the two of them are up to some shenanigans once more.

So beware my darling girl. I worry less about Ryan than I might, knowing your fine husband is with you and would likely box him about the ears should Ryan try to cause you harm.
Eat well for the baby, darlin, and do write me with news of your running of the railroad. I am ever so proud of you.

Your loving Granny

Aileen rose and gazed out at the street from the place where she and Jedidiah had made their home above the store. She had stayed here, rather than return to Troy, in hopes he would return as soon as possible. She dropped the letter back into the gray tin bowl on the table.

But my fine husband is not with me, Granny. I am pregnant and alone.

In her mind, Jedidiah had been taken and was being held. As soon as a ransom note appeared, she would do whatever she had to to raise the money to free him or find a way to do whatever his captors demanded.

Maybe he's been put in prison for helping a runaway? Should I ask the sheriff?

She had hired two young men from local farms, Daniel and Harry, to help her manage the store, make deliveries, and allow her brief afternoon rests when possible. She joined Daniel on the front porch as he swept yesterday's soot.

"Another new mills' opened Ma'am. It'll be good for business."

"Yes, I suppose it will. Daniel, did you see that Max, the Coffey's gardener, was taken south by slavers?"

"I did see that, yes, Ma'am, and a sorry thing it is."

"Did your grandfather fight in the Revolution, Daniel?"

"No Ma'am, he had a bad leg, but my great uncle John Coffey did. He was given the land we live on today for fighting with Washington. I'm told he hated the Brits."

"What do you think he would have said about Max being taken in the night after fighting for American freedom?"

"I don't rightly know."

"You see the Irish love freedom and hate the Brits as well Daniel, but. . ."

"But," he finished the comment for her, "The Irish didn't win and they don't pretend to be the hope of the world now do they?"

She smiled at him with a knowing glance. "My Jedidiah believes America's the hope of the world. I hope he is right."

"I hope so, too, Ma'am." He replied, tucking the broom into a corner of the store. "My father says we may have to fight to make it so."

One afternoon in mid-June, she climbed the stairs slowly to accommodate her growing belly and curled herself under a light, summer quilt that Sara had given her for their wedding. The few light pains of that morning were growing into occasional stabs that made her draw in her breath. As she was about to drift to sleep, she heard the familiar voice of a man coming from below.

"I'm looking for the proprietress of this establishment." It was unmistakably the voice of Joseph Ryan, and her eyes snapped open.

"It's imperative that I speak with her." She heard his demand being brought down upon Harry, the considerably more timid of the two boys she had hired.

Not you. It's enough struggle to deal with the aches of pregnancy and the loss of Jedidiah. I can't face you, you evil creature. Go away.

"Where is she?" Ryan demanded, and she could imagine sweet Harry quaking in his boots.

Unwilling to let him abuse the boy, she slowly hoisted herself from the bed and lumbered carefully down the narrow stairs. The pains were returning every few moments but were not excruciating. Emerging into the store, she faced Ryan.

"Harry, go to the post office, won't you, to see if any letters have arrived?"

He hesitated, sensing something was amiss, but proceeded out the door.

She glared at him and asked, "What do you want here?"

He was sizing up her form. "So, you're carrying a child."

"It's no business of yours. I've no desire to see or speak with you, not now or ever again." She crossed her arms over her chest.

Ryan seemed to be fishing for more to say. "I want to tell you that I have found God. I am a believer now and I shall never again be the man you once knew in Ireland. I wanted to say that to you."

She wanted to say, "You can burn in hell," but knowing that would be a sin, she said, "You have said it. Now you can leave."

"There is something else you need to know," he continued undeterred.

She was growing impatient, more so because the pains had not ceased, and her back was hurting now.

"I've told you we have family history. That history, well, it binds us. It means we belong together." He appeared to be pleading now and she stepped further away from him.

"I must make up for my father's sins by taking you as my wife."

"I have a husband and a fine one, too." She shot back at him.

"Just listen, please. My grandfather, Dan Ryan, was a great man. My Da, well, he was not."

Where is he going with this?

"It was my Da who foiled the united uprising, just as your grandmother always said, but now I know why."

"Grandmother has a certainty about people and memories. She did not favor your father, that's for certain."

Why is he looking for reasons to stay? I should be lying down.

She felt a strong twinge in her back, and it made her draw a sharp breath.

"My grandfather, Dan Ryan, was your grandmother, Betha's, lover for many years. He never lost his yearning for her, just as I have yearned for you. Betha helped him build a weapons cache during the uprising. When my Da was a boy he snuck around, discovered their secret, and took to hating the two of them. He talked of this to me before he died. He begged me to make it right, get absolution for his sins, love you the way his father wanted to love her. He admitted it all, that he told the Brits where they hid the weapons, that he ruined the uprising and ruined their lives. Though he confessed to Father Murphy, he died with that on his eternal soul."

Another pain seared across her back, this time more intense. It took her breath away and she felt dizzy for a moment, but she remained attentive because what he was saying made sense and she wanted to understand the whole of it.

She knew her Grandmother had secrets. She had told Aileen about the weapons and the uprising. She was bitter that the uprising failed and had always laid the blame at the feet of Joseph's father.

Now she was beginning to understand why she saw Betha sobbing so often while sitting sadly on the low stone wall. Grandmother, a married woman, had loved Dan Murphy. Infidelity was practically a death sentence for a Catholic woman in Ireland. If her dalliance became known, she would have been forever shunned. Her fear of Father Murphy and the fact that Grandfather's name was never spoken made James' revelation quite plausible.

"So, what if this is the truth. Why is it of any importance now?"

"Because we belong together."

"That's a tale for the fairy books, Joseph. It's not real. I don't love you and never have."

When he looked up again, he stared at her protruding stomach.

"I asked you to go. Now I'm telling you."

He was stalling. "I'll just pay for some tobacco and leave you be. . . unless. . . ."

His voice trailed off and he looked at Aileen again. This time a familiar sneer crossed over his face.

"Unless you need someone to help you through this difficult time. Then, you know, I'm the man for that."

Oh, there it is.

Sweat was now beading on her forehead and the pains were getting worse.

He always has a devious motive. I somehow have always known, and Grandmother knew, that he's a bad man, a violent man.

"I'll thank you to make your purchase and leave. I have a good man in my life, a trustworthy man. I am married to a man who has nothing to apologize to anyone for."

Harry had returned with no letters in hand and, clearly not knowing what else to do, stood behind the counter, mute.

Joseph turned to face her, and a furious scowl climbed over his face. He reached into his pocket and threw something metal and heavy at her.

She stepped aside, avoiding the object, and took a moment to register what she was looking at on the floor in front of her a medallion engraved with keys, the one she had placed in Jedidiah's vest pocket the night he disappeared. Fire raced up her neck.

In her mind's-eye she saw the terrible images from a scene she been fighting to avoid for months but now could not repress.

Jedidiah surrounded and dragged off in the dark. . . the men pulling at him, beating him, tearing his jacket. . .Joseph Ryan there with them, retrieving the medallion. . .maybe even being the one to place the rope around Jedidiah's neck or pull the trigger. . .

When she looked up at Joseph in horror his expression turned sheepish, then angry again.

"Alright, so you don't want me. You always thought better of yourself than you ought. He died whimpering, your Jedidiah. What does that say about your so-called man?"

The rage that struck her turned the room yellow and red with light.

"You murdered him! You murdered Jedidiah! And then—what?— you come here to see if I'll have you? Something is very wrong with you. You are a bastard, the devil incarnate, Joseph Ryan!"

Clear now that she would never have him, he struck back at her with his words.

"I came to see if what I'd heard is true, and it is. You're big as a studded cow. Come to think of it, why would I want you with a filthy coward's child in your gut?"

Small bags of carpentry nails were stacked on the counter. She grabbed one and hurled it at his face, striking him on his right cheek- bone. He swore as a bloody red line climbed down his cheek. Harry stepped in front of him.

"And here's me, with fresh news about your brother and sister," he said with bitterness, "but you'll not hear a word of it now, damn you and your coward's ugly brat."

"Get out!" she raged at him, straining her voice.

He hurried out of the store, leaving the medallion on the floor.

Harry stood frozen, staring.

Sudden severe pain made Aileen double over and seize her stom- ach with both hands. "Go get the sheriff, and the doctor, Harry," she managed to breathe out. "I need them both."

Another pain ripped through her, and a gush of water spilled from beneath her dress onto the floor. "It's the doctor I need first. Run, Harry."

When the next pain came, it nearly knocked her down, and yet it was not as great as the agony that wracked her heart knowing now that Jedidiah was never coming back.

17

PETERBORO

Sara set bolts of calico next to the store's sewing supplies and turned to see Aileen intently reading a letter she had pulled from her worn leather satchel. It had been four months since she gave birth to Bessie. She named the child Elizabeth, after her grandmother, and settled on this as a nickname. Sara could see that her energy was returning, and that comforted her.

Another bright autumn was turning gray as surges of cold wind and freezing rain descended from Canada. The storms pelted the red tin roof of the store, creating a fast, noisy drumbeat above their heads and making customers happy to rush inside and warm their hands by the stove.

"You won't come back to Troy with me? John and Keating would love to have a little one in the house. You wouldn't be so alone."

"I'm not alone. I have Bessie." The little girl, with her perfect little bow of a mouth and Jedidiah's eyes, was asleep upstairs.

"I've made plans."

The wind picked up quickly and frost appeared on the windows. Aileen handed the letter she had been reading to Sara.

Dear Aileen,

Mr. Smith and I beseech you to come and stay with us in Peterboro. There is much work to be done on abolition, philanthropy, land acquisition and agriculture. We know that our causes are dear to your heart and, having lost four children, I can tell you with certainty, that hard work is a healing balm for grief."

Sara looked up at her, "You mean to accept her invitation then?"

"Yes. I made my decision this morning. In addition to the causes, she's taken on the care of eight children born to Mr. Smith's cousin whose wife recently passed. Ann is a good and patient soul, but that may be too much even for her. I'd like to help."

"I see a bit of fire in your eyes again," Sara said, smiling. "That's good."

"I take after my grandmother, Betha, I believe." Aileen pulled Sara over to sit with her at the maple table surrounded by spindle chairs in the corner."

"Strong, fiery women, your granny and my mum," Sara replied with a smile.

"Why did Annie leave for America at such a young age?"

"I don't know. I asked my father about it long ago. I sensed he knew her secret but wasn't revealing it."

I don't hold all my granny's secrets either, but I do know there are some to be had."

They both laughed and Sara changed the subject.

"Is it true Gerrit Smith's niece, Elizabeth Cady, frequents Peterboro?"

"Yes, do you know of her? She spends her summers there."

"We haven't met but I've seen her leaving the Willard School for Women in Troy."

"Ann says she's read all of her father's law books. I envy her that."

"Well, you should have the chance to tell her so. What of the store, Aileen?"

"I'll ask Keating and John to come and sell it."

Sara looked surprised.

"I can't be here without Jedidiah, and it should fetch a good price."

"I see. I just want you and Bessie to be safe."

"I'm not safe here. This is where Joseph Ryan found me. He knows I'm alone" she added bitterly. "The bastard made sure I'd be alone."

"Did you tell the Sherrif he admitted the crime? I don't want you or Bessie anywhere near that man."

"The Sheriff listened but little else. Bessie will be safer in Peterboro. With the protection of the Smiths, and all of those children to play with, it'll be grand for her." She hesitated for a moment and added, "If I'm to stay here, I hope I can grow some of the faith Jedidiah placed in this country."

Sara's eyes moistened. "Our Jedidiah, he just refused to be helpless in the face of evil, didn't he? We miss him so."

Aileen could hear the baby stirring in her crib above them and Sara headed for the stairs. "Let me get Bessie if she's waking. I may not have the chance to hold her for a while." She paused with one foot on the lowest step. "What of your search for Michael and Molly?"

"I'll never give up. Michael, by one account, is working and doing well for himself operating locks on the Canal, though the man who saw him there never returned. It's Molly I'm most concerned for. I'll not give up until I've found her. I have a new lead but it's too fresh to hang hope on."

The following week, Danny helped lug her last few cases to the dock of the feeder canal at the edge of Fayetteville. Most of her and the baby's belongings had been sent on ahead. She hitched Bessie up onto her hip, slipped a few bills in his hand, and watched his eyes widen in gratitude.

"Here's something for Harry, as well," she said, placing a few more bills in his fist.

Keating had relayed to Aileen during a visit last month that Gerrit Smith was transformed by Jedidiah's death and the refusal of those he'd once considered good citizens, to allow free speech on the subject of slavery. His news made her anxious to go to Peterboro.

"Smith now repudiates all half-measures and welcomes radicals, like John Brown, to his home," said Keating. "They have joined their hearts and finances fully to abolition. I sat at their table with Oneida natives, escaped slaves, and intellectuals all debating the issues of the day."

Keating's admiration for the Smiths and a post-script on Ann's letter convinced Aileen to leave Fayetteville. The post-script read:

Slaves wandering in the night are making their way to freedom with the help of people lining the Erie Canal from Albany to Buffalo. Stephen Myers, Harriett Tubman, Frederick Douglass, Jermain Lougen, and Reverend Samuel May are all working on the cause. Join us, Aileen, and help to provide the comradery, hope and sustenance they deserve. It is a long, frightening journey to freedom, and we need your help.

Canastota's lift bridge allowed packet boats to pass beneath and dock at Canal Street where captains unloaded people, packages, and animals. This morning, muck farmers were bringing giant bags of sweet-smelling celery and spring onions to the water's edge. A young man in a large cap and an unusual plaid jacket was fishing off the pier. He offered Aileen a big smile and hearty wave, lifting her spirits.

"If you were any longer, you'd be late!" pronounced a voice from behind her.

"Jimmy!" she exclaimed, turning. "Is this even possible? The Lord must be playing tricks on me! Can it be you? I'm not dreaming now, am I?"

Bessie buried her face into Aileen's coat lapel. Aileen tickled her cheek and said "Bessie, don't be shy girl. It's my friend, Jimmy, from Cork."

"So, I see you've been exercizin' your powers of perception, Aileen." The witty sarcasm was the same, but his brogue had faded in the years since they bade one another farewell in the harbor at Albany. She almost hesitated to wrap her arms around him because, a full foot taller and immensely cleaner, he now cut a fine figure of a man. Throwing caution aside, she gave him a one-armed embrace that brought tears to her face.

He instantly became alarmed by her distress. "Now," he said, stepping back to take stock of her and Bessie, "what has this spectacle of a country done to you? Never mind the answer. Your little girl is the spit of you. She must take a load of suffering away."

"She's the spit of her father, really," Aileen said somberly.

"Right." Jimmy's exuberance waned a little, and not knowing what else to say, he offered, "Well then, let's chat about all of it while I drive you up to the Smiths."

"How is it you know where we're going?"

He wrapped a blanket around her shoulders against the cool air and helped her and Bessie onto the wagon. "Missus Smith herself sent me. I do. . .some things for the Smiths," he said, with a wink. "I work in the glass plant by day and, you might say, deliver packages and the like by night."

She understood immediately. Jimmy would be the perfect fellow to help runaways in the dark. He knew poverty and loneliness and his bright spirit no doubt lifted the weary travelers when they were sore of foot and soul.

"Have 'ya heard from dear Rose, and did you ever find the wee ones?" he asked, as he turned the horse and wagon uphill."

"My heart worries for our Rose, Jimmy. I've written a dozen letters to Saratoga and even sent someone there to try to find her and have heard not a word back, all this time."

As he drove the wagon carefully up the steep hill she explained her journey to Palmyra, her father's death, Michael's departure, and finally her marriage and the horrifying death of Jedidiah.

"I haven't run on like this with anyone since Jedidiah died. Now let me know your story."

He described his stint on the railroad in Schenectady as "dirty work for low wages" and explained how the work had inspired him to study at the new Rensselaer School of Engineering where he met his wife.

"Now," he said proudly, "I am a machinery supervisor at the glass factory right here in Peterboro. We haul the sand up the Oxbow Road from Sylvan Beach on the Lake of the Oneidas. We fire a window as lovely as today!" He swept his arm around emphasizing the natural beauty that surrounded them.

"All the way from Cork we've traveled. Now here we are, on a sweet green hillside with the looks of Ireland," she declared with satisfaction, glancing uphill toward the Smiths' estate.

His boyish exuberance had matured, she'd noted, and he asked, "so you've learned nothing at all of Molly's whereabouts?"

"The letter from Father said Molly had been sold in New York Harbor. There was talk she was taken in by a family from Vermont, people by the name of Noyes. Their son, John Humphrey Noyes, is a utopian socialist. I have recently heard the name mentioned along the Canal. He fancies himself free from sin, can you imagine?"

"I'm sure the lights of glory shine all about him," Jimmy said, with a wry look. "That's what these men, and there's many of them in these parts, would like us to believe."

Jimmy pulled into the oval carriage path in the front of the Smith estate and slowed the animals. Six pillars fronted the striking white, three-story home. To the west, nestled beneath trees with draping branches, stood a tidy brick structure with twelve-paned windows. The sound of moving water could be heard along with many bird calls she had never heard before. On the other side of the home was a fountain surrounded by fragrant trees and several smaller structures.

If you've been trapped all your life in slavery, it must seem like you've arrived in heaven when you come here.

"Ann's lost four babies, dear woman," said Aileen as her eyes landed upon the square of fenced-in grave markers. "I hope I can be of help to them. Jedidiah always said he could smell the breath of love here in Peterboro."

"He was a romantic, then?" replied Jimmy. "Well, there's much to love on this hilltop. Gerrit's father built this fine home and made a tidy fortune in land. Mind you, unlike Gerrit he built the home with slaves and acquired the land by swindling the natives. His eldest son, Gerrit's brother, Peter, started the glass factory where I make my wages. He goes in way too much for the drink, poor fellow. However,

Gerrit and his wife, Ann, show kindness and consideration to all. It's them that puts the sweet scent in the air hereabouts, that's for sure."

"Join us for dinner, won't you?" Ann invited Jimmy with a smile, as she and Gerrit came down the front steps to meet them.

"Thank you, but no, Ma'am. I've equipment at the glass house to tend to tonight," he responded, suddenly adding, "and I'm feeling sure there is not a single thing, even eating at your fine table, that could top the glorious day I've had till now."

Jimmy jumped to the grass and held Bessie as Aileen stepped down. Lifting the child high above his head, he made her giggle before returning her to her mother. Aileen beamed at him as he slapped the horse's reins and rode away.

Surveying the landscape, she saw natives deep in conversation on the Smiths' portico and Negroes speaking with white residents on the Village Green. A stunning, bright white church with a clocktower poked out over the trees. Gerrit Smith was every bit as impressive as she recalled from the abolitionist meeting in Utica. Ann's demeanor was warm and kind. Aileen watched as Jimmy, in his plaid jacket, disappeared from view. Turning to the Smiths, three images mixed and flooded her mind.

She saw the Irish travelers in the bowels of the Dublin Packet emerging to dance on deck. She envisioned Negro escapees traveling north and the Oneida natives going west to Wisconsin.

All of these souls, pulled like roots out of the ground, are seeking freedom. Will America make a place for them?

It was evident to Aileen from her first week in Peterboro, that Gerrit and Ann had created a hilltop hideaway of peace in an era of tumultuous change. There were no posters offering rewards for escaped slaves. The women here looked less downtrodden and overworked than those she had met anywhere else, and one could frequently hear singing from the workers at the glass factory down the hill as they walked the roads home after a long day of work.

Ann welcomed Aileen into her home with extraordinary kindness and allowed her to navigate her role as a grieving widow, new mother, and abolitionist at her own pace.

There were days when Aileen failed to descend the stairs from her room until late afternoon and others when she stood talking with the house manager, Viny, in the kitchen at sunrise. She soon learned that Viny possessed wisdom, and she was drawn to her. Aileen particularly admired the way Viny held herself—back straight as a board and a kind smile for everyone.

Bessie played at Aileen's feet on those mornings, in the kitchen, crawling after the turnips that fell and rolled noisily across the wide-plank wooden floor. At ease in this setting, Aileen sometimes exposed her melancholy. With Viny nearby, Aileen found that her healing could take place.

Several weeks after her arrival, she sat on a rose-colored chaise in her room and began a letter to Sara about her new home.

The gentle, tolerant environment here spills out onto the village square. The native Oneida people converse on the lawn. Former slaves who are now free, own cottages, and shop, trade, and share news of the weather with local farmers.

When the sun beckoned her outside, she strolled onto the square with Bessie on her hip. The scents were damp and candy-sweet, and her baby girl's face turned pink with the joy of it. A slight breeze tilted the small, young leaves of the maples that lined the village streets. She closed her eyes and conjured the smell of Irish hillsides in April.

Grandmother, how glorious it would be for you to meet your name-sake, my own little Elizabeth.

Tucking the ribbons of her baby's bonnet neatly into the sweater that covered her muslin pinafore, she imagined Betha hoisting her great-granddaughter high into the air and eliciting raw, uncomplicated laughter.

I'll raise her with your strength and determination.

American women were stoic, and in this respect, she had clearly become American. She knew that carrying a child on her hip made her the kind of woman that many people failed to notice. It did not concern her. Since Jedidiah's murder, a veil of hardness often crossed her face, and weariness was visible in her gait.

The hard life of this new country can be painful, but it offers possibilities that were unthinkable for a woman in Ireland.

She had learned from Viny that many women were enrolled at the nearby Clinton Female Seminary. The Oneida women in her midst showed a level of leadership and composure she had seen exhibited only by the very wealthiest European women.

In the coming weeks, she would make plans with Jimmy to drive her to Canastota where she would board a packet boat bound for Oswego. There she would deliver messages to John Edwards, Gerrit's partner in the port city, regarding the arrival of escapees and the need to secure their passage across Lake Ontario to Canada.

"*Ann Smith*" she explained in her letter to Sara, *shares her knowledge of natural medicines and cures with me. She carries arrowroot on her frequent trips south to Philadelphia during the winter months. She taught me to bundle it with ginger and rhubarb root to help the sick, sometimes starving escapees hiding in the barn.*

She wears white clothing. I think it shows her dedication to cleanliness and enhances her well-deserved saintly reputation among the people of Peterboro.

I notice only one source of tension in their marriage. Gerrit refuses to provide Ann with her own store of financial resources, and she resents having to ask him for funds to make contributions to the causes she cares deeply about. He does seem to adore her though and writes to her every day when she is away."

After posting her letter she climbed the wooden stairs to Martin's Mercantile and overheard a conversation between an old, bearded man with bright blue eyes and a strong young farmer in much-repaired overalls who was hoisting bags of supplies onto his wagon.

Leaning against the store's front porch railing while reading his paper, the old man shouted to the farmer, "Charles Darwin. . .he's returned to England on the HMS Beagle."

The old man was bent over, most likely from decades of hard labor, and Aileen noted that he was chewing a particularly sweet-smelling tobacco.

"And how about John Ruggles?" The young farmer, now sweating from the labor of loading the buggy, responded. "He was granted the very first United States patent for inventing traction wheels that allow trains to go uphill."

The man's hopeful tone reminded her of a conversation she'd had with Jedidiah at breakfast one morning in Troy after reading the Sentinel. She stopped and became almost wooden for a moment. Memories of Jedidiah like this sprang forward without warning and sometimes took her breath away. She looked up and saw the sun come out from behind a dark cloud.

He's glad I'm here. This is where we belong.

18

FACES WET
WITH TEARS

"You're Mrs. Tracey, aren't you?" A pretty young woman with brown hair piled high and wearing a lace blouse buttoned closely around her neck approached Aileen, her hand outstretched.

"Yes?"

"I am Elizabeth Cady, Gerrit's cousin. I am so pleased to make your acquaintance. Let's share a bench and talk."

"I've looked forward to meeting you," responded Aileen, eagerly moving to a seat on the square. "Ann told me we share ideas and interests that are, shall we say, uncommon for women of our age."

They traded the sleeping Bessie back and forth while discussing abolition, a woman's right to vote, temperance and education. Aileen related the sad story of Jedidiah's murder and her plans to arrange Lake Ontario passage for escapees to Canada. For her part, Elizabeth Cady recanted an extraordinary conversation she recently had with an escapee who had been secreted away with her in the attic of her uncle's home.

"We whispered for hours, shared our secrets while cousin Gerrit fed the slave catchers food and spirits in the dining room below. Harriet Powell is her name. She had to bid farewell to everyone she loved to find freedom. I could feel the weight of her grief and her determination. She made it safely to Kingston."

"It's a terrible trade they have to make."

"Her courage—well, she was full of it."

"I wish I had more courage."

"I'm told you have plenty, crossed the Atlantic on your own, did you?"

"I did. But you. . .I am envious of your education in Troy and the access you've enjoyed to your father's law library. My grandmother was courageous, but I was taught to listen to Father Murphy, do penance and follow the ten commandments, not to get an education and question authority."

Elizabeth Cady stood, allowing baby Bessie, who had awakened, to attempt a step or two with her arms raised high and her pudgy hands clasping hers.

"What brought you to America?"

"I came here to try to make right something terrible that I had a hand in creating. With Jedidiah, I thought perhaps I could."

"What precisely did you come here to do?"

"Find my half sister and brother. As tiny children they were sold to a ship captain bound for New York."

Her companion gasped, and as a show of sympathy, took hold of Aileen's hand, prompting Aileen to share every lead, strategy, and false hope regarding Molly and Michael that her search had unveiled since she arrived in America.

"What is the family name you just mentioned? The Vermont family that may have rescued Molly from the man who bought her on the docks of New York Harbor?"

"Noyes. They were prominent I was told. The father a congressman and the son a preacher."

"Noyes you said?"

"Yes. Thank you for your kindness, Elizabeth. I must get Bessie back to the mansion now. My girl needs to eat."

"Aileen, I think you may be able to find your sister even without Jedidiah. Perhaps I can help."

"If you can or cannot, I am grateful to know you." As she departed, Elizabeth remained seated, motionless, appearing to be deep in thought.

Several days later, the fresh air inspired Aileen and Viny to help the laundress by hanging sheets out of doors. Bessie lay sleeping in a large basket of braided sweetgrass while butterflies gathered in clusters on the milkweed behind the laundry.

"Who is that?" asked Aileen, watching a beautiful native woman walk toward the forest behind the mansion.

"Her name is Leah. She's an Oneida princess," explained Viny, pointing to a graceful Oneida woman followed by a white dog and balancing a large platter of food.

"Why does she look forsaken?"

"She's losing her family. The Oneida are leaving for Wisconsin. More go away every week."

"Like Ireland." Aileen continued watching her closely. "The ports are full of boats heading west, and crowded with women whose faces are wet with tears."

"Mr. Smith says the Oneida are a noble people," explained Viny. "Their warriors fought with Washington and the patriots. They took food to him when his army was starving at Valley Forge. They were lied to and had their land stolen by the State of New York. The first day I arrived here Mr. Smith advised me to honor the Oneida and learn from their customs. I've gained wisdom from watching Oneida women."

"Where do you think she's going with that food?"

"Maybe to a green corn ceremony or community death feast. They honor their ancestors by sharing their traditional foods—venison, corn mush, berries, and the like—and offering a platter to those who have passed on."

Aileen's throat became dry. "Jedidiah would have loved that tradition."

"You look so sad when you say his name."

They watched Leah disappear into the woods.

"You'll find the joy again, Aileen. The Oneida believe the Creator brings people into your life to guide and teach you when you need it most. That happened to me, and I believe it will happen to you."

The following week, Elizabeth Cady rode up to the Smith estate on horseback pulling a saddled mare behind her.

"Let's have an adventure. Do you think Viny would watch your daughter?"

Aileen looked longingly at the riderless, chestnut-colored mare and emerged a few moments later wearing her first big smile in months. She mounted the horse with relish and trotted happily around the grounds. It felt as if her heart was beating again, and blood was finally moving through her veins.

She followed Elizabeth down a steep trail marked by waterfalls of different sizes. In the distance, a large lake became visible through the trees. A fat brown woodchuck lumbered out from behind a huge, granite-streaked boulder, and songbirds chittered at their arrival around each bend of the trail. Elizabeth Cady stopped at a massive basswood tree near a stream and dismounted.

"Before we go farther, we have to talk."

Her serious tone broke the spell of their near perfect outing, and Aileen joined her on a large, flat rock protruding over the creek. There, they pulled their legs out from under their corseted skirts and allowed the sun to warm their thighs.

"Noyes is a preacher. He is bringing a 'utopian' community here. Do you know of these?"

"I visited the Shakers once in Watervliet. They seem to have a special covenant with God and sublimate themselves for their community."

"This is different."

"Jedidiah was intrigued by the Shakers and their happiness, though he couldn't accept their total surrender of their personal lives."

"Do you know of Charles Grandison Finney?"

"By name and reputation. He's a fiery preacher who holds revivals. He lets women speak at his services."

"Noyes is magnetic like Finney, but his ideas about women are different. He believes in something he calls complex marriage."

"The Shakers are celibate."

"His community is not. In his community, every woman is the wife of every man and every man the husband to every woman."

"They have no real marriage? No intercourse?"

"They have intercourse but not with a marriage partner, per se.

Noyes thinks that by not forming allegiance to a single partner, or a primary family, selfishness and jealousy can be dissolved. Even the children only remain with their mother until they can walk, and then they're placed in a common nursery."

Aileen immediately comprehended what Elizabeth was trying to tell her. If Molly had been raised with children who knew only communalism, she may have forgone seeking her biological family years ago. If all children belonged to everyone in their society, then with Noyes she was not an orphan or alone. If she had somehow landed in such a community, it might be most comforting to her. Even if she were to recognize Aileen, Molly might not want to bond with her or become reattached. She might even consider herself unfaithful to her society should she do so.

"Noyes has come here with a sizable group, and I'm told there are many young girls among them. They are building a great stone mansion nearby. I wanted you to know all of this so you can decide if you want to investigate this further."

"I understand, and yes, yes I do."

They remounted their horses and rode for almost an hour toward Sherrill, where they came to a clearing with two large cabins left by the Oneida people surrounded by several small farmhouses and a sawmill. The footings for a large, new structure were roped off, and both women and men were industriously engaged in construction.

It was a curious sight. The women had short haircuts and wore pants under their dresses. They worked alongside the bearded men quietly and efficiently and all performed their tasks with the intensity and instinct of a hive of honeybees.

"Would you recognize Noyes from drawings?"

"I'm uncertain. Would you recognize Molly?"

"Perhaps. She would be twelve now."

They meandered closer to the group. There were more than a hundred people carrying rakes, shovels, and pails on the property, which was full of puddles from last night's rain. No one looked up to greet them. A man wearing a straw hat was reading to some children under a shady elm.

"What I know about these people I learned by hiding and listening to my uncle and his friends after church. I must say I was stunned. You will be stunned as well so if you want me to stop. . ."

"No stopping, tell me everything."

"Alright. They remarked on Noyes' desire for women to experience pleasure and also their desire for women to become educated, gifted in the arts, able to choose their occupations, and, of course, not have to worry about pregnancy at all times."

"But how?"

"Apparently the men are taught to control, you know, the release, by practicing with older women who can no longer conceive."

This last piece of information was altogether too much for Aileen, and she urged her mare forward toward the group of children. Her eyes rested on a thin girl with curly blonde hair. Her eyes were downcast, and she was pulling on the threads of her pantaloons.

"Molly?" Aileen called tentatively. She dismounted and stepped slowly toward the girl. Her heart was pounding, and a bead of sweat ran down her neck. She imagined the bubbly child in Ireland, the one who twirled herself in carefree circles with the stain of black pudding on her frock.

A man stepped in front of her. His face was angular, and his posture erect. With what appeared to be a forced smile, he turned to the children and made a sweeping motion with his arm, directing them toward one of the barns.

"Go," he ordered, his voice brusque.

Aileen would not be diverted from her quest. Her face became red with shame as she thought about all of the information she had inadvertently shared years ago in that Irish confessional. She marched past the man and yelled frantically to the child who might be Molly.

"Molly dear? It's Aileen. Your sister."

The girl, her heart-shaped face looking back, kept moving away quickly with the rest of the children.

"Miss, I am afraid you've made a mistake."

"Molly, Michael sent me—your brother Michael, who sings and plays the mouth harp and who cries for you every day. Michael is fourteen now Molly."

The girl stopped, turned, and glared at Aileen. Her eyes filled with hate and her hands curled into fists. She fell to the ground and began frantically pounding the muddy soil. Then she emitted a sound like that of a frantic sow being dragged to slaughter.

Elizabeth dismounted and hurried to Aileen who had fallen into a state of shock, standing like a tree, feet planted, staring at the bleating child, and with both hands covering her mouth.

An older woman from the construction site calmly gathered the screaming girl into her arms and began to lead her away.

"No, no, no, no, you will not take her!" Aileen called out, desperate. "She was taken once from the Town of Kildare in Ireland. She'll not be stolen again."

Pausing, the woman seemed to understand. She ran her bony fingers across Molly's head four times, stared into her face, and spoke something Aileen could not discern.

The man who had blocked her path was rushing now toward one of the log cabins.

Elizabeth Cady raised her arm around Aileen's shoulder, and they walked slowly toward the woman and child.

The woman gave Aileen a silent expression of understanding so deep that it made Aileen cry. Only a woman who had lost a child could have looked at her that way. Aileen gathered her strength, kissed Molly's filthy hand, and sank to her knees.

"Won't you please forgive me Molly? I did not want to shock you. Forgive me, dearest, and let me please, oh please let me bring you home." She reached out to lay a hand on the girl's arm.

Molly recoiled and her eyes flashed with anger. "I don't know you. I want to stay here. They're good to me here. I will stay right here."

The woman who had rushed to Molly before Aileen leaned her head close. "The man who bought her was terrible to her before Mr. Noyes was able to free her and bring her here."

There was a long pause, and the three women stared at the ground, bound together in the pain Molly was experiencing, something they knew they did not understand.

The girl had wiped her tears on the back of one hand, looked over her shoulder and spoke furtively. "You can visit me and tell me of Michael. Not now. I have chores to do."

Elizabeth Cady looked around. Many of the workers had stopped and were watching them with blank faces—not menacingly, but discomfiting, nonetheless.

"Aileen," she prompted, "let this be a good start. It is said that runaways, even those desperate for freedom, fear the new and unknown. It holds them back at first."

Aileen faltered. Indecision was wracking her senses. *Have I come this far only to fail? Maybe I should tread carefully. She's no longer a little girl who can simply be told what to do.*

She noticed a slight hint of curiosity in Molly's eyes.

"Alright Molly, I will be here, certain as the sun rises, to see you tomorrow."

As they departed on their horses, Aileen looked back and saw a tall man in a dark suit walking hurriedly toward the barn. Elizabeth also caught sight of the man, and with some alarm in her voice said, "There is another reason you must return for her tomorrow."

"Tell me."

"Those who are allowed to procreate in this society are carefully chosen and paired by the leaders. Molly may soon be of age. Noyes takes the young virgins for himself."

Elizabeth's voice drifted off and she looked into Aileen's eyes, watching as she absorbed this last piece of horrible, frightening information.

Aileen's face became stone-like. She stopped her horse and responded calmly, but bitterness exploded from her words like the dust of aging sumac flowers pulled harshly from a tree.

"Ah, how these new evangelicals twist the rules of decency for themselves alone. Catholics reject marriage for the clergy because they want priests to refrain from loving one individual above Mother Church. The Shakers are celibate, as well. What you describe here seems the opposite. This so-called utopian community seems designed to satisfy the lechery of old men. And to think it's the Catholics not allowed to vote or make a decent wage in this country."

"Molly would be twelve now?" asked Elizabeth.

"Yes," replied Aileen as they resumed their ride back to Peterboro, "and I'll take her away from Noyes, this wretched 'first husband' of young girls."

19

UNFAIR

As promised, Aileen returned to Molly at the Oneida Mansion House construction site the next day and every day thereafter in October.

Carrying a tattered quilt and a basket of apples, Aileen generally made a place for them beneath a basswood tree. The sun often baked through the chilly air and made the leaves shrivel into curvy shapes and shout the color orange. As the weeks progressed, the raw anger Molly had expressed on the day they met had shifted into a heavy silence. She seldom made eye contact, smiled, or contributed to conversations into which Aileen valiantly and repeatedly attempted to breathe new life. Her once lustrous, blonde curls resembled straight, oily-brown ropes, dangling over her bent forehead and shadowing her cheeks. In the distance, members of the Oneida Community, women with short hair and pantaloons and men with beards, suspenders and black hats, continued the construction work.

Today, as was her habit, Molly sat cross-legged several feet away from the hem of Aileen's skirt, looking down, and picking at the threads from the quilt with the nubs of her deeply bitten nails.

"We have the same father, dear," Aileen started. She always used her calmest voice when speaking with Molly. "Do you remember him? We both lost our mums, you and I, but Thomas O'Malley, he was our da, yours and mine. His face was lit with a smile most days."

To Aileen's surprise, Molly curled gently and began rocking and humming. Detecting something vaguely familiar in the muffled monotone sounds, Aileen began to hum with her.

All at once, Molly sat upright again and stared into Aileen's eyes as the older sister sang:

> "Dream, dream, grah mo chree
>
> Here on your papa's knee
>
> Angels are guarding
>
> and they watch o'er thee."

Throwing her dirty hair away from her face, Molly's eyes brightened as she continued to stare at Aileen.

"Are you recalling this song, Molly?"

Then Molly's expression went flat, and she looked away. "Unfair."

Aileen took this hard, singular word, spoken with such misery, as progress—an opening—and began talking quickly.

"Unfair it is, yes. Unfair all that was done to you, torn from your home, and sent across the sea. Taken from your father and brother and then," she hesitated before deciding to plunge forward full speed. "Perhaps you were sold, Molly? The people who took you, they, they were not good to you?" Aileen flushed with excitement at this long-awaited moment.

Slowly, Molly nodded. "Is he dead?"

"Father? Yes. He caught the fever of the Montezuma Swamp."

Fearful that this news would shut her down again, Aileen resumed talking, almost frantic and breathless.

"You were a darling girl. Father loved you. You gave him a smile the size of Connemara. He pledged three years of labor digging the Canal so he could come to America to find you and your brother. He thought of little else. He asked me to help him. That's why I'm here. His last words were of you, sweet Molly. I'll show you the letter handed to me in a church in Palmyra."

Molly pulled herself closer. The two of them leaned forward at the same instant and fell into the quiet comfort of a sisters' embrace. Holding one another in silence for several minutes, Aileen could feel the fragile girl's shoulders relax and drop and her breath reach deep into her lungs. As she ran her hands over Molly's head and rubbed the ruffled apron bands on her shoulders, she thought of the single word the child had used to describe everything that had befallen her. . .

Unfair. Unfair indeed.
Unfair that I spoke too freely to Father Murphy.
Unfair that my baby girl's father was murdered.
Unfair that Grandmother cried by the low stone wall.
Unfair that Rose was raped by her husband's father and the Negro woman drowned in the Canal.

Taking Molly's face in her hands Aileen asked, "Oh Molly, why did we believe that it would be fair? Would it hurt this badly if we had not?" She gently raised her sister's chin.

"Molly, would you come with me tonight to Peterboro? I want you to meet Bessie, your niece, and Elizabeth Cady who brought me to you, and my friends, Billy, and Viny. Will you come with me, please?"

"No. I will not."

20

CANAL MAGIC

Several weeks later, Aileen's face felt hot as she lifted her sister onto the back of her saddle. Molly had finally agreed to go with her to Peterboro, but only for one night. Feeling the tentative embrace of Molly's thin arms around her waist, she looked to the sky and smiled.

Thank you, dear Lord. Make me worthy of this.

They trotted forward into the darkening woods in complete silence.

Viny, looking serene and wearing a perfectly pressed dress of ticking fabric, greeted them warmly and walked to them from the back porch of the mansion. Bessie was perched on her hip.

"Welcome home, Miss Aileen. This little one's been the starlet of Peterboro this afternoon, cooin' at the birds and inspirin' Mr. Gerrit to leave the land office for the house just to peek in and see what she's up to."

"Viny, I want you to meet my sister, Molly. She stays with the Noyes community. She is our guest tonight."

"Well, Glory be."

Viny studied the girl closely and appeared to grasp the gravity of the moment and the pain in Molly's eyes. She reached up and placed her hand on Molly's arm.

"You come with me, child. I've a mind to wash that hair of yours and find you a pretty dress to wear."

Molly stared at her in disbelief.

"There's nothing a body can do to divert me once I'm set upon something."

"Just a moment, Viny," said Aileen as she helped Molly down from the horse.

"Molly, meet your niece. This is Bessie."

She lifted Bessie from Viny's hip and placed her squarely in Molly's arms and felt relief wash over her when Molly did not recoil or resist. Rather, she cuddled the baby and ran her forefinger under her chin until Bessie graced her with a peaceful smile.

"I've held little ones before and rocked and bathed them," Molly turned to Aileen. "But I've never touched a child who shares my blood."

Aileen's eyes bulged and burned, withholding salty tears.

"Mr. Noyes says it doesn't matter," Molly continued. "He says every child is everyone's child, that we shouldn't think of them as our own. Perhaps he is mistaken."

"We should love all children certainly, Molly," responded Viny.

"But this does feel," Molly's voice trailed into a whisper, "different."

"Yes, you hear a little music when you look on one of your own," Viny added, "and you feel your chest crack in two when they are taken away."

Without warning, Bessie slapped her pudgy hands loudly onto each side of Molly's face and emitted a squeal so impertinent that the three women spontaneously burst into laughter. "Molly, this is Viny, my friend. This grand house, well, she makes it work. She is not a servant nor a slave. It's her job. She holds Mr. Smith's trust and mine."

Viny placed her arm around Molly's shoulders and started for the back stairwell. Looking back at Aileen she said, "Mr. Gerrit wants to see you, Aileen. There is a Mr. Myers here—a Mr. Stephen Myers—who wants to speak with you both."

"Stephen Myers? Thank you Viny, I will join you upstairs presently."

Molly followed Viny up the back stairs with Bessie on her hip as though she had made the trek a thousand times. Watching them, Aileen breathed a sigh of relief. Every hint of a smile on Molly's face was bringing her deep satisfaction.

I did my penance, she mused. *I fulfilled Father's last wish. Bless Elizabeth Cady for taking me to Sherrill. Bless Viny for quelling her fears. Perhaps this is how this was all meant to unfold.*

"Hello, Miss O'Malley."

To her right, in the doorway, stood Stephen Myers, the dignified man who had shepherded her, Rose, and Jimmy up the Hudson and who, more recently, trusted her enough to accept her help assisting escaped slaves reach Canada.

"Mr. Myers, this is a surprise!"

"I've come to see Mr. Smith about the Florence Settlement. You know his plans. He'll give free Negroes land there, enough land to qualify them to vote. I want to help. I'll bring my wife and children here to farm in Florence on land I own."

"What of our work in Oswego?"

"Let's discuss that, as well."

Aileen felt her heart divide. All she wanted at this moment was to comb Molly's clean, wet hair and tuck her safely into her bed beside her. She had longed for this precious night for years, desperate to know her sister was sheltered, and warm, and safe beside her. Each moment away from Molly this evening would physically hurt.

"Perhaps we can discuss this tomorrow?"

"I'm afraid that isn't possible. There are packages in the barn."

Aileen balked at that. It was a cold night for hiding in the barn on the Smith Estate. She knew the escapees would be frightened and hungry and that catchers might be in close pursuit. She thought of the bleeding feet she often bandaged in the barn.

"Of course, Mr. Myers. First, we'll speak with Gerrit in the drawing room."

By the time they crafted a plan to assure the Oswego route of escape from Albany would remain open, and took food, blankets, shoes and medicine to the barn, Aileen knew Molly was likely to be asleep. She had seemed exhausted. There would be no quiet conversation as they lay next to one another under the warm blankets that evening. As she ascended the stairs, however, she felt at peace.

Moonlight was seeping through the cracks in the curtains and it created a bright gleam on the brass headboard above the girl's tousled hair. The soft, steady drumbeat of Molly's breath gave Aileen a sense of steadiness she had not felt since before she boarded the ship in Cork. She stood erect, listened intensely, and reveled in the sound.

This is no longer about sin or penance. This journey is about love. I will find our brother. Molly, and I will see this through together.

She reflected on how she'd changed since coming to America. She had come to find her father, half-sister and -brother. What she found was family at the Rawson's, love with Jedidiah, and now purpose as an abolitionist.

Walking softly across the room to her dressing table, she reached into a carved wooden box and removed the necklace engraved with keys. Since the day James Ryan threw it at her she had not worn it. She recalled sewing it into Jedidiah's vest, thinking it would protect him from the violence she sensed was coming his way. Running her fingers over the metal, she was reminded that it had not protected him.

No object or faith that can protect someone from harm. Rosaries and necklaces are meant to soothe our souls. We hope our last breaths will be as peaceful as hers this night. There's no harm in them but no power in them either. Who gave this necklace to Annie Eustace, and why did she have it sent it to Grandmother upon her death?

She placed the necklace back in its box, turned back to the bed where Molly lay sleeping, knelt beside it, and prayed.

Dear Lord, Your spirit is here along this Canal. It makes the Shakers dance and the preacher's bellow. This artery of freedom, as Jedidiah called it, makes magic from the languages of immigrants and the cries of escaping slaves. May the magic bring me peace, Michael, and the wisdom of the Haudenosaunee.

Climbing into bed next to Molly, she fell into a deep, satisfied sleep.

21

WOMEN
OF INFLUENCE

The smell of cornbread and rich, brown coffee wafted up the stairs from the kitchen the next morning. Aileen recognized the loud voice in the hallway to be that of Gerrit's brother, Peter Skenandoa Smith. Peter was named in honor of his father's friend, Skenandoa, the Pine Tree Chief of the Oneida. Sadly, Peter drank heavily and possessed few of the great leader's legendary strengths.

Aileen slipped out of bed onto the cold floor planks and saw Molly standing near the frosted window looking out at the fountain which had been disabled due to the cold. She joined her at the window and saw footprints in the icy mud leading from the barn to the woods.

"Who is that?" Molly pointed to a beautiful Oneida woman wearing a blanket shawl and walking across the yard. She was followed by a white dog.

"My friend Leah Shenandoah. She's lovely, isn't she?"

"Yes."

"Oneida women are powerful and respected within their nation. You can tell by the way she is walking, can't you?"

"She's proud." Molly was clearly intrigued.

"Women in Ireland don't walk with their heads held high like that, nor do married women here in America, unless they are wealthy, and even then. . ."

"There's so often sad sagging shoulders on women—even the women at the Mansion."

"My grandmother in Ireland had land and rights only because her husband died. Even here, widows can own property, but married women cannot. We lose the right to our property, finances, even our children when we wed."

"But you wed."

"I was fortunate to marry a good man in Jedidiah."

"Mr. Noyes believes in group marriage."

"Are women treated well there?"

"I think so. I am not owned by anyone, but my choices are few."

"Are you treated well there, Molly?"

"I don't know what that means."

"With kindness. Does anyone hurt you? Make decisions for you? Touch you?"

"They decide who I will lay with, yes. I'm not keen on that."

Aileen felt a surge of anger but kept her horror from sounding in her words. "Surely you're too young to lay with any man."

"The man who took me from the docks. He touched me, hurt me, kept me like an animal. Mr. Noyes saved me from him."

"I'm glad of that."

Molly was not ready to end the conversation. "The men decide. What's to happen. Who's to lead."

"That's the way with the Americans, as well. My friend Elizabeth and I speak often about this. Our men could learn much from the Iroquois."

"I thought she was Oneida the woman with the white dog."

"She is. Hers is one nation of the Iroquois Confederacy, just as New York is one state within America."

"Tell me more?" Molly's eyes were bright with curiosity. Aileen pulled her close and spread a blanket over their laps to continue. This was the longest conversation she had ever had with her sister, and she had no desire to cut it off.

"Leah taught me how the Iroquois honor women. They work in the fields together and own their own property. There is no beating of women in the Iroquois longhouse. Wise old women, like my granny, Betha, in Ireland, are called Clan Mothers. These women choose which men will be chiefs."

"Women choose the leaders?"

"Yes, and it's so sensible. They observe boys from childhood and select leaders who are most likely to keep their sacred traditions alive. Their attention is to moral qualities and character, not wealth."

Looking thoughtful but confused, Molly slipped out from under the blanket, reached for her clothes and realized they were missing.

"Don't worry. I have others you can wear. Viny has likely taken yours to the laundry."

Reaching into her closet, Aileen extracted some items and laid them on the bed. Observing Molly's discomfort with this arrangement, she hastily added, "I will go to see about yours right now."

"My community with Mr. Noyes, we are Bible Communists," Molly pronounced, sounding as if the word "Bible" was sufficient to avoid criticism.

Understanding what Elizabeth had told her about Noyes' sexual practices with young virgins, Aileen decided not to inquire about Bible Communism and instead smiled warmly at her sister as she left the room.

On her way to the laundry, she heard the Smith brothers arguing loudly in the parlor. It was rare to hear outbursts of anger in the Smith Mansion.

She entered the laundry and found Viny stirring a wooden laundry bat into a copper boiler bubbling with water and lye. Aileen loved the laundry with its wooden box mangles, steamy scents, and strings of clothing hanging in front of the wood fire. Viny shot her a broad sparkling smile.

"I'm working on her body linen. There are stains that may require ox gall." She handed Aileen a glass bottle. "Can you get this filled at the butcher?" Aileen nodded and departed quickly. On her way, she saw Jimmy and called gleefully to him. "Molly's here, Jimmy!"

As he came forward, she could see that something was wrong. There were dark circles beneath his eyes and his clothes were disheveled and torn. His appearance startled her because it contrasted so greatly with his normal cleanliness and cheer.

"What is it, Jimmy? What's wrong?"

He ran to her. "The plant foreman, Jon Hudson. I don't want to offend you, but I caught him raping the factory's night maid. I attacked him and drove him off her. It were a bruising scuffle."

"Bless you Jimmy!"

She's unmarried, that girl, and without money she'd have no chance for justice. He complained about me to Peter Smith who just this day has fired me. I'll have to leave."

"I overheard Peter arguing with Gerrit this morning at the Mansion."

"He's not a bad man, Peter. He's just in the drink so much he has difficulty sorting people."

"Don't be packing yet, Jimmy. Wait to hear from me."

Fury rose in her breast as she rushed into the store and asked the butcher to fill the jar with gall-bladder fluid from an ox, a liquid used to remove stains from clothing. Glass container in hand, she ran frantically back to the laundry on the Smith estate, all the while ruminating on what approach she should take with Gerrit to save Jimmy's job. Then she heard Jimmy call after her.

"I'm happy you found your Molly, Aileen!" *That's Jimmy. In the crisis of his life and yet finding space in his heart to be happy for me.*

She recalled his mischievous smile the evening he gave her shelter in front of the fire when she was homeless in New York City.

Leaving the ox-gall with Viny, she raced up the back stairs to find Bessie cleaned, dressed, and bouncing on Molly's knee.

"Thank you, Molly."

"You seem upset. Have I done something wrong?"

"Oh no, I have a friend in trouble. I'm not sure how to help him."

"I have something to tell you, but it can wait. Go help your friend while I play with my niece."

What was it that Molly had to tell her? Aileen felt impatient that it had to wait, but it did.

She found Gerrit alone in his study.

"Good morning, Sir"

"Good to see you. You met with some success yesterday? Must have been hard leaving your sister to work with me and Mr. Myers last night."

"It had to be done."

"Your work with Mr. Myers and my Oswego agents is brilliant. You are dedicated and wisely discreet."

"I hope you will not find me impertinent, but I must ask for your help for a friend of mine."

Gerrit Smith's face came alive. He put his newspaper on the table and gave her his full attention. This was just the kind of request he relished. Even his term in Congress and abolitionist activities did not satisfy his devotion to aiding people who needed help. A steady stream of people arrived at the mansion each week giving him that opportunity.

"Tell me your friend's need."

"It's Jimmy. You know him, he's the engineer in your brother's glass factory. He came upon the foreman debasing a young woman who cleans the factory at night, and he dragged him off her."

"Debasing?"

"Forgive my plain speech. He was raping her, Sir."

Gerrit's eyes darkened.

"This was done in a factory that bears my name?"

"Yes, and the man Jimmy thwarted, Jon Hudson, he lied to your brother about the incident. Mr. Smith's fired Jimmy."

Gerrit nodded thoughtfully.

"I am blood-certain about Jimmy, Sir. He would never lie about this."

"So, Hudson's the one who should be traveling down the Oxbow Road, not Jimmy?"

"Yes."

"I'll correct this presently. You can tell Jimmy we want him here in Peterboro. His job will be returned to him." Smith retrieved his newspapers from the table and added, "It was the right thing to do. You often act courageously, Aileen. Jedidiah loved this quality in you."

This last remark raised a lump in her throat, and her voice softened. "Thank you so much, Sir."

Turning to leave she paused, needing to tell Gerrit more. "When I come home here, the lanterns on this porch, high on this hill, always bring me clarity—clarity of principle. I hope all who see these lights are as inspired by them as I am."

"Thank you, Aileen" He stood to take her hand. "We can make a country that lives up to its creed."

"Once we dig out the poison in the furrow of these freshly plowed fields."

"Poison, yes, and planted deep. Sojourner Truth and Frederick Douglass will visit soon. I've heard from them both. We'll root it out, all of us together."

Encouraged, as she always was after speaking with Gerrit Smith, she went to find Molly and Bessie. She found them playing a game of jacks in the kitchen.

"Viny is having your garments wrung out to dry, Molly. Shall we go find Jimmy? He's the fellow I told you about who played the harmonica to the pigs in order to come to America. I have some good news for him, and I want him to meet you."

Molly nodded, more out of obedience than with enthusiasm, and they donned their bonnets and coats and walked toward the square.

When Bessie spotted Jimmy coming toward them, she began giggling and clapping her hands. His face was still clouded with worry. He took Bessie into his arms and twirled her around in circles. A tiny trace of snow began falling from the overcast sky.

"I spoke with Gerrit. Your job is yours, Jimmy."

He stopped twirling with the baby and still seemed wary. "And Hudson?"

"I don't think you will see him here again. Now I want you to meet Molly."

A huge smile exploded on his face. "So pleased to meet you, Molly O'Malley. Your sister's lived for this day."

She nodded, but said nothing, and Aileen wondered if she had been told not to speak to men outside the Community. It had dawned on her that Noyes and the other men considered these women to be their property.

A tide of ice was coming in. "Let's bring Bessie back to the fire." Aileen reached out her hand to catch some snowflakes and asked, "Molly, do you think you could stay another evening?"

"No."

Her response was firm, plain, and clear. Jimmy appeared startled by it and looked away. Aileen wondered why Molly was so adamant to leave on this frigid night.

"I told you I would come for only one night." Her voice was defensive.

Every taste of happiness that Aileen had been savoring since the previous day when Molly agreed to come to Peterboro faded. Fighting back her emotions, she responded in the kindest tone she could muster.

"Yes, you did, and I'll honor that, of course. Why don't you take Bessie to the drawing room, and I will find a horse and wagon and drive you back."

She remained stunned when she entered the laundry. Viny, recognizing her expression, tread carefully.

"She's thinkin' she'll return then?"

"Yes, yes. I had hoped. . . ."

"You'd hoped she'd stay. You hoped she'd feel what you feel."

Aileen slumped into a cane chair at the folding table and dropped her head onto her forearms. Viny's patient and loving hands rubbed her shoulders and back.

"The child's been told, that's certain."

"Told what?"

"Not to trust you and that she must return."

Aileen looked up in confusion while Viny rolled Molly's clean garments into a soft leather bag. Before completing the task, she held a thin piece of cloth normally worn under pants and skirts up to Aileen's face.

"She's a woman now. By the look of the stains I took out of this, she's a woman now. They won't let her go. I've heard they do experiments. Select people to make perfect babies. She is young and beautiful. They've likely chosen her."

22

THE STORM

Aileen stretched her spine to see above the horses and onto the path that wove into the rapidly darkening forest to the Oneida Mansion House. The snowfall, still light, flew sideways and bit into her cheeks, stinging like the pain in her chest. She glanced at Molly, covered in rough-looking barn quilts and leaning so closely to the left seat rail that Aileen feared she would fall or jump.

The argument that had begun as soon as they were on the road echoed in her mind as she drove the two mares carefully down an embankment and onto the frozen leaves of the lower trail.

"I don't know you!" Molly had said with fire in her voice. "I never did. I don't know why you've come in search of me." Her eyes had flashed with contempt as she assailed Aileen. "You look at me so strangely—it's uncomfortable. I am not your salvation. We were never really sisters. I would know you in my heart if we had bonded when I was a child."

Startled by her wisdom, Aileen considered telling her why she had been abducted.

"Whip up these nags and get me back. You said you would. I can rely upon the people at the Mansion. I want no more mysteries, no more questions without answers. I only need to know what is right before me, what to expect."

Aileen, exasperated, finally responded to her taunts. "Did you expect to be paired with someone not of your choosing? Did you expect to have your body touched by an old man?"

Molly hesitated. "Yes, they told me it would be so. They said the act would not fill me with a child and it has not. It can be comforting, at times pleasant. Once it was," she bit her lip and looked at the ground, "thrilling."

Aileen had felt her heart beating rapidly, and she finally let out a scream so loud that it startled the horses. "That is disgusting, sinful, they've twisted you!"

"No one hurts me there. The people there are not cruel. No one withholds food or shelter or beats me. No one owns me there."

Furious with herself for committing to return Molly to the community on this dark, cold night, Aileen switched at the horses' flanks.

"So be it."

The wind was breaking thin limbs off the trees and whisking them into the creek. The rushing waters froze as waves pushed up onto the trail.

"This is a treacherous night, let's not make it worse." She reached over and rubbed the back of Molly's hand. Now she had to shout to be heard.

"We won't be far from you, Bessie. I don't believe God's mapped it all out for us. I believe we decide. You've decided, Molly. I have decided, as well."

As they approached the broad stream at the edge of the Community, a loud cracking sound made the horses rear, revealing that the water had risen over its banks and turned this portion of the trail into an icy pond. Alarmed, they halted the horses. A distant, plaintive song and drumbeat seeped into the air.

At the same time, a voice came back to her—Jedidiah's—and she remembered what he had instructed her to do another time when she was driving their wagon, and the ground became uneven and difficult.

She loosened her gloved grip from the leather reins and balanced them softly between her thumb and wrist. The horses murmured to one another, then snorted.

Jedidiah's voice came back again. "Let go, Aileen, loosen your grip."

"I don't know how to pull back," she had said then. Nor did she know how to pull back from trying to rescue Molly now.

"Let the animals move at their pace. Loosen the reins. They have a wisdom that helps them make their way."

"I will," she said quietly. "I will let go. I cannot control this situation any more than I could keep Jedidiah alive." The horses began stepping gingerly back from the cracking ice.

Molly jumped out of the wagon and lead the mares toward a clearing away from the stream. Aileen joined her and hurriedly untied the wagon's bellyband and loin straps.

"We will leave the wagon here. Can you ride without a saddle?"

"I think I can stay mounted."

Aileen slapped a quilt onto one of the horses, hoisted Molly onto it, and circled the animal's neck with a heavy rope she found in the back of the wagon. She mounted the second horse after fashioning reins from the wagon assembly and began the long, slow trek to Sherrill as the storm raged and Molly followed behind.

She fell back into her defeated musings as the horses adopted a steady gait and the snow swirled like tornadoes near the ground.

"Just a few more miles, Molly," said Aileen flatly.

"He's God's representative on earth, Aileen," as if reading her thoughts about Noyes.

Molly was reminding her of the way her grandmother supplicated herself to Father Murphy, practically groveling, and spicing the tea precisely the way he liked it.

It was his power and wealth that made her cater to him, not his faith or hers. Jimmy and Rose, not a shilling between them, but they're the ones who deserve the making of a lovely cup of tea. People one could trust.

Aileen and Molly were drained and exhausted when they arrived at the Mansion.

Molly went to her small, spartan room, and Aileen was shown to the chaise in the library for sleeping. The stars cast shimmering strips of light onto the loden green carpet beneath the skylight. The smell of leather-bound books comforted her a little as she pulled a soft woolen blanket to her neck. As she fell asleep, she could hear the same plaintiff wail and soft beat of drums she had heard near the creek.

Someone is in pain, and the Oneida are drumming and chanting to heal them. Perhaps they are drumming for me.

23

———

THE WATER
THAT RUNS NORTH

The morning was far too beautiful for her dark thoughts. The ice-laced trees made her stop and stare at the forest. Naked, gray trunks stood in stark relief to the crisp, white snow, and birds on gnarled branches sent their songs floating onto the blue winter air. Though grateful for the borrowed saddle beneath her, Aileen's shoulders slumped forward as she began her long ride home, leading the second horse. With the roads and trails icier than the night before, someone would have to be sent back for the wagon.

Why didn't I mask my sadness when I said goodbye to her? I only made her more irritable by showing my pain.

Molly had indeed seemed more perturbed than sorry to see her riding away from the Oneida Community. Aileen's heart felt as cold as the frosty morning.

I disappoint those who are dear to me. Father suffered when I went to live with Grandmother. Even as a child I saw his pain. Grandmother made a life for me in Ireland, and I left her there alone. Jedidiah might still be alive had I not humiliated Joseph Ryan. Michael's vanished, and now Molly, dear Molly, would rather live with strangers than reside with me.

A wolf stepped out of the woods, planted its feet firmly on the path ahead, and snarled at her agitated horse, which began to shy and buck a little. Too drained and exhausted to be startled, she reined in the scared creature and considered her situation.

If I get any closer or shout, he might attack.

The wolf did not move, but kept bristling and snarling, and the stand-off continued for many minutes. She waited in stillness and once again heard drumming on the crisp morning air. She thought of her friend, Leah, a member of the Wolf Clan.

She said wolves are pathfinders; that they'll guide us to live the way the creator intended.

The animal's piercing blue eyes appeared kind. Then the animal turned and strode back into the woods.

There is another route to Peterboro, the one past the Falls. It's longer, but I'll take it. It'll be good to see the Falls before arriving home.

She yanked at the reins of the mare she was riding, and guided the one she was pulling along behind her as she followed her instincts toward Chittenango Falls. The pounding sound of the falling water grew louder as she approached.

The falls' name, Chittenango, was an Oneida word meaning "the water that runs north." As she emerged at its base, she marveled at the two-hundred-foot drop of roaring, partially frozen water.

Jimmy had led her here last December, behaving as if he were bestowing an early Christmas gift upon her. She recalled riding alongside a rushing feeder stream as the growing roar sounded in the distance.

Once again, Chittenango Falls lifted her spirits with a sense of wonder. Its torrents struck a dozen or more limestone pedestals of different heights and widths and tumbled into a foamy basin surrounded by huge flat stones.

If God can make such wonders as this. . . .

Reflexively, she reached into her pocket for her rosary and recalled she had not carried it for weeks. No, more like months. What good did it do? Her exhilaration fell quickly. She stared at the rocky ledges of the ravine then let her head fall into her palms and sobbed out loud.

"I've lost everything that matters. My country, my husband, my faith, and now Molly, as well."

The damp air crept beneath her cloak and into her bones. A movement on the precipice above the falls caught her eye.

A curl of gray smoke was rising into the shockingly blue sky. The falling water brought with it the scent of corn husks and sweetgrass. Standing at the top of the falls, she saw it was Leah wrapped in a red blanket. Her long, black braid reached across her breast from over her shoulder.

She felt a slight dose of happiness enter her solemn mood, and Rose came to her mind.

Ah, Rose, how I long to take tea with you again, my friend.

Through Leah, she'd gained great respect for Oneida women. She witnessed their sorrow at the western migration of their families and marveled at their competence with farming and managing tribal and family life.

Aileen noted and appreciated how native men treated women with respect.

When Leah saw Aileen watching her, she stood silently. They exchanged stares.

Rose would urge me on. She would tell me to reflect on whatever good I've found in America instead of what I've left behind. Rose would be right.

She rode to the top of the Falls where she found a solitary, beautifully-constructed, bark-covered longhouse.

Three Oneida women stood with Leah. As she dismounted, they offered her heated nuts rolled in maple sugar. She swallowed them gratefully, so deeply in need of kindness and warmth this morning.

"You are welcome to sit by the fire and warm yourself," said Leah, arranging her blanket over Aileen's shoulders.

She moved with the women inside the longhouse which smelled richly of tobacco. Sap was boiling on a hot stone fire, and sunlight slipped between shafts of bark creating glints of light on the earthen floor. Benches of tied saplings lined the walls which held baskets, blankets, and canoes. Abundant fronds of dried corn and herbs hung from the ceiling.

Aileen turned to Leah. "I'm grateful."

Leah's smile was enigmatic, as if she knew something she was not saying.

Heavy animal skins draped across the doorways at either end kept out the bitter cold. Aileen felt safe and began to regain her strength before the ride back to Bessie and Peterboro.

There was nothing in her experience in Ireland or America that remotely resembled the political power and grace of these Oneida women. Leah's friends at first appeared disinterested and slightly amused by Aileen's presence.

Then Aileen noticed that the women were saying something in low voices to one another, looking at her, and nodding.

She asked Leah, "I heard singing last night when my horse was stopped on the ice and again later at the Mansion House. Was that all of you?"

The eldest, a silver- haired woman, asked Leah to give her message to Aileen.

"Sister wants you to know that it is time to uncover your burden."

"Burden?"

The old woman gazed into Aileen's face and placed a string of purple and white beads into her hands.

Leah responded, "Sister knows. It's time to find your good mind once more. These beads will help."

Aileen had no idea what was meant by the old woman's comment, but when the women gracefully sat down on the soft animal skins surrounding the fire and made a place for her, she joined them.

Why do I hesitate? These ceremonies and symbols are kind and respectful. In Ireland, I prayed to a symbol of a bleeding human heart wrapped in thorns.

Outside, the wind rose a little, sending discordant musical sounds through the ceiling and quiet groans through the walls. The central fire guttered and rose, and she mused on the challenges before her. Taking deep breaths, she fingered the purple and white beads intensely as she had so often done with her rosary.

I must convince Molly to leave that place, find Michael, carry on Jedidiah's work, and try to love this land as much as he did. Could I ever become as peaceful and wear my strength as gracefully as the women around this fire?

"The purple oyster shell beads represent blood," Leah explained, "injury you may have caused yourself and others. The white beads are for clarity of mind."

She continued to knead the beads with her fingers.

I was jealous of the children, feared Da loved them more than me. My stupidity allowed their capture. Those babies suffered for my failings.

Her stomach erupted and she vomited into a wooden bowl that Leah had hastily placed next to her.

"Your brother will find you, Aileen." said Leah softly. She stroked Aileen's curls and held a mug of herbed tea to her lips.

The women quietly began reciting the "*Ohenton kariwahtekwen.*"

"These are the words that come before all else, Leah explained. They are said at the beginning of everything. Especially healing."

Just as she finished telling Aileen the story of Aiionwatha, a warrior who went insane with grief but learned forgiveness and returned to reason, they were startled by the sound of clopping hooves. They rose and emerged to investigate.

"Are you Aileen O'Malley?" The rider was a middle-aged man with a beard, not someone she knew.

He does bear a resemblance to a co-worker of Jimmy's at the glass factory.

"Yes, I am she."

"I was sent to find you, Ma'am. Mrs. Smith said you like to ride by the Falls, and I should try taking this route. Something awful has happened."

Aileen thought of Bessie. Her heart began racing, and she stood motionless in the snow.

"I was headed down the Oxbow to get supplies in Canastota." He hesitated, unsure how to proceed. "I saw something bright in the snowbank. It was a plaid jacket. It was Jimmy, Ma'am, killed by Jon Hudson's knife. Mr. Smith said to find you. Said you were friends, you and Jimmy."

Her face became burning hot and sweat dripped from her head and neck. Leah came to her side.

Aileen stared up at the man on the horse in disbelief. She imagined Jimmy as she had first seen him; filthy, teeth missing, and barking orders on the wharf in Cork as though he were the captain of a fleet. Now she understood Molly's stoic agony, why she often couldn't cry or even speak. The pain was so overwhelming it shut her down.

She silently mounted her horse, and pulling Molly's empty mare behind her, followed the stranger down the road lining the steep cavern that held the Falls. Her hands were shaking now, and the purple and white beads were taught between her fingers.

PART FOUR

1840-1852

"I am now safe in old Ireland,
in the beautiful City of Dublin."

In a letter from Frederick Douglass

to American friends, 1845

24

JONAH

Jimmy's senseless murder haunted her for years. She had written letters to Rose containing the dreadful news and sent them to several different addresses in Saratoga but heard nothing in return.

Hudson was tried and sent to Auburn Prison. During the trial, Aileen sat silently in the courthouse and wept. After the trial, she had gathered her strength and begun plotting her future. Although the Smiths were exceedingly gracious to her, most of Jedidiah's resources and the money from the sale of the store in Fayetteville had run out, leaving her concerned about finances. She still wanted to obtain a proper education for herself and was determined to obtain one for Bessie. She would not ask Gerrit Smith to finance that goal.

She spent most days working in the Land Office, a small, brick structure with paned windows that stood with simple prominence on the center of the west lawn. This was the nucleus of Gerrit Smith's massive land business and the point of entry for visitors to the estate. Aileen worked on land transactions and managed the "begging letters" Gerrit Smith received each week. His reputation for making discreet grants to individuals had spread resulting in hundreds of requests each month.

Glancing out the window on a bright June day, she saw five-year-old Bessie toss a stick and run alongside Riley, the tri-colored foxhound they had adopted from a litter left in a tin pail next to the Canal in Canastota.

"That pup makes a fine mate for Bessie and Frolic," injected Gerrit, joining her at the window and referring to his own dog, a shining bronze Irish Setter, now prancing forward from the barn to join the fun.

"Even the animals know that this is a grand place to live, Mr. Smith. Look, here comes another unexpected guest. You've hosted over thirty this month. I'll get about crafting your letter to the Cramer family."

Dipping her quill into the desk's indigo ink well, she emitted an unconscious, satisfied sigh. She reveled in these mornings in the Land Office, with sunlight streaming in the windows, the press of important work before her, and the scent of leather and last night's candles in the air. She retrieved a letter from her pocket. It was addressed to her in her grandmother's hand and held the green wax stamp she recalled from the sideboard in their cottage in Kildare. She placed it carefully in sight on her side table, smiled, and began her work.

Soon, a light-skinned negro man knocked at the door, and Smith welcomed him inside. He wore a faded blue military jacket and carried an air of confidence, despite his youth. She judged him to be approximately eighteen years old.

"My name is Jonah, Mr. Smith. I've come from Oswego with a message for you from Mr. Edwards."

Smith owned much of downtown Oswego, including its wharves and docks. The delivery of a message from Edwards in this personal fashion was highly unusual. Edwards, as Gerrit's representative at the port, had broad authority and wrote to Smith daily detailing his transactions.

Jonah pulled a poster from his bag, unfolded it and displayed it to Smith. As Aileen looked up, she could detect surprise on Smith's face.

"Aileen, you had best come closer to hear this."

Crossing the room, she felt a rush of anxiety when she saw the pen and ink drawing of her brother Michael's face on the poster in Jonah's hands. She and Jedidiah had created and distributed this along the Canal many years ago. Despite the offer of Smith's generous reward, the poster had failed to produce a verifiable lead on Michael's current whereabouts. The Lockport lead that Jedidiah tracked down before his death had been genuine, but Michael had departed by the time Jedidiah arrived, and no one knew his destination.

"A ship captain from Sacket's Harbor saw this poster in a pub on the Oswego docks. Seeing your name on it offering a reward, he came to Mr. Edwards claiming that a young man, older than the fellow in this image but with the same face markings and brows, works in the shipyard there."

A stream of fire raced up her shoulders to her neck. Last week, with no prompting, a liniment salesman told Aileen he had encountered an Irishman with the last name O'Malley on a Great Lakes schooner headed for Sackett's Harbor. She stood and leaned back against the front of her desk. The sound of two flies frantically circling one another and snapping against window glass became insufferably loud. She placed her hands over her ears and took a deep breath.

Sensing her shock, Smith stepped in.

"Thank you kindly, Jonah. My friend, Sam Hooker, lives in Sacketts. Can you deliver a note to him tomorrow? I'll request that he investigate this with all due speed and send word back to me."

"Yes, I can do that, Sir."

As Smith began writing his note, Aileen vaguely noticed Jonah exploring book titles on a shelf.

He can read.

Whenever emotions swept over her, she had developed the habit of reaching into her pocket and rubbing the beads given to her by the Oneida women along with her jade rosary. She hinted with her fingers for the white beads.

Clarity, these beads represent clarity.

She moved to the window and allowed herself a daydream, imagining Michael as he would look now. She envisioned the two of them riding high in their saddles, triumphantly entering the Mansion House and freeing Molly. With Michael present, Molly might finally depart the place. Michael would be eighteen years old now. Molly was sixteen and becoming a beauty. Closing her eyes, Aileen imagined Molly running to them with an open, radiant smile and reaching for Aileen to lift her onto her steed. She imagined Michael's grin as her arm became heavy with her sister's grasp, and she swept the girl up closely behind her in the saddle.

"You'll be staying with us for dinner then, Jonah." Smith interrupted her musings with a statement, not a question.

Jonah stared at Smith, speechless. Although he was a free man, he had never shared a meal at the same table with white people and knew of nowhere in America where this occurred.

"Please go over to the big house. You must be tired from your travels. Viny will show you a place to wash and rest. We'll see you at supper."

Startled by Smith's kindness, Jonah looked to Aileen seeking validation of the offer. When she nodded, he left the Land Office and walked across the lawn to the Mansion.

She watched Jonah and reflected upon who else might be joining them for dinner that evening. The previous week, a spirit medium and his daughter from Corning, a Seneca sachem, three deaf children and their mother, an escapee from Hagerstown, Maryland, and John Brown, a fiery abolitionist from Ohio, had all made appearances at the Smith table. She snapped herself back to the present.

"Might you excuse me for a short while, Mr. Smith?"

"Of course, Aileen, take the time you need."

She retrieved her grandmother's letter from the side table, walked down the road, and entered the clapboard-sided Free Church of Peterboro. Smith had created this church out of frustration with Christian denominations that refused to condemn slavery. He was devout and believed strongly in the separation of church and state. His views aligned well with Aileen's own spiritual evolution. She was grateful that Christ no longer required her to be a Catholic to achieve salvation, yet still held dear many of the teachings about Jesus that she had grown up with in Ireland. She bristled at anti-Catholic sentiment and found solace in the bible readings offered here on Sundays. Her belief in a benevolent God was strengthened by observing the customs of her friend, Leah, who found God in the natural world around her.

Seated in the last walnut-stained pew of the church, she murmured, "Akshotha," the native Oneida word for grandmother, and opened the letter.

The creaking sound of wooden floorboards in silent surroundings interrupted her as someone entered through a side door and knelt quietly before the altar. She returned to her letter and gasped at the first sentence.

My dear girl,

I am about to die. Perhaps not tomorrow or next week, but there is business I must reconcile before the Lord calls me home, and I will do some of it here. Your letters about your work with the abolitionists have prompted me to tell you something more of the united uprising and how it shaped our lives.

I had the fire of rebellion in my soul when I was a girl. My marriage to your granda was arranged to quell my restless spirit and train my attention to cleaning and making children and stew. Marriage failed to quiet me.

One day I saw a farmer being mercilessly beaten with the sharp end of a hoe about his head and shoulders by a cruel foreman. His brothers were standing by in witness, yet failed to come to his aid, fearing his fate would become their own. Before my eyes, the lot of them, particularly the beater, became smaller, lesser beings. From that day forward, I am outraged by any show of unchecked violence and power. I joined a unit of the rebellion. I was as passionate for freedom and humanity in Ireland then as you are in America today.

Aileen recalled a similar experience, watching the violence done to the hoggee in Watervliet.

Then I met and came to admire Josephs Ryan's grandfather, Dan Ryan. He was a brave and charming fellow. The poetry fell from his lips as smooth as glass. I was captured by the romance of our mission to unite and free Ireland and thrilled at his rebellious ways.

We carried on and gathered weapons, hiding them in the cellar behind the pig barn at O'Donnell's farm. We were discovered stealing a kiss there one rainy afternoon by his son, John, Joseph's father. The boy's anger drove him to tell the Brits where we had spirited the weapons, and the scoundrel also told Father Murphy that he had found us in one another's arms.

Only with my promise to walk away from Dan Ryan forever would Father Murphy agree not to tell your grandfather what he knew and make waste of me in the town.

I recommitted to my life with your grandfather. He became a good husband for a time, until your mum started growing in my belly. The priest must have put the sin of jealousy in his soul with falsehoods. Claiming your mum was not his own, he cursed me and never spoke a kind word to me again. He treated your mum like a stranger as she grew, never accepting the truth that she was, in fact, his child. When she died giving birth to you, he was swallowed up with the guilt.

That is why, years later, he took the tidy sum he had accumulated by stealing liquor from the docks in Dublin and placed it in the hands of Father Murphy to keep safe for you. He filed papers saying the money was yours and that my hands should never touch it.

The funds, still held by Father Murphy, are rightly your own. Do not be deprived of them. Murphy wanted you to marry Dan Ryan's grandson, Joseph, so he could keep control over the two of us and continue to hold the money. By leaving for America and refusing to marry Joseph, you denied him the power over you that he held over me all these many years.

I love you child, and I miss you more each day. Carry on the fight in America. Find your voice. Claim your inheritance. Slavery, false piety, unchecked power, and senseless violence all need to be vanquished from this earth. Its women the likes of you who will do it.

Your own gran,

Betha

Her heart was pounding as she folded the letter and placed it back into her pocket. Now, so many mysteries became clear, particularly the many times she had seen Betha crying at the low, stone wall.

I have an inheritance? That's Bessie's education and perhaps my own. But how. . . .

Suddenly, Lily Ostrander, a pretty woman with a foul personality, and the only Peterboro resident Aileen truly disliked, interrupted her thoughts by noisily pushing open the heavy pine door at the side entrance to the church. To Aileen's dismay, Lily spotted her in the pew. The woman's scowl contrasted terribly with her bright yellow frock and straw hat. She walked toward Aileen and assumed a haughty expression before speaking.

"I understand Elizabeth Cady's off to London with Stanton, her new husband, then?"

"Yes, and I miss her good company, Lily."

"What business has she there?"

"I think you know."

"Oh, yes, the World Anti-Slavery Convention in London. What's a girl from Peterboro have to offer there? Never mind, I'll be off now."

Betha's written words were ringing in Aileen's ears.

Carry on the fight. Find your voice. She insulted your friend!

Aileen rose and followed Lily out of the church, gathering her strength. She spied one of Elizabeth's blue velveteen hair ribbons, soiled with spring mud and caught in the undergrowth of a forsythia bush. It gave her strength.

She shouted happily at Lily's back. "Smile, Lily! Elizabeth goes to London for all of us—for you and me, for our daughters and their daughters, for our enslaved brothers and sisters, for our country, and for the world."

Lily hurried away.

Suddenly, Aileen knew what to do. Her spirit remained high for weeks following the letter and her confrontation with Lily. She reread Betha's letter a dozen times and waited anxiously for Elizabeth's return. When Elizabeth arrived, she found her friend deeply disappointed at the insult she and other women abolitionists had suffered at the World Anti-Slavery convention.

"Where is the logic that permits men, who profess their faith in freedom, to refuse abolitionist women a seat at the table? We were allowed to watch and listen but not take part in the proceedings. Garrison, bless his soul, joined us in the gallery. I'm crestfallen, but I did meet a like-minded sister in Lucretia Mott, a Quaker from Philadelphia."

"You'll see her again?"

"Yes, we agreed."

Aileen recounted the events that had taken place during Elizabeth's absence, including her confrontation with Lily, the visit from Jonah, the evaporation of yet another lead on Michael's whereabouts, and her grandmother's stunning letter.

"I know my mind and my path now. I'm told that the man who bore a likeness to Michael from Sackett's Harbor left as part of a crew on a Great Lakes brigantine heading west toward the Welland Canal."

"Perhaps it truly is Michael and he'll return."

"No one knows. Dinner at the Mansion stunned Jonah."

The women giggled having seen this reaction to dinner at the Smith table before.

"Jonah's smart as can be. He lives here now, in Peterboro,

working at the glass factory. He's teaching Molly to read."

"A colored man is teaching her to read?"

"He was taught by a Quaker in Potter's Corners. Molly's taken a liking to him. She's almost seventeen, and it's time she learned to read. She wouldn't let me teach her."

"I'm happy for her."

"I take him with me to the Mansion House when he has a day free from the factory. After our visit they work together in the library."

"And you, Aileen? What is next for you?"

She glanced at the late-flowering sedums and Black-eyed-Susan's on the square and rose to select a stem.

"I will stay here. Jedidiah would want me to raise Bessie here, where she'll know the likes of you and see the possibilities of life. But if I am to remain in these protected surroundings, unable to free Molly from that cult, I must do more."

"Gerrit says you are invaluable with the land transactions and delivering messages to ship captains on the arrival of escapees."

"I need to do more."

"What then?"

"The slave trade ends this month in Britain. A reckoning is coming. I've found my voice. I've ideas for new ways to help slaves seeking freedom."

25

SECRET
OF THE KEYS

Her work was risky, and she was successful. This would be the third year that Aileen would disguise and accompany freedom seekers to the port of Oswego. With the trails dry and the Canal about to reopen, she was excited to resume her own brand of smuggling.

Peering out the dusty window of the Land Office, she saw a tall Negro man with a muscular frame striding purposefully across the lawn. He wore a serious, defiant expression and a gentleman's jacket.

It must be Douglass. Gerrit said he was coming.

She knew Frederick Douglass had not arrived for the purpose of escaping to Canada. Still, she assessed him and quickly surmised that, despite his light skin, the rugged countenance and chiseled arms of this man would never allow him to be mistaken for female. Even her fullest cloaks and most deceptive hats would fail to disguise him. Gerrit hurried to the door to greet him.

"Mr. Douglass, welcome to Peterboro. Your narrative made a deep impression. You're moving us forward. Your story, your oratory—they're powerful."

"Thank you. I'm honored to make your acquaintance."

Aileen noticed that his right hand was bandaged and slightly deformed.

"Yes," he said, noting her glance, "this injury happened last year in Indiana. Still bothers me when I write."

"Mr. Douglass, this is Aileen Tracey. Her husband, my friend Jedidiah, was murdered by a mob of haters."

"I'm sorry."

"She and her daughter, Bessie, reside here now."

"Jermain Loguen speaks enthusiastically of your exploits, Mrs. Tracey. I am pleased to make your acquaintance."

"Aileen, Mr. Douglass is planning a trip to Ireland. We want him out of reach of Hugh Auld, his former owner for a while."

Aileen shook Douglass's hand.

"You'll find a different form of slavery in Ireland, Mr. Douglass. The chains are absent, but the oppression is there for all to witness. I wish you well on your voyage."

"How does one recognize Irish oppression?" Douglass asked.

"Some things are the same. You'll see hopelessness in the eyes of children, poverty, and famine. The sense of desperation will be familiar to you. My grandmother writes to me of it."

"And how will I be received?"

"You will be treated like a man in Ireland, and not offered insult as you are here. Women, however, do not receive similar respect in the British Isles."

"Mrs. Stanton told me as much. Such an insult she bore at the

London Convention. So stupid to discount one-half of the moral and intellectual power of the world." He hesitated for a moment, then added, "Eternally foolish."

Pleased with this response, Aileen took his arm and walked him to the mansion. They enjoyed companionable conversation on the lawn until Aileen noticed Viny descending the steps from the back of the house.

"Viny, meet Frederick Douglass."

"I know of 'ya, Mr. Douglass." Viny took his hand in hers.

"He's about to visit Ireland. Mr. Smith may help him start a newspaper when he returns."

As Viny showed Douglass to his room, Aileen considered her grandmother's letter with regard to her inheritance. The funds were still at St. Brigid's rectory under the control of the now ancient, but still irascible, Father Murphy.

Could Douglass possibly retrieve the funds? Could he meet Betha? Could he tell her of Bessie and bring her some solace before she dies?

Smith shared Douglass' frustration with William Lloyd Garrison's insistence upon "moral suasion" to gain freedom for slaves. Douglass had experienced enough violence to understand violence would be needed to gain emancipation. John Brown had recently convinced Smith of the same.

Aileen entered the house to check on Bessie.

"Peterboro is all in clouds this morning, Bessie, my darlin'."

Almost ten years old, Bessie placed her porcelain-faced doll on the table and raced to the window to witness her favorite morning spectacle. Steam rose slowly from the bright green lawn and rolled like a tumbleweed across the square, obscuring the woods that surrounded the village on the hill.

"It's like the northern lights, mum—only in the daytime. Mr. Caldwell at the General Store showed me an engraving. He says the northern lights doomed the Franklin expedition. What's an expedition?"

Aileen loved her daughter's curiosity. Resembling Jedidiah both in physical beauty and spirit, her thick red hair, unlike Aileen's own dark curls, now fell in a bright, stunning braid down the center of her back. Her lace bloomers and black and green flowered pinafore, pressed to perfection, made a lovely picture this morning.

"Let's scour Mr. Smith's library to learn more about expeditions."

Smiling, they entered the musty-smelling, book-lined room, and saw Douglass seated, leaning over a round oak table. Yellow tulips filled a simple white vase, and a map of Ireland was spread out, occupying his attention.

"Mr. Douglass, I would like to introduce you to my daughter. Bessie, he is about to cross the sea to Ireland."

The child gazed at him in wonder. "You are beautiful, Mr. Douglass."

Douglass appeared embarrassed by Bessie's enthusiasm. He expressed his appreciation with a warm smile.

"My Gram lives in Ireland. I'm named after her, but she's called Betha, not Bessie like me."

"I would be honored to meet her, Bessie."

Presented with an opening that she could not have scripted more perfectly, Aileen leapt at this opportunity.

"Go to the kitchen for your porridge, darlin'. I need to speak with Mr. Douglass for a moment."

Bessie skipped happily toward the kitchen, turning to give Douglass a radiant smile as she exited the room.

Aileen reached into her pocket, withdrew her grandmother's letter, and presented Douglass with a document signed by her grandfather, Grayson Dooley. It stated, in a scrawling hand, "Inheritance for Ms. Aileen O'Malley, from her grandfather, Grayson Dooley, is held by Father Murphy, St. Brigid's Parish, Kildare, Ireland." The deeply creased and yellowed paper bore the signature of a Magistrate named Maloney.

"What would you have me do with this?"

"I would have you carry it. No, I beg you to carry it, please, Mr. Douglass, to St. Brigid's in Kildare and present it to Father Murphy along with a letter that I will compose."

Douglass looked confused.

"Not far from St. Brigid's lives my grandmother, Betha Dooley. Have you a grandmother, Sir?"

"I don't know. I was taken from my mother, sold away when I was a boy."

"Of course. So stupid of me to ask. You must know better than most, the longing, the ache in your soul to love and connect with and comfort your family."

"Yes, I know that feeling."

"My mother died giving me birth, so my grandmother raised me as her own. She was a freedom fighter for Ireland, a woman to admire. She is aging, Mr. Douglass, and will soon die. Could you please visit her and tell her of this place on my behalf?"

"Why?"

"If you could, tell her of Peterboro, of all of the good people here, those who rise and risk all to fight for freedom. If she understands that Bessie and I live in such a place as this, then," Aileen's eyes moistened and she coughed to clear her throat, "then, I believe she will die in peace."

Silent for several moments, Douglass carefully considered her request.

"And the letter?"

"It is for a priest in Kildare. It could release my inheritance and provide an education for me and my daughter."

"I hesitate only because this is so unknown to me. I am an American slave about to cross the sea for the first time and meet people I may not understand."

"You will be held in esteem in Ireland, Mr. Douglass. I am sure of that."

"Alright, yes, I'll do this. A coach comes for me this afternoon, so please pen your letter to the priest right away."

Back in the Land Office, she dipped her pen into the inkwell and wrote two letters to Father Murphy. For the first, she used a piece of Gerrit Smith's finest business stationery.

Father Nathan Murphy
Church of St. Brigid
County of Kildare, Ireland
18 August, 1845

Dear Father Murphy,

I pray this visit from the highly-esteemed American, Mr. Frederick Douglass, finds you in good health. I am enclosing here two documents.

The first pertains to my inheritance and is signed by my grandfather and Magistrate Maloney. As I am sure you will recollect, the bullion was entrusted to you for safe-keeping until such time as I required it. I require it now.

Please send a bank draft and all records concerning my inheritance to the Bank of New York in care of Gerrit Smith. Mr. Douglass will retain the first document and return it to me. The second document is a personal note from me to you. Please read it carefully and consider it fully.
Yours in Christ Jesus, Our Lord,
Aileen Tracey (O'Malley)

She decided to write the second note on the black-rimmed mourning stationery Keating Rawson and Sara Tracey had given to her following Jedidiah's death.

Father Murphy,

It's a sad trail our lives have taken to arrive at this reckoning. My friend, Sara Tracey, daughter of Annie Eustace, recently found and shared her mother's journals with me. Now I understand why Annie fled Ireland so suddenly and I understand the cruel message carried in the medallion you placed around her neck before her voyage.

It is a despicable priest who uses the sacrament of Penance to further his own desires. You used my confession to do Joseph Ryan's bidding. Molly and Michael were kidnapped with the words of my confession. You used Annie Eustace's confession to subject her to acts not fit to be written by my hand.

You forced the keys medallion upon her to ensure her silence and to remind her of your power to hurt her. Before she died, Annie sent the medallion to my grandmother without explanation. Perhaps she thought returning it to Ireland would finally unlock it's hold upon her.

I wore your cursed medallion back to America and it made me sick. It also failed to protect my husband who wore it to his death.

Father Murphy, I tell you this: your medallion will not silence me as it did Annie Eustace. I write to say that your dark power is gone.

Consider carefully the actions you now take. It would be a tawdry scandal and sorry state of affairs should Annie's diaries fall into the sacred hands of the Bishop—or even worse, the Dublin Journal.

Aileen Tracey (O'Malley)

She folded the personal note, placed all three documents in a large envelope, and raced to give them to Frederick Douglass who was waiting in the carriage near the barn.

"Thank you, Mr. Douglass. Thank you with all my heart."

"I am pleased to be of service," he replied, appearing uncertain, then added, "I am grateful to have Aileen O'Malley for a friend."

26

OSWEGO MAIDENS

His field-hardened hands fit tightly into the woolen mittens embroidered with pink roses. She was pleased that she had decided upon these the night before. It was easier to disguise men as maids in the cold weather.

The raucous clattering of wooden masts rocking in Lake Ontario's wind dominated Oswego's wharf. White caps pounded onto the piers from the huge horizon. The soft-blue sky belied the knife-cold air cutting into their skirts and cloaks as they stepped from the canal packet up onto the deck.

Her expertise was sharpening. She had abandoned arsenic complexion wafers for an herb and honey lotion created by Leah to lighten the facial skin of those in her charge without accompanying illness. When time permitted, she taught the men to knit, a solely feminine pursuit that foiled pursuers and served as an outlet for their anxiety during travel.

This morning, she led William from the wharf wrapped in shawls. His hair was covered in a close-knit cap enclosed in a wool bonnet, and he swayed his hips slightly as instructed. They walked to the West Third Street home of Gerrit Smith's business partner, John Edwards.

"My master told me abolitionists were cannibals."

"Wise you were not to believe him, William."

Edwards met them at the front door, and they quickly entered a windowless room in the rear of his modest clapboard home.

"I've procured your passage with a load of salt headed to Cobourg. With storms ahead you'll have to wait here a few days."

"Thank you, Sir."

"You'll find William a good house guest and a brave man, John. He has strength and imagination. He evaded his trackers in Pennsylvania and made his way to Peterboro alone. I have your clothes here, William."

She pulled his shoes, shirt and pants from a package and placed them on the table. Next, she rolled the hat, rose-embroidered gloves, and feminine cloaks together tightly and slipped them into her bag.

"Soon you will have your freedom."

William, appearing overwhelmed, fell into his chair. Edwards held a newspaper as he walked her to the door.

"Gerrit's concerned about the trackers in Scriba last week."

"I'm aware."

"And unafraid?"

"If men like William can quell their fear, I've no choice but to do the same. Theirs is the greater burden. I fear for my Bessie though, growing up in a country that may go to war. Any rumors on Michael?"

"Sorry to tell you, no. I'll continue to inquire. Have you read the coverage on Douglass's trip to Ireland?" He placed a newspaper in her hands and bid her farewell. "For your trip home; may it be a safe and happy one."

She relished the fourteen-hour trip back to Peterboro. The gliding packet boat kindled happy memories of her time on the Erie with Jedidiah and offered precious time for reflection. As she boarded, she noticed fresh lumber and new construction on the remains of a flour mill that had burned to the ground the week before.

In America, things move fast. People, crops, buildings. They regrow like lightning. Why is it new ideas do not?

She opened the paper to read a description of Frederick Douglass' triumphant trip to Ireland. After being made to sleep in steerage while crossing the Atlantic, he was now giving speeches to huge crowds and receiving great acclaim for the Irish edition of his "Narrative of the Life of Frederick Douglass, An American Slave."

The Irish are liking Douglass. They love a good speech about a great public wrong. I wonder, has he seen Grandmother? Has he presented my letters to Father Murphy?

Tired and pleased to have helped William accomplish the second-to-last leg of his arduous journey, she propped her head against the green velvet settee inside the packet lounge, wrapped her cape over her forearms, and drifted off to sleep.

When she arrived at the Smith Estate the next day, Bessie bounded from the front door to greet her mother. The weather was warmer here than in Oswego, and the child's long, red curls danced in the sunlight. Aileen jumped from the wagon and swung Bessie in full a circle off the ground before burying her nose in her daughter's neck.

"You smell sweet, my love."

"Mommy let's have a picnic. Can we ask Viny to come? Let's do it, Mommy. I'm hungry."

Sadly, it was precisely this kind of exhilarating moment with Bessie that tore at Aileen's heart. Bessie 's joy reminded her of who Molly might have been without the kidnapping.

She was grateful though, that Molly now bore no resemblance to the morose, shrieking girl with dirty hair that Aileen had found many years ago at the Oneida Community.

"Perhaps, dear. Let me get settled."

Soon Bessie was chasing their puppy around the yard, and Aileen went upstairs to unpack and rest.

An hour later, Aileen found Bessie devouring blueberry crumble in the kitchen.

"Shall we go see Aunt Molly? We can invite her to picnic with us. It's Sunday. With the Glass Factory closed, Jonah might drive us."

"Oh, yes, Jonah will drive us! He loves Aunt Molly, and I love him."

"You do?"

"Yes. He whittled a sparrow for me from honey-colored wood."

"Have you noticed Molly smiles more and asks more questions when we visit her lately?"

"Yes, it's Jonah. He makes her happy. She walks straight up now, not all hunched over like a turtle."

As Bessie predicted, Jonah responded enthusiastically to Aileen's request to drive them to see Molly at the Oneida Mansion House.

Aileen quizzed Viny gingerly as they prepared a basket of food.

"Jonah's been kind teaching Molly to read, hasn't he?"

"Yes." Viny smashed some strawberries onto a biscuit. "She deserves kind, poor child. The day I found stains on her panties I started praying for her freedom."

Bright groupings of late summer phlox lined the road to Sherrill. Jonah, Aileen, and Bessie chatted over the snorting horses and rustling leaves. When they entered the circular stone pathway to the Mansion's front door, a serious-looking man scowled at Aileen and tipped his hat, with familiarity, to Jonah.

"You know him, Jonah?"

"I know him some. I'll park the wagon out back and meet you in the library."

The massive front door swung open to reveal Molly walking toward them. She wore a cream-colored dress with a lace collar. Her shining hair fell in gentle curls around her shoulders and her face was flush with excitement. The smell of wood burning in the Mansion's fireplaces rushed out of doors as she entered the open portico.

"Molly!" exclaimed Bessie, reaching for her aunt from the seat of the wagon. Jonah lifted Bessie and gently placed her in Molly's arms. He carefully avoided looking directly into Molly's eyes.

"Hello, sweetness," Molly responded, snuggling Bessie. Then she gave Aileen a much more reserved embrace and they started down the hall to the library.

As they traversed the long corridor, Bessie chattered and held Molly's hand. Aileen mentally revisited her first, agonizing trip to this room. She recalled staring out of the skylights at the stars and crying her heart out.

I found her and had to let her go. She may never reconcile with me, but I still want her to leave this place.

A tall woman named Claire, with a somber expression and wearing a long dark dress, approached them.

"Where is Jonah?" she directed her question to Molly.

"Planting the wagon. He'll be right along."

The woman faced Aileen. "We enjoy Jonah's visits here. He has taught our Molly to read. Mr. Noyes wants all of the women here to become educated, you see."

"I think I do see."

She recognized the positive features of this experimental community but recoiled at their mind-control and sexual practices.

Molly rose as Jonah entered the library. He was a handsome, virile man. Aileen noticed an almost imperceptible touch of his hand to Molly's as he sat next to her on the davenport. The conversation soon went to the topic of Frederick Douglass' travels in Ireland, and Aileen retrieved the newspaper article she had read on the way home from Oswego. Handing it to Jonah she asked, "Could you read some of Douglass' words to us, Jonah?'

He hesitated for a moment. Then in his deep baritone voice, he slowly read.

"Instead of the bright blue sky of America, I am covered with the soft grey fog of the Emerald Isle. I breathe, and lo! The chattel becomes a man."

Aileen detected a single tear trailing down his face. Molly saw it as well and openly reached for his hand. Aileen's thoughts raced.

Oh no, this is what I've feared. There are laws against this, even in the north. Is Noyes encouraging this? Is he recruiting Jonah? Could this be another of his eugenics experiments?

Jonah could lose his freedom, or be hanged, or sent to the deep south. Molly could be broken, again.

Quickly studying Jonah's facial features, hands and biceps, Aileen vowed to herself that she would never allow Molly's spirit to be crushed again. Studying him further, she asked herself, what kind of hat might work?

27

THE INHERITANCE

She was leaving with Bessie to visit Elizabeth in Seneca Falls when Douglass returned. This trip had become a summer sojourn for them since Elizabeth and her husband, Henry Stanton, made their residence there. Gerrit called Aileen into the Land Office and praised Douglass' success overseas.

"Do I understand that your supporters there raised the money for you to buy your freedom, Sir?" Gerrit asked.

"Yes, they did. They did indeed." Douglass looked older and more confident than when he had departed. He revealed an uncharacteristic smile as he described his exploits.

"My driver was my first surprise. He said, 'this is a land of thinkers and debaters, Mr. Douglass. You'll find yourself fitting right in.' It was just as you predicted, Aileen. I was treated well. No one seemed disturbed by my dark presence in Ireland."

He also described the impoverished families he had seen there. "Filthy they were, whole families with gaunt eyes and faces, leaning against alley walls. The scent of death was present everywhere."

"How were you received by Father Murphy?" Aileen had been waiting for weeks to ask him this. As she sat on the edge of the bench in Gerrit's library, she could almost smell the tobacco and wood wax of St. Brigid's rectory.

Douglass responded slowly. "I was surprised by the grandeur of the priest's lodging. All the window lace and gold chalices seemed out of order with the suffering on the streets. He was small, bald, and very sickly in appearance."

Aileen imagined the contrast between the two men.

"His hands trembled when I handed him your papers and announced who they were from. I showed him the bequest document and retained it as we planned. Then I handed him your letters, and I told him I would return in several days to hear his decision. He was shaken, no denying it."

"And more shaken after he read them, I surmise."

"Yes, when I returned, he appeared quite ill. He said to tell you the bank draft would be on its way to Smith's account in New York."

Aileen breathed a deep satisfied sigh. "And Grandmother?"

"I was grateful to have met her." Douglass grinned at the memory. "She had molasses cookies on the table when I arrived. We visited by the fire."

"Her health?" Aileen asked anxiously.

"When I spoke of you and Bessie, her cheeks pinked, her hands rose to her hips, and she even danced a twirl. She was failing, but her memory was not. We spoke long into the afternoon, and she gave me this to bring to you."

He reached into his sack, pulled out a package wrapped in linen and unfolded the bandana her grandmother had worn in the uprising.

"When I reached Dublin, word traveled to me that several days after my visit, Betha Dooley," he hesitated, "she drew her last breath. I'm sorry to bring you this sad news, Aileen."

Aileen's body went numb. "She's gone? Grandmother is gone?"

"The women in town took care with her services and burial. If you return to Ireland, you'll find a fine stone for her there."

Aileen could not speak. Her chest suddenly ached. The threat to send Annie Eustace's diaries to the bishop had unlocked her inheritance, but this news, that her grandmother, the invincible Betha Dooley, had died was all that mattered this day.

"Thank you, Mr. Douglass, I am forever in your debt. You gave my grandmother some happiness, some peace, before she died."

Douglass stood to leave and thought better of it. Instead, he sat and recited, in detail, his conversations with Betha the night before she died. "She passed a contented woman and grateful to you, Sir," he turned his head to Gerrit, "for all you have done for her granddaughter."

Aileen envisioned the cottage, with its scruffy plants, low stone wall, and view of the River Liffy. This brave woman who had taught her to love and to fight and to make the perfect pot of tea. Betha was gone from this earth.

28

SENECA FALLS

The canal ride to Seneca Falls was always pleasant, as was staying in Elizabeth Stanton's raucous house, full of children and agitators. It felt like visiting family, a sense that Aileen needed badly after the loss of Jedidiah and Betha.

Elizabeth always shared her mind and heart fully with Aileen. It had strengthened their bond over the years.

"Cousin Gerrit's unwillingness to accept that the urgency of our movement equals that of abolition is infuriating."

"Gerrit's a great man. He tries diligently to understand your differences. Abolition is paramount to him that's all. He did say he's pleased that Douglass will speak at the convention Friday."

"I am grateful to you both for that. Douglass will speak for suffrage, and hundreds are aware of our declaration of sentiments by way of his newspaper."

They stepped onto the porch to watch Bessie and the Stanton girls jump from a window in the barn loft and plummet a considerable distance onto a pile of hay. Bessie enjoyed keeping up with the bigger girls, and the sight made Aileen happy.

"Come, let's get about our preparations," said Elizabeth. "Lucretia will be here soon. She's been visiting the Senecas."

The three-day convention stirred a fury of emotions in Aileen. The ninety-degree heat had failed to wilt Elizabeth's power at the pulpit. She spoke vehemently in defense of the social, civil, and religious rights of women, gesturing with her arms and articulating each sentence as though it had been buried in her heart for centuries.

Lucretia Mott also inspired the audience of three hundred women and one hundred men, as did Frederick Douglass's endorsement of the right of women to vote.

With Bessie dozing against her shoulder, she hoped the canal ride home would be uneventful so she could carefully consider all that she had seen and heard.

While disembarking to take on supplies and passengers in Lyons, however, she quickly realized this was not to be. Two of the three Fox sisters were seated on a raised platform and had just completed one of their infamous "tapping" performances near the docks. They claimed to be receiving messages from the afterlife and were attracting large crowds all along the Canal.

"Bunk," Keating Rawson had said when first hearing of the Fox sisters. "These immigrants will believe anything that takes them a few miles farther into the heartland."

As she made her way through the crowd, a cold chill shot through Aileen's chest. Squeezing her arm around Bessie's shoulder, she located a bench and hurried toward it.

"What is it, Mama? What's wrong? Are you ill?"

"No, dear, I just had a chill. So strange on this hot day. I want to sit a moment, that's all."

What is wrong with me?

This sensation was totally unfamiliar to her. It was an acute awareness of her surroundings, as if her eyesight had sharpened.

Her eyes were drawn to the front window of a mercantile shop across the street. A gray shadow appeared, and a face stared out at her.

It's grandmother!

Betha wore a satisfied grin. Her eyes were piercing, appearing lighter than their surroundings. Just as quickly the image disappeared.

It took a long time for the crowd to disperse completely, and when it had, Aileen grasped Bessie's hand and rose to return to their packet boat. Behind her, still seated on a raised platform, Kate and Margaretta Fox remained, as if the trance they had been in had not returned them completely to this realm.

Walking briskly toward the Canal, Aileen suddenly felt strangely compelled to look back at them. They looked to be twelve and fourteen. One had a dark braid that fell to her waist and the other a bun pinned firmly on the back of her head. Despite the heat, they wore dark, heavy cloaks around their shoulders.

What are they doing? Waiting for another crowd to gather?

The younger of the two sprang up suddenly, pointed directly at Aileen, and shouted "There's a message for you, Irish woman."

The words struck her. Few people marked her as Irish by sight. Her hair was dark and her cheekbones high, mimicking the Irish of Spanish descent and hardly recognizable as Irish in America. How had she known?

"You'll do well to heed me," the girl shouted louder. By now a dozen people were watching this exchange.

"The boy you are seeking, Michael, he's talked to me from the other side. Abandon your search."

It was as if thunder struck her.

Pulling Bessie close to her skirts, Aileen wheeled and stared at the girl. Everything in her surroundings—the people, the trees, the girls on the platform—began to spin and she thought she might lose her balance. Opening her mouth to speak, she found that her tongue would not move.

Bessie began pulling on her mother's skirts.

"Mama, come! We need to go now. I don't like that lady in the black cape."

A movement caught her eye, and she shifted her gaze from the shouting girl to a solemn-faced woman in a black dress who was hastily departing from the scene. Aileen ran to get a closer look at the woman with Bessie hustling behind. Confirming her suspicion she recognized Claire, the woman from the Oneida Community who seemed to hover over Molly whenever she paid her a visit.

She paid the sisters to play this hoax on me! They know if I find Michael, Molly will leave them. Has she been following me?

Aileen was not prepared to debunk the whole spiritualist movement that was growing wildly all along the Canal as a fraud. She had, after all, experienced the appearance of her grandmother in the window. Turning her head back to the Fox sisters, Aileen stated calmly but audibly, "In America, we are free to believe and worship as we please, but in any religion, it is a sin to bear false witness for money."

As they walked back to the packet boat, the crowd grumbled and dispersed. She sat at the back of the boat with Bessie on her lap and thought of Betha. Her grandmother's visage had been kind and reassuring. As she stared into the wake trailing where the boat had passed, she determined to take up the cause Elizabeth had advanced at Seneca Falls and find the secret behind the woman, Claire's, strange obsession with her sister.

29

A GUEST FROM SACKETT'S HARBOR

She was doing important work, helping to organize this first convention of fugitives, free men, free women, and abolitionists, and she loved it. Aileen admired the bold lettering: "LIBERTY, EQUALITY, FRATERNITY!!!" on the abolitionist weeklies she would take to the post office that afternoon. The large headline did justice to the urgency of Gerrit Smith's message calling for the convention in Cazenovia to thwart the Fugitive Slave Act expected to pass Congress the following month.

She thought of the terror she had witnessed the week before when a young Negro boy was pulled from his mother's arms, shackled, and thrown into a wagon. Onlookers had been paralyzed, and the sound of the child's wails could be heard through the streets as the wagon kicked up dust and headed south.

Sweat poured from her brow on this unusually humid August afternoon in the Land Office, creating water spots on the yellow parchment papers she was handling and tightening the curls on her forehead.

Peering out the window, she became amused by the birds on the property, floating from their branches and languishing at the fountain on this steamy afternoon. She could hear, just slightly, the clink of the front porch swing where Bessie napped with her dog, Riley. This provided her with some of the quiet hours she needed to prepare for the convention.

Bursting into the Land Office, Gerrit's eyes contained uncharacteristic anger. He reviewed the last sentences of the notice she was holding.

> *Will not they of the "old guard" delight to look each other in the face once more and renew their vows upon a common altar? Let them come from every quarter—free men, free women, and fugitives! They are bid a most cordial welcome by the good people of Cazenovia. There are friends, meeting houses and beautiful groves there! Let all come who have a heart and can!*

Reading his own words seemed to calm him.

"The notice, it's working," he said, emitting a loud breath. "They push too far with this Act, stealing fugitives, even in the north."

"Agree, Gerrit. People are coming to Cazenovia. Those who aid fugitives could be sent to jail for six months."

"I call it the bloodhound bill. Rewards inspire captors to lie. Free Negroes will be afforded no trials. A mockery of our Constitution."

Aileen's spirits sank lower.

What will this mean for Jonah, for Molly?

In recent months, Molly and Jonah were obviously happy in

one another's company. Aileen recalled their faces when they shared Christmas gifts, small paintings of birds on birchbark they had crafted for one another. Grateful for Molly's more frequent visits to Peterboro and her growing independence from the Oneida Community, Aileen often stopped to watch the couple play with Bessie on the lawn and walk companionably while chatting on the green.

She reached into her desk for several pieces of correspondence. She reported to Gerrit.

"Douglass will chair the proceedings. The Edmonson sisters, Joshua Loguen, Samuel May, and Angelina Grimke will all be here. What's bothering you?"

"The village expects to double in size for three days. If two to three thousand arrive, we'll have to move from the church to Grace Wilson's orchard."

"I spoke to her yesterday. She agreed. Will your friend's brother from Sacket's Harbor, arrive for the convention? I want to question him on sightings of Michael."

"Yes, Terry Greene will be here on Friday. His Lieutenant, Ulysses S. Grant, has given him leave."

Gerrit leaned back in his chair and mellowed, thinking of Greene's older brother and long-time friend, Jacob. An outpouring of boyhood memories, of scaling the waterfalls and ravines of Madison County, washed over him. They had each attended Hamilton College. When both Jacob and his father died unexpectedly of typhus, Terry joined the infantry. His letters from the Mexican War were stored in a tin box beneath the Smiths' four-poster bed, a testament to the esteem in which he was held in the Smith household.

After dinner on Friday evening, the guests moved into the parlor to discuss the next day's convention proceedings. A welcome breeze flowed from the floor-to-ceiling windows of the mansion, moving the curtains like dancing, ghostly apparitions.

Aileen found herself drawn to Greene, a muscular, compact man with an impeccable uniform and ready smile. Noticing her attention, he moved closer to stand near her settee.

"Gerrit regards you highly."

"And I him."

To her astonishment, she felt an unmistakable flush of attraction, but quickly suppressed it.

"You fought with Grant in the Mexican War?"

"It's been my good fortune to serve with Grant. He's quiet, quick, and resolutely kind to his troops."

"Would he be comfortable visiting this abolitionist haven? I understand his wife's family owns slaves."

"He set free the only slave he ever owned and did so when he was penniless."

"Then he might visit us?"

"He's pledged to temperance and not much for mixing. But perhaps, if the invite included a game of checkers."

Aileen unrolled the old poster of Michael as a child.

"Mr. Greene, I've been told that a young man by the name of Michael O'Malley may have worked in shipbuilding in Sackets Harbor. Does the name or this likeness from years ago have any familiarity for you?"

He looked closely and with great interest at the drawing of Michael's face.

"Why, yes it does, Miss O'Malley. It does." Then he went silent.

She looked at him anxiously, wishing she could drag an answer from him worth chasing.

For several, long moments, he rubbed his eyebrows and looked at the ceiling before redirecting his gaze back to the poster. This provided Aileen with the opportunity to appreciate his dark-brown eyes and smartly shaped moustache.

"I'm sorry. I cannot lay claim to the place where I saw him, but I know I have."

Viny entered the room and rushed over to whisper in Aileen's ear. "It's Miss Molly. She looks a fright and wishes to speak with you right away."

"I'll say my farewell, Mr. Greene. Some urgent business has come up."

The poster bearing Michael's likeness fell to the floor as she rose. Greene retrieved it and placed it gently in her hand.

"Shall I call upon you again if my memory serves me better?"

She paused mid-step. "Yes, please do, Mr. Greene. I'd enjoy seeing you."

He was trying to keep her there just a little longer, it was obvious. "This gent is someone special to you, is he?"

She did not want to stare at his handsome face, yet she did want to, and so she looked down. "Yes, he is. He is my brother."

30

MOLLY'S ESCAPE

Molly looked wilted sitting in the straight-backed chair that had been placed in the center of a circle of community members. Not one of the somber white faces staring at her showed the slightest hint of kindness or understanding. Their eyes were either impassive or reproachful.

Nervously, she fingered the small painting of a house wren on birch bark in her lap.

Noyes paced around her twice, and she could feel his glare.

"Molly has exhibited serious faults. I've watched her try to cure herself. She appreciates the home we have given her, but it has become clear that she has succumbed. . .succumbed to the temptation of selfish love. She desires Jonah, exclusively, a non-believer who turned a deaf ear to our entreaties to join us. I ask all of you, is Molly capable of the sacrifice required in our community?"

The accusations flew at her like arrows, each criticism more stinging than the one before: she was not devout, had "excess egotism", failed to isolate herself from Jonah, visited Peterboro too often, worked not enough, failed to convince Jonah to join the community, and most egregiously, she resisted participating in stirpiculture which was designed to create more spiritually and physically perfect children.

Tapping a reservoir of strength, Molly took the insults without cracking. She was determined not to cry and not to apologize for loving Jonah. When they finished, she raised her head, stood, and pointed her finger to the skylight.

"You deny love? You will not succeed with this shaming. All that is good here, all that is kind and loving and industrious will fail should you persist in denying love."

Noyes walked close, took hold of her arm, and lowered it, scowling at her.

"Do you not understand that we can only achieve perfection if, as a family, we embrace Christ's ministry on this earth? Can you be cured of your selfishness, Molly?"

His face was close to hers now, his breath hot on her cheek, and his eyes were bloodshot with anger.

"Apparently," she said, in a level voice, "I cannot."

She left the room, with gasps and murmuring following her out the door. While preparing her travel sack, she realized that nothing in her room was hers to take. The clothes on her back and shoes on her feet were communal property. But the house wren, lovingly painted by Jonah, was hers. She folded it into a small piece of muslin and tucked it next to her breast. She then placed extra socks and shoes into a satchel and went to the kitchen for provisions.

I will pay them back for these things. I know the road to Peterboro. Aileen said it is a four-hour walk. I can do this.

She left through the side door, stopping temporarily to look back at the mansion where she had known joyous, confusing, and even some soulless experiences. These people had rescued her from a savage man. She was grateful, but now she was going home. If she could set eyes upon her brother, Michael, again, she could be truly happy.

The woman Claire emerged from the woods and stood on the road in front of her.

"Thank you," said Molly, "but our time together is over."

"May God protect you," Claire responded, tears streaming down her face.

Aileen knew instantly when she saw Molly, sweaty and bedraggled in the kitchen, that her most fervent prayer had finally come to fruition. Molly had left the Noyes community.

"There's no need to say a thing, dear. Come upstairs with me. We'll get you cleaned up, rub some salve on those tired feet, and have you share a bed with Bessie. This will make for a happy morning for the two of you."

Grateful for Aileen's warm, uncomplicated welcome, Molly smiled and followed her upstairs. Something critically important needed to be said right away, though, and she stopped and pulled her sister's arm.

"Aileen, I am with child. I know not the father. It could be Jonah or one of the men from the community. If they were to learn this, they might have prohibited me from leaving. They will consider my child their own."

Weighing the importance of this revelation, Aileen placed her hand softly on Molly's face and leaned close to kiss her cheek.

"We'll work this through, Molly. Trust me."

"I do. I do trust you."

The stories in the morning papers that Aileen purchased at the general store reinforced what everyone feared; that conflict between the northern and southern states was likely to ignite. More and more slaves were escaping to find freedom. Those that were caught and returned to their masters received brutal beatings and were often sold into the deep south. Some had a foot cut off in punishment to ensure they would never run away or run anywhere again.

Southern newspapers were calling the upcoming meeting of abolitionists in Cazenovia "Gerrit Smith's Convention." Although financed by Smith, the gathering represented a new, inter-racial coalition of men and women, both free men and fugitives, and persons of every religious sect and political party, united in outrage by the pending Fugitive Slave Act. Frederick Douglass was elected president of the convention.

The proceedings began with the robust voices of Mary and Emily Edmonson, fifteen- and seventeen-year-old former slaves, singing the hymn "I Hear the Voice of Lovejoy on Alton's Bloody Plain". Their voices silenced the surroundings. Even the leaves in the orchard seemed to have stilled to listen to their song. It recounted the death of Elijah Lovejoy, a white abolitionist as passionate as Jedidiah had been, at the hands of a pro-slavery mob. There would be no glossing over the risks abolitionists faced at this conference.

With Bessie at her side, Aileen walked slowly to the clearing where Jonah and Molly were seated. Their expressions showed alarm. The speakers were truthtellers, and they were striking fear into Molly and Jonah's hearts.

She watched Gerrit hold himself immobile with Douglass and a group of radical abolitionists, preachers and escapees, permitting Erza Weld to make a daguerreotype commemorating the occasion.

Terry Greene offered to drive Aileen, Bessie, Molly, and Jonah back to Peterboro following the second day of the convention. She enjoyed sitting next to him as he drove them through the sun-dappled woods. She listened for the distant roar of Chittenango Falls, and her thoughts harkened back to Jimmy and Leah. She told Greene the entire story of her reckoning at the falls and Jimmy's murder.

"They did help me find 'my good mind' again." She explained. "Thank you for listening."

He had listened closely to every word of her story. "Leah said Michael would find you?"

"Yes. I've been happier since she told me that. I haven't seen him, but I believe her."

"So do I." He smiled warmly at her.

She noticed Molly speaking feverishly to Jonah in the back of the wagon and thought better of interrupting them. Instead, she lifted Bessie to her side, and they sang together most of the way home.

When they arrived at the Smiths' estate, Jonah and Molly occupied the front porch swing, and Greene took the wagon and team to the barn. Aileen walked upstairs to put Bessie to bed. She gazed at her daughter's moon-lit silhouette against the crewel-trimmed pillowcase and emitted a deep, satisfied sigh.

It had been a day of righteous work, family, and friends. Douglass had even taken a moment to speak with her about Betha, recanting how her grandmother's skirt had twirled with delight upon hearing of the letters she had written to Father Murphy. Terry Greene's admiring eyes had lightened her step, and Molly appeared stronger and more independent than ever before. She heard Molly call to her.

"Aileen, can you speak with us?"

"Certainly, I will be there in a moment."

When she joined them on the veranda, their eyes were anxious and troubled.

"We need your help. Jonah and I want to leave here and make our lives together in Kingston."

Jonah took note of Aileen's shocked expression, held Molly's hand, and took over the conversation.

"Here, in Peterboro, I am a free man. Here, I do not hide my literacy, my curiosity or even my love for Molly. But soon even Peterboro will not be safe for a colored man. Douglass himself may soon leave for Canada."

Aileen knew he was right. She had admired him from the moment they met in the Land Office. Jonah was a good man, intelligent and kind.

"I understand why you want to leave, and yes, there is a growing community of escapees in Kingston, but I shudder to think of it. Here, I feel I can protect you."

"You cannot. Molly is with child. Should Noyes learn this, he will try to retrieve her and keep the child unto their community."

Although she accepted the logic that was being presented to her, she could not refrain from panic. Stepping close to Molly on this now humid and silent night, she pulled her to her feet, and wrapped her in a tight embrace.

"We haven't yet found Michael. Am I to lose you before we do?"

The two women pressed against one another tightly. Aileen ran her fingers through Molly's hair, allowing their curls to mingle and their tears to dampen one another's shoulders.

"Father Murphy's treachery tore you away. Now, finally, I have you with me, and you are strong and capable." Aileen began to cry.

"You are finally your own person, listening to your own heart, free from the torment of your stolen childhood. Am I truly about to lose you once more?"

Molly drew back her face and, revealing genuine anguish, responded.

"Yes."

"I'll long to see Bessie and Riley running on the lawn. And you, I'll long for you, the person who fought to allow me to find happiness. But I must leave. Just as you left Ireland. It's my only path to freedom. Will you help us to reach Kingston?"

Aileen breathed in the soft scent of peppermint that often drew up from the factory in Clockville on the evening breeze.

"Of course I will."

Aileen crossed her arms in front of her and began pacing the veranda, deep in thought when Terry Greene emerged from the hallway to join them.

"Forgive me. I overheard the latter part of your discussion. I may be able to help."

"I'd be so grateful. I'm ruling out Oswego as a point of departure. Although Mr. Edwards is there, as well as access to shipping, the city's been crawling with federal marshals of late. They've been absconding with free men as well as bondsmen."

"There's a family on Stony Point, south of Sacketts, with a small fleet of schooners. They ply the St. Lawrence with lumber. Our quartermaster knows them. Find your way there, and I'll see to it they help you cross to Wolfe Island and on to Kingston."

"Thank you, Terry. We'll travel first to Florence and stay with Stephen Myers. Then to Starr Clark's tin shop in Mexico and onto Stony Point from there."

With a new sense of confidence and resolve, Aileen abruptly stopped planning and began issuing instructions.

"Molly, get to sleep now. Jonah, see that a healthy, well-rested team of horses is available. I'll find Leah. She can guide us along the old trails. Terry, will we see you at Stony Point?"

He nodded yes, clearly impressed with her every word.

She squared her shoulders. "We should do this tomorrow, before I change my mind."

31

———

BROKEN DREAMS

Aileen knelt before her sister and fastened her five-button shoes.

"These are sturdy. Should last a year. It will be cold in Kingston. I added a muff to your bag."

Her chatter suppressed the anxiety she felt about their pending trip and the inevitable farewell that would mark its conclusion.

What will we encounter on the way?

Beyond their personal mission lay bigger questions. As the nation pulled further apart on the issue of slavery, would there be war?

Their plan was to forego the speed and comfort of the Canal to avoid attention. Jonah would drive the wagon on the old Oneida trails under the guidance of Leah. Should anyone inquire, they would simply say that Jonah and Leah, both employed by Gerrit Smith, were driving Aileen and Molly to visit their cousins in Sackett's Harbor. Heavy luggage would belie their tale, so they took care to pack few belongings. Gerrit's oversized hands squeezed some gold coins into Molly's palm and provided Jonah with letters of introduction to start their new lives in Kingston.

Molly handed Aileen a small envelope containing two of the coins given to her and a handkerchief trimmed with lace.

"Please take this to Claire at the Oneida Community Mansion when you return. She was kind to me, pulled me from a beast of a man, fed and clothed me."

Aileen nodded and drew her sister close. "Da would be so proud of the woman you have become."

"He was good to send you after me. Will we ever reunite with Michael, do you think?"

"I do," she replied with more conviction than she was feeling at the moment.

An hour into their journey, they were still riding high on the rolling escarpment where Peterboro stood. They broke into a clearing with a northern view so shockingly beautiful that Jonah stopped the wagon to stare. Leah turned, rose, and shouted. "It's Kanadario, the far lake, the shimmering water. It'll take Molly and Jonah home."

It was true. The sky was so clear and their view so perfect, they could see both of the lakes to their north. Lake Tsioqui, named Oneida by the settlers, stood at the base of the hill. It was flanked by a great brown plateau that the pioneers named "Tug Hill" to describe the difficulty of bringing wagons and goods over it. The plateau was crowned by the massive Lake Kanadario, which appeared like an endless, soft, cloudy-blue ocean melding into the sky.

"My ancestors dwelled here, overlooking all of this."

She pointed to three, six-foot-wide circular depressions in the ground. "Here are the grain pits. Over there are the graves."

Her words united the foursome in solemn silence. Each thought of their own ancestors as they gazed at the site before them.

"The Canal sliced your homeland like a knife to the heart," said

Jonah, voicing what they all were feeling. Then he clicked the reins and drove on.

The Iroquois name, Tsioqui, described perfectly the expansive, notoriously fickle lake that now lay before them. The word meant "white waters." Warm and shallow, storms could transform these waters from peaceful slumber to raging fury within moments, catching packet boats and canoes unaware and placing them in peril. They would not risk plying these waters. Leah directed Jonah to a trail on the lake's eastern edge that would allow their wagon to bump along on a northward route toward Florence.

A loud crackling sound in the woods startled Aileen. A bear? A wolf? She had grown increasingly uneasy since waking from an unsettling dream in which she envisioned Molly, frightened and swimming after a cormorant that had fallen from the sky into a lake. She knew from Leah to place stock in dreams and planned to speak with her about it as soon as they were alone.

Soon a doe and fawn appeared and stared, flicking their tails in annoyance at the wagon full of intruders. Aileen's heartbeat returned to normal. Jonah rubbed his blistered fingers on the stubble of his deeply cleft chin and waited for the animals to move into the brush before urging their horses forward. He quickly stopped again.

"I forgot to bring beans for the feeding chaff."

Aileen felt another surge of alarm. She felt attuned to every possible mishap or misstep that could put them in danger.

"We need the horses strong. The beans would help."

Leah climbed out of the wagon and began releasing one of the horses.

"I'll ride back to Morton's in Bernhards Bay to purchase a supply."

Knowing Leah could ride swiftly and without a saddle, Aileen pressed some coins into her hand. "Thank you. Please be careful."

As Leah climbed the rickety steps of the store porch, she noticed three horses, laden with rifles, bedrolls, and leather satchels, tied to the hitch post in the alley. The animals were unlike those owned by local farmers and seeing them made her hesitate. The Oneida had many good relationships with local settlers. Her tribe's loyalty to Washington during the Revolutionary War was well-remembered in the region. Vagabonds, however, were always a threat to native women and the law offered no protection or punishment.

When she turned from the counter to leave with her bag of crushed beans, the three men blocked her way and began taunting her. They stunk of horses and sweat.

"We ain't found no niggers on this trail, but here's a squaw to take with us."

"I get her first," said one of them, grabbing at her arm.

A crash startled them all.

The shop keeper had tipped over a heavy tin of horseshoes that resided on a shelf behind the counter, sending it spilling and thundering to the floor.

Leah ducked beneath the distracted men and made a dash for the door. Outside, she leapt onto her horse, and galloped off with lightning speed.

The one who had tried to grab Leah had run out the door after her, but the shopkeeper called out.

"Give me a hand here, gents, won't you?"

Muttering and swearing, the three men gave up the thought of retrieving their prize.

"We'll give you a hand with this mess if you tell us something."

"What?"

"We're looking for niggers. Runaway or otherwise. Been deputized to catch 'em and bring 'em south. Heard there were a bunch of 'em around here. You know anything about that?"

"Oh, yes," said the shopkeeper, sounding agreeable, even eager. "You want to go south of the lake to find them. Take the trail back southeast, that's your best bet."

As they departed, the shopkeeper made the Sign of the Cross and returned to his work, having sent them in the wrong direction.

Florence was busy. Seventy families of negro farmers were thriving south of the Salmon River Reservoir that fed the Canal. Gerrit Smith was proud of the community. He had provided enough land to ensure the residents could vote, and the trusted Stephen Myers had successfully promoted it.

Even without his trademark upturned collar and handsome necktie, Aileen recognized Myers' dignified carriage as he approached their wagon.

"Greetings, Aileen. Gerrit sent a messenger. We're pleased to shelter you and your friends."

Aileen was always happy to see Stephen Myers, and this was no exception.

"I have something in my possession for you from Saratoga. It was addressed to my wife's parents near Albany and forwarded on here."

Saratoga? Rose! Could it be from her?

Aileen had tried unsuccessfully for years to locate Rose. Keating Rawson had even taken her to Saratoga to search for her before her wedding to Jedidiah. Wanting desperately to share her happiness with Rose, she had knocked on doors and questioned shopkeepers for three days but failed to unearth a single lead on her whereabouts.

Often, when Jimmy was alive, he would join Aileen and Bessie on the porch after dinner, and they would reminisce about Rose, her strength of character, uncanny penchant for irritating Captain Mick, and the way "Sara-TOOO-GA" rolled from her lips.

"What is it, Aileen? You've lost your color."

"I'm fine."

Her mind reverted, as it did several times each day, to Molly's pregnancy.

"Get settled, Molly, and have some water. Stephen, could she nap somewhere near?" She looked up to find Myers staring curiously at Jonah, who had lowered his hat, shading his face.

During the previous hour, mountainous alabaster clouds had developed dark gray underbellies. Now the wind was pushing the formations furiously across the sky, presaging a destructive storm.

"Take the animals there," said Myers, pointing Jonah to a large barn a few hundred yards away.

Aileen hurriedly assisted Molly from the wagon, and Harriett Myers waved the three women toward her from the porch of her modest log home. Once inside, the darkness descended rapidly. Hail began clattering on the roof, and soon the wind shrieked through the crevices beneath the door and around the rafters. Aileen's eyes settled upon a wooden box jutting out from a burlap postal bag on a small table near a window.

Leah quickly jumped up the wooden stairs and into the cabin. Her frightened face brought a swath of fear across Aileen's chest, so powerful that she slumped into a rickety wooden chair from the force of it. She locked eyes with her friend.

"Trackers are hunting Negroes near here. We are not safe."

Aileen absorbed the import of Leah's experience at the store in

Bernhards Bay. All of Florence was now at risk. Jonah and others could be abducted and sent south. They were about to travel miles of woodland trails to reach the rocky shores of the Stoney Point Lighthouse. An ambush was not only possible in this isolated environment, if one were to occur, they would be out of reach of help.

Leah began humming a melody and wrapped Molly's shoulders in a maize and blood-red-colored quilt. Soon they were napping peacefully on the bed. As the storm settled into a steady rain, Stephen joined Aileen and Harriett and placed fresh-caught bass into a flat iron pan. Stephen and Aileen cupped hot tea, sat in adjoining rockers, and fell into the kind of deep conversation that had marked their friendship for years.

"When I first came here," Stephen said, "I believed so much was possible."

"You have made so much possible. Seventy families here, living on land they own, in homes they built, starting businesses."

"It won't last."

His teeth clenched, making his high cheekbones more prominent. She had never seen him like this. Stephen Myers and Gerrit Smith had instilled in her a stone wall of faith in the inevitable triumph of their cause. This unshakeable faith had sustained her since Jedidiah's murder. She stared at her friend in disbelief.

"You cannot mean that, Stephen! You plied the Hudson with slaves hidden in barrels. You built the eastern Underground Railroad."

"It doesn't matter."

"It does matter. It has to matter. Look around here. You've made a place for Negroes in America."

"If I had done that, Jonah and your sister would not need to escape to Canada."

"Do you know Jonah? He's a free man who works in the glass factory in Peterboro."

"I knew him as an escapee. Harriett and I sheltered him years ago in Albany."

Stunned by this information, she quickly forgave Jonah's lie. Why wouldn't an escapee hide his identity? Perhaps the Quakers had freed him. If not, now the mission to see Molly and Jonah safely to Kingston could truly be a matter of life and death.

"The Fugitive Slave Act destroys the dream."

He stood and looked dejectedly out the doorway at the curling street of tidy homes and shops nestled into the wilderness.

"No one will stay here or remember what was done here. We've already been threatened by marauding gangs. Self-deputized marshals are everywhere. I have sentries on watch this very night."

"What will you do?"

"Return to Albany. I've family and friends there. Many of the families here will go north to Canada rather than risk being sent south."

For the first time since Jedidiah's murder, Aileen felt despondent. Her dead husband's unwavering faith in America had seeped into her soul. Now, she was feeling it slip away.

The abolitionists, farmers, and shopkeepers she had come to know had bolstered her faith in this new nation. Pioneers speaking different languages, inspired by the passion of Finney, had broken with their old religions and built cities and social experiments all along the Canal. Equality had come to feel possible here, for this generation, even for women and former slaves. She'd borne witness to Jedidiah's dream in Gerrit Smith's Peterboro. There, every day she saw Oneida natives, former slaves, and farmers work together to raise barns, heal one another's sick children, and haul loads of sand up Oxbow Hill to the glass factory.

"Stephen, this nation is full of invention and ingenuity, not just in the way people live and the tools they use, but in the way they care for one another. The Canal itself speaks hope to immigrants who arrive in America with no hope at all. Surely there is hope for the Negro race here as well."

He slowly rubbed his forehead with the gnarled, bumpy fingers of his right hand.

"I wanted to believe that. Life has proven me a fool. The Canal your da helped build made opportunity for some. It also broke into pieces the homeland of your friend and banished her people from the graves of their ancestors. You know this."

He returned to the table and stared into the tea leaves at the bottom of his cup.

"They send us away. Our dark skin is glaring evidence of America's sin. Its mortal sin. We horrify simply because we exist."

Aileen squirmed in her chair, repelled by the haunting truth of his statements. He continued.

"This nation can't look at us without hate, pity, or self-loathing. Most of us are too dark to be out of sight. There will be no peace for us. Even Peterboro will change when monied men who are less than Gerrit Smith have the power he does today. Laws will be made that will keep us apart."

"War may change America, bring emancipation. Is war inevitable do you think?"

"Perhaps war will come, even emancipation." He inhaled deeply. "Our grandchildren may feel the breath of freedom. But not us, not here, not now."

She thought she saw a tear race down his face. Then he resumed his trademark erect posture and announced, "I am going to find that package from Saratoga."

The azure lace of her mother's shawl slid between her fingers as she reached into the gray paper box from Saratoga. Aileen stood petrified, staring at it.

Was Rose dead? Why else would this package be before her?

Then the scent of rosemary and the essence of safe, sensible Rose lofted into the cabin's evening air. Aileen closed her eyes and smiled, thinking of her first, true friend.

"This is from Rose. Recall her? She was with me on the Hudson steamer when we first met, along with a young boy."

"I do. Her face, a scar? Her eyes were kind."

They spotted the letter beneath the shawl at the same moment. Aileen, relieved, sighed and reached to retrieve it.

"Have your privacy with this."

He led her to a solitary, moss-laden bench on the front porch. The rain had stopped, the air was rich and wet, and the woods were strangely silent, amplifying the sound of the bench feet scraping on the uneven, gray wood floor, and her swiftly-beating heart. She tore open the letter.

Dear Aileen,

See before your very eyes that my cousin, Charles, taught me to write in my own hand! I am sending this, my first letter, to the family of our Hudson steward, Mr. Myers, with a prayer that he or his acquaintances on the river will know how to reach you. I want to share with you, at long last, a bit of my American adventure with hope that I shall someday learn some of your own.

Here in the Adirondack mountains, God has given me safety, family and love. These blessings may have passed me by had I failed to encounter the likes of you and become your friend.

I was damaged and sad, and you were young and afraid when we crossed the sea. We had no mums, no paths to follow, just our friend, Jimmy, and the trust that grows between women who share their pain. We found our way to laughter and schemed our way to freedom on the streets of New York. I thank you for this precious shawl. When you placed it around my shoulders in the Port of Albany, I felt your respect, and it made me able to start anew.

Cousin Charles' wife passed soon after I arrived in Saratoga, so I never went to work at the Springs. Instead, we moved to a farm outside Ballston Spa. There, I helped to raise his four darling girls.

Two years ago, I wed Danny Callahan, the postal delivery man in the village. He's the one who told me that my letters to you at the Rawson's never found their way. We've moved, Danny and me, to Glens Falls where he works in logging and paper. It's a comfortable cottage we have on Green Street, with a fine stove and garden. My Danny is as good a man as God ever made, bringing me tea in the morning, and reading to me by the scent of a pine-log fire as the sun sets over these ancient mountains.

Have you found the wee ones and forgiven yourself for their plight? Has Ryan, that rogue from Cork who tried to force you to become his wife, let you be?

Should you receive this, come to see me, Aileen. Our visit is long overdue. Until then, may your mother's shawl settle back upon your shoulders, cover you with strength, and provide you with the protection you deserve.

With deepest affection
Rose

There it was. Rose had given her the affirmation she needed to believe, once again, in her own strength. Only understanding what is truly right, feeling it in her bones, and acting upon it would get her home safely to Bessie.

Thank you, Rose, thank you.

She stood, tied her mother's shawl firmly around her waist, and called into the cabin, "What maps and guns do you have for me, Stephen?"

32

THE MIGHTY
ST. LAWRENCE

They studied the route from Florence to Stony Point by kerosene lantern. It would take at least sixteen hours tramping along wet, uneven trails and through dense forest to reach the lighthouse on Lake Ontario's shore. To travel undetected, their noisy wagon would have to remain in Florence.

Jonah wiped sweat from his forehead repeatedly as Leah pointed to old Oneida footpaths that would provide the best chance to avoid slavecatchers. "The route from here to the Salmon River, it's dangerous," she explained. "The men from the Bay, they'll know they were tricked. They'll be here by tomorrow night if they take this trail north."

Aileen looked at Stephen, frightened by this news.

Myers turned to look out the window and fell into deep thought. "We have enough men here in Florence to fight them off, but you three, alone on that trail." He went onto the porch to consider their predicament.

Several moments later he returned and looked at Leah.

"Take your wagon and a sledgehammer from the barn. Drive the wagon down the road south of here, break one of the wheels and leave it there."

He shifted his gaze to Jonah.

"There's a cemetery due north bordered by a ravine. Go there. Hide until I arrive. I know abolitionists in Redfield. I'll get reinforcements and a funeral wagon to take you to Stony Point."

Everyone snapped into motion. Myers spoke hurriedly to two of his neighbors before departing. Molly joined Aileen and Jonah who were exiting via the back door holding a lantern and the map.

Several hours later Jonah, Aileen, and Molly arrived at the cemetery. Fog descended upon their surroundings. Stones engraved with the names of early pioneers and their children appeared every few feet. They stopped and stared at each one, as though they were discovering their own family's remains. Then they turned off the lantern, huddled against a fallen tree trunk behind the graves, and listened for horses and men.

An owl shrieked and they huddled closer together. Aileen tried to envision the hours and days ahead. They would be cramped riding in a funeral wagon. There would be delays at Stony Point depending upon the mood of the great lake's waters. She thought of her daughter, glad that she was likely tucked safely into Viny's bed at this very moment.

She heard the sound of twigs snapping beneath the step of what? a wolf? a mountain cat? No, these were human steps she was hearing. A flash of fear flew up her arms and settled on her chest.

"Aileen, it's Leah."

Her breath released noisily from her lungs. She stood and waved to her friend. "Here, Leah, over here."

"This may work," Leah whispered hopefully. "When they see the broken wagon, they may think we are all in Florence and look no further up this road."

Aileen looked at Jonah and realized what a minor role she was playing in this escape in comparison to his. She was sacrificing a few nights away from home. He was leaving a job and place that he loved to keep Molly and her child safe from Noyes. He had already driven a team through woods rampant with slavecatchers, scoundrels who could send him to the deep south. He was leaving everything he knew and cared about without uttering a single complaint.

It disgusts me. This proud, capable man is being made to run, hide, and escape.

The clattering sound of wheels against rocks and snorting horses flooded their surroundings. Five men with torches and rifles on horseback arrived behind Stephen Myers. His calm voice pierced through the din. "Back up here."

He directed the driver of a long funeral wagon bearing two caskets toward a clearing and waved Jonah, Aileen, and Molly forward. "This is Asa Johns. Here's water. Climb in. Aileen and Molly, you share a box. There are breathing holes in the caskets. It'll be uncomfortable, but safe."

Molly and Jonah embraced before she climbed into a wooden box with Aileen. Stephen gave Aileen a long stare before closing the lid. Sadness hung about him like a veil.

"I will see you in Albany, Stephen."

He nodded solemnly.

"Thank you."

Aileen patted Molly's blond curls as they nestled closely in the coffin. She whispered in her ear, "I love you, Sister."

The rumble of Myers and his companions heading south toward Florence faded into the distance.

"I wish Michael were with us."

"He was spotted on Lake Ontario, not once but twice."

Soon they heard the sound of a horse arriving from the north. Their wagon came to a halt and Molly's breath caught in her throat.

"Who do you carry there?" The voice was unfamiliar, loud, and challenging.

Aileen felt her body stiffen, and she tried unsuccessfully to restrain her tears.

Their driver responded calmly. It's the Sampsons from Redfield. The blue death got them."

Aileen marveled at his ingenuity. Cholera came from drinking contaminated water and was a messy affair. The victim's corpses often turned blue from dehydration. The stranger would be unlikely to inspect their hiding places for fear of contamination.

"Go on then," the stranger barked.

Aileen whispered in her ear, "Molly, I swear to you, Canada will be your home."

The roar of waves echoed through the casket as the wagon pulled to a halt. Grateful that sleep had come over them toward the end of their journey, Aileen shaded their eyes from the sun as the lid of the casket opened to the smiling driver. Asa Johns was clearly proud of himself for getting his charges to the safety of the Huntington home near Stony Creek.

Jonah was already standing near the wagon. He was speaking with a woman with gray hair tied severely into a bun. The wind whipped fiercely around them, reddening their faces as they stepped from the wagon.

Molly took in her surroundings. "It's an ocean! It's the sea!"

Aileen felt relief at Molly's happy wonderment, having feared Ontario would trigger memories of her first trip across the Atlantic as a small child huddled in fear with her brother. She turned her face toward the white caps that were pounding onto the shore, breathed deeply, and smiled.

"We are going to make it, Molly. Da would be proud."

The woman turned to Aileen.

"I'm Zina Johns. My husband, Asa, drove you. You'll be with us until weather permits safe passage to Wolfe Island."

They walked on a pedestrian footbridge over the creek and past a grist mill and lumber yard. Soon, Henderson Harbor appeared before them.

"What glory!" sighed Molly. She planted her feet apart and gazed forward, clearly mesmerized by the horseshoe-shaped basin of blue water rimmed by forest and framing the endless horizon of Lake Ontario.

They walked to a large cobblestone house on a bluff. Looking down at the water, Zina explained, "This is the ancient portage from the head of Henderson Bay to Stony Creek. It saves travelers the treachery of rounding Stony Point. Even with the new lighthouse, it's still a route to be avoided."

They entered a kitchen where sunlight poured through paned windows. Aileen and Zina began scaling salmon and chopping turnips on the long, battered wooden table in the center of the room.

"You live here alone, the two of you?"

Zina's face scowled. My cousins, the Huntington's, built this place. They became Mormons and traveled west with Smith. Two of their girls became his fifth and sixth wives."

"Religions sprout like corn here in America."

Zina poured a glass of water from a speckled, blue pitcher and handed it to Aileen before responding. "That they do. All I know is when those of one faith spew hate upon those of another, they've lost their way. I'm no pure child but I know God wouldn't have us hating each other."

Aileen smirked and placed the turnips in a pot near the woodstove. "When people have faith, the leaders have control. They favor the tasty meals dropped at their door, the lonely widows, and the confessions of sin. Some like the power too much."

"Go and take a walk on the point Aileen. The lake will clear your head. I'll send Molly for you when the meal is ready."

As Aileen stepped down the trail toward the lighthouse, she became grateful for Zina's suggestion. Layered limestone cliffs rose sharply above the water and sun-bleached tree roots spilled artfully from the stone. The pounding rhythm of the lake and cleansing breezes transported her to a rare, peaceful state of mind.

That evening Asa explained that Captain Nathan Nickels from Henderson Harbor, known for his adept use of the hygrometer, had assured him that Tuesday would be the most fortuitous day to sail to Wolfe Island. Aileen, Jonah, and Molly prepared for the journey while enjoying the good food and company of their hosts.

It was a clear morning when they departed on the lumber schooner. Jonah whistled a tune as they left the harbor. Aileen noted the relief on his face. As they entered the St. Lawrence River, the sky suddenly turned gray.

The wooden spar extending from the ship's bow disappeared from sight as the boat rocked forcefully up and down across the waves toward Wolfe Island. Jonah and Molly huddled together beneath the deck, clenching each other's hands with a mix of fear and determination. Aileen attempted to walk about the cabin but was thrown around awkwardly as the ship lurched from side to side. She had ruled out the option of staying behind because her commitment to Molly, no longer fostered by guilt, was absolute.

A great wash of spray came over the deck and poured down the hold. Aileen could hear the piles of lumber straining against the ropes that kept them balanced on deck. Alarmed, Jonah placed Molly squarely in Aileen's arms, tied the women together with a rope and placed them above the hold. He climbed up the ladder. During the next five minutes the schooner lurched violently forward and back. Aileen became increasingly convinced they were going to sink and die.

The temperature had fallen dramatically, and black clouds could be seen between the masts. She heard shouting then an ear-splitting crack followed by the rippled pounding of falling wood. The ship heaved to one side. Aileen looked up and glimpsed the mainsail falling down into the waves. Grabbing Molly, she dragged them to the edge of the tilting vessel and tied their rope to the metal ring of a huge barrel. An iron fitting flew their way, catching Aileen on the left brow and rendering her unconscious.

33

———

REUNION AND FAREWELL

The soldiers said they found her unconscious lying across her sister's breast. Jonah was found a mile south of where they had landed, dazed and with a severe cut on his shoulder. Terry Greene let her know that Stephen Myers had left for Albany and the pioneering Negro farmers of Florence departed soon after for the safety of Canada.

Julia Grant became a friend as Aileen recovered in Sackett's Harbor. She came to help Terry Greene when she saw him rushing across the lawn carrying a woman to the infirmary. She warmed the shivering Aileen with blankets and hot tea and sat by her bed that entire night.

"Is my sister alive?" Aileen asked, looking up at her in the morning.

"Yes. It's a miracle. The two of you tied to a barrel that wouldn't sink!"

Julia stayed by her side for four days, then introduced her to Captain Grant and others in the Village. Aileen marveled at her kindness and her ability to make her sober-faced husband a cheerful companion, particularly over a game of checkers.

This morning, she touched the strands of gray in the dark curls that framed her face, then lifted and sniffed the rosemary plant she had placed on her vanity the day before. Mornings and the scent of rosemary always brought memories of Betha, the particular flavor of her tea, and the shape of her arrow-straight back walking down the hill to the Village. As she reached for her cape, she heard Julia tap on her door.

Will you join us for breakfast, dear?"

"After my walk, yes."

She strode up the embankment outside the Union Hotel to the spot where the view of the sunrise over the St. Lawrence was spectacular. She stared at the jagged rocks below. She knew those rocks had torn many a ship asunder.

Staring down, she relived the trauma of reaching for the long, frozen clumps of Molly's hair spilled haphazardly on the sand. Her sister had been near, face down, and frighteningly still.

We're back on the American shore. Molly is dead!

She recalled her heart racing as she tasted the sand in her throat and the vomit that came after. She'd crawled closer to Molly, finally turning her over. Drawing in a deep breath Aileen lifted her eyes to the morning sky and relived the total joy that had swept over her when she spotted a lifting motion on Molly's chest. After that everything had gone blank.

Aileen returned to the hotel and breakfast with Terry Greene and the Grants.

"You're one of the sisters then?" a young soldier asked as she walked into the foyer. "One of the O'Malley sisters? I've heard the tale, been stationed here with Michael."

"Yes, I'm his sister, Aileen."

"He's told us all about you. How you came from the old country to find he and the little girl. How you searched all these years."

Her face flushed.

"Pleased to meet you, that's all ma'am. I wish you well."

"Thank you."

She relived the moment when Molly and Michael first reunited while she walked slowly through the paneled hallway to the dining room. The infirmary had been sunlit and quiet. The smell of camphor was in the air and the man gazing down at Molly, who was lying in the bed next to hers, was undeniably Michael O'Malley. His resemblance to their father was profound and tears were rolling uncontrollably down his face.

She heard him say, "Hello, little sister."

"Michael, Michael—is it you?" Molly's face had frozen in shock.

Recalling Molly's breakdown when first they met at the site of the Mansion House, Aileen intervened and began speaking to her in a low even tone.

"Breathe sister, breathe. Leah said Michael would find me. Look here, Molly, after all of this, finding us is exactly what Michael has done."

Michael eyes widened as he looked at Aileen for the first time.

"I don't recall you very well. I was so young. Greene found me after you showed him your poster. When my schooner docked, he told me about you, both of you." His gaze returned to Molly.

"I'm so sorry, so sorry Molly. I couldn't protect you. I wanted to.

I tried to. I pulled you from that man on the dock, but they clobbered me. Then you were gone. You were gone!"

Aileen pulled herself out of bed and grasped his hands to comfort him and steady herself. They embraced before leaning together over Molly. Then they were all crying, hugging, and running their fingers through one another's hair. Molly was laughing with excitement through her tears.

Returning to the present, Aileen moved toward the dining room. She saw Terry Greene and the Grants sitting at a lace-draped table in the corner. Grant and Greene stood, and she walked over and placed herself into the singular empty chair.

"Let's not discuss war this morning." She reached for the raspberry jam.

"Agreed," responded Grant. He grinned behind his beard and took Julia's hand. "It's a grand morning for your journey to Wolfe Island and Kingston. I'm pleased for you."

Terry Greene added reassuringly, "Michael has everything in hand."

"He's the right man for this job," added Julia.

An hour later they were all standing at the dock in the sunny, well-protected harbor.

Aileen chatted with Captain Grant before boarding the boat. "My grandmother fought in the united uprising. Perhaps I'll take up spying for the Union should the need arise."

She could hear Michael reassuring Jonah and Molly. "There's no slave catchers on Wolfe Island. We'll get you there quickly and on to Kingston. There's a community for you there."

The short trip to Wolfe Island was smooth and uneventful. The weather was glorious when they stepped onto the shore. Aileen took

Molly's hand and led her to a little beach. They took off their shoes and perched on top of a multi-layered rock shelf jutting out into the lake.

The water was warm and clear, and a brilliant array of multi-colored rocks were just beneath their toes. The bottom of Aileen's dress became wet when she reached down and pulled a fist-sized pink and black granite stone out of the water. "Betha," she named it and reached in again. This time she pulled out a flat gray stone adorned with rust-colored circles. Turning it over she saw a fossil in the shape of a key. "This is Annie, Annie Eustace who I told you about," she said to Molly.

Carrying both rocks, she walked to a sandy section of the coastline and urged Molly to join her. Feeling girlish, she twirled her skirt in a circle in the wind. With a thin piece of driftwood, she drew Ireland in the sand and placed the rock that was Betha squarely in the center. Next, she drew the shape of the American continent. Molly gathered gull feathers and Aileen carefully placed them across the northeast section. "The Iroquois." Molly clapped her hands, thoroughly enjoying Aileen's antics.

Aileen laughed with satisfaction when she found a heart-shaped stone for Jedidiah, and hummed when she discovered a pure white oval for Rose, and salmon-colored nugget for Sara. "My friends," she explained to Molly.

Next, she shaped a large mound from a pile of wet sand. "Peterboro," she proclaimed. Molly helped her place pebbles representing Gerrit, Ann, Viny, and Bessie on its crown. She raised a square piece of green sea glass to her eyes. "Frederick Douglass," she said and tucked it into a notch on the southern shore of the lake.

Now, fully immersed in her project, she fashioned New York City, the Oswego wharf, Troy, and the Oneida Mansion House from pieces of bark. She created Chittenango Falls by directing water channels over small piles of limestone shards and placed a stone named Elizabeth near Seneca Falls. She carved the Hudson and placed Stephen in the center on a boat-shaped leaf. She handed Molly a stick. "You can dig the Canal," she suggested while placing a freckled rock near Schenectady and naming it Jimmy.

Her mood suddenly darkened. She looked at Molly then stood erect and stared down at the assemblage. "I don't know how to mark Port Byron or Palmyra." The horror of the suicide she had witnessed in Port Byron had never fully left her mind.

"Palmyra is where you leaned of Da's death?" Molly asked.

"Yes." Aileen imagined the waxy hands of the ancient nun who told her of her father's death. Before she could continue, a two-foot wave came crashing over her masterpiece, pulling her carefully constructed world out into the lake, and leaving twisted scraps of sticks and muddy pebbles in its wake. She looked up to see Molly staring at her curiously.

As she looked down at the ruined sand-map of her life, she prayed that just a smidgeon of the confidence she had carried as a pretty, privileged, Irish girl, would mix with the wisdom she'd gained in America and make for a good life.

"The wave reminded me of leaving Cork where I said goodbye to all I knew and loved. It was just, swept away."

Molly threw her arms around Aileen's neck. "You left to find us and now you have. There'll be no more tearful farewells for us, Aileen. We'll be together in the years ahead, you and Michael and me."

Aileen responded by running her hand over Molly's belly. "I may take up some work with the Union Army if there's war, but we'll visit,

Michael and I. We'll soon be playing with this wee one you have on the way."

Kissing Molly tenderly on the cheek, she held her close and whispered softly while looking over her sister's shoulder at the St. Lawrence, "Betha would call this a grand moment, and right she'd be. We've taken the last step of our long flight to freedom."

AFTER THE WAR
(AUBURN 1865)

Aileen and Bessie strolled arm in arm along Genesee Street, which was lined with redbud trees, stately mansions, the new Greek Revival Courthouse, and blocks of stunning Romanesque Revival buildings.

"Auburn already feels like home. It was a hotbed of abolitionism before the war. I'm anxious to get settled and begin teaching."

"I hated being apart during the war, mother."

Aileen stopped mid-block and turned to face her daughter. Bessie's red curls and yellow silk dress were bathed in sunlight. She had stayed with the Smiths in Peterboro during the war, while Aileen was in Virginia, serving as a spy for the Union Army.

"Viny's letters were full of praise for you Bessie."

The Smith's household manager and Aileen's good friend, Viny, had written to Aileen every week while she was away.

"She told me how you organized the aid society, the canning and sewing, mending blankets and making medical supplies." She felt a catch in her throat. "I'm so proud of the woman you've become."

Bessie lowered her eyes. "I cried a lot during the war. I worried about you, but then I got to work."

"Indeed, you did," said Aileen. She kissed her daughter on the cheek. They leaned into one another as they resumed their stroll, grateful to be together again.

Soon they passed a group of soldiers, laughing and playing a game of hoop and stick on the sidewalk. The men's glances at her daughter made Aileen aware of how her beauty now attracted attention.

"Will Mr. Greene and Mr. Douglass visit us here?"

"I expect they will. Perhaps sometime this summer."

As they turned onto South Street the Seward Mansion came into sight.

"How did you become so close to Mrs. Seward?"

"Elizabeth introduced us years ago. She's a good woman, brave, an abolitionist. We met at the Convention in Seneca Falls. I'm glad she invited us for lunch."

They opened the iron gate which was framed by azaleas and flowering vines and stepped onto the narrow walking path leading to the grand home. They were shocked to find an aging soldier in a dirty blue uniform sobbing uncontrollably on the steps leading up to the front door.

"What is it sir? Can we help?"

"I just delivered a telegram to Frances Seward from Washington. It's the most awful thing."

He was shaking as he blurted out, "They took him. . .the angels took Mr. Lincoln! John Wilkes Booth, the actor, he done it. It was a plot. Another scoundrel attacked Mr. Seward the same night. He is barely alive."

"Sir, I cannot comprehend. . ."

"He stabbed good Mr. Seward's face! It was a conspiracy! The rebels wanted them all gone, Lincoln and his best men." He was shouting now.

Bessie put her hand on the man's shoulder in an attempt to comfort him. He shot her a look of gratitude and began running his fingers repeatedly through his disheveled gray hair.

He caught his breath, calmed himself and continued. "He beat Seward's boy, Frederick, with his gun and hurt Augustus, too! We don't know who attacked Seward, but we will. The scoundrel. He even pushed Seward's daughter, Fanny, to the floor. Poor child saw the whole terrible thing."

Aileen and Bessie stared at the man and then at one another with dread. The world that had seemed so hopeful and vibrant just moments before, fell instantly into darkness.

Aileen's thoughts raced frantically. *Impossible. Three of her children and her husband attacked? Would they live? And Lincoln, Lincoln is dead? Impossible.*

She raced into the home and up the stairs to see Frances. When she entered her bedroom, the drapes were closed, and she saw a figure near the window in the shadows. Leaning over from the waist with her hand pressed against the wall and crying quietly was Frances. Aileen reached for her, gently pulled her upright and rocked her in her arms.

In the days that followed, news of the assassination swept over the City of Auburn like a brutal wind before a winter storm. Black bunting was draped from balconies, flags were lowered, and stores were closed. Aileen and Bessie helped Frances as best they could, greeting dozens of visitors who arrived to express their relief that William Seward had survived the assault and their shock and grief over the loss of President Lincoln. This morning Aileen and Bessie sat in the basement kitchen, near the fireplace that stood from ceiling to floor, to have a quiet moment together. Bessie poured their tea.

"Have you seen Mrs. Tubman, Mother?"

"Yes. I attended church with her Sunday. The place comforts her. She wishes she had met Lincoln when she had the chance."

"Regrets. I wonder, do nations have regrets?"

"I hope so child."

"I'll miss you while I'm visiting Peterboro."

"Yes, but I am glad you're going. The Smiths need you. Please give them my love. Ask them to understand why I must stay here, won't you?"

"They'll understand. Will you write to me, Mother, and help me to understand? Often, since the assassination, I can't sleep."

"I'll write to you, Bessie, just as soon as I have a clear thought to share."

After several weeks, Aileen retrieved her dip pen from the side table in her bedroom, found a quiet spot in the parlor, and wrote the letter she had promised to Bessie.

My Darling Girl,

A priest in Ireland once told me, "Families require sacrifice." His words brought me to America. After this great Civil War, now we know, bitterly, that countries require sacrifice as well.

My heart is with you, along with our dear friends in Peterboro. Mr. Lincoln heard the cries for abolition that sang out from our village on the hill. He lead us through the war, and emancipated the slaves. It's an utter cruelty that he has been stolen from us by an assassin's bullet. I lament Lincoln's murder like a screaming wolf when I am alone in the comfort and solitude of Fort Hill Cemetery. I am crying for my country.

In Ireland, violence was the child of poverty. There was monarchy, limited land, bad crops, and cruel repression. I saw many a child with hollow eyes edged in fear, seeking scraps in the alleys and animal feed in the barns.

Here, there is enough for everyone. Here, we are guaranteed the right to worship as we please. Here, we change our destiny. We build cities, educate women, carve a canal through our heartland and welcome people from all nations to our shores.

But remember child, we took this land from the Iroquois who loved and respected it. This land was theirs. We took it from them with violence and nothing good ever comes from that. Had we sought to understand their culture and learned some of their ways, we would be better for it.

Your father was eternally hopeful for America. I draw upon his faith at times like these. He believed we would have Negro leaders one day and that educated American women would lead our country into the finest, most enlightened era the civilized world has ever seen.

Today, though I try mightily to taste his optimism, I fear we are cursed by our violent, obstinate past. I cannot explain to you why, with all this abundance and possibility, and the gift of democracy, our President's life has been taken by a bitter-hearted man holding a gun.

I wonder if violence is now baked as mercilessly into this American soil as it was in Ireland's. I wonder if murder will prevail everywhere when men with strong wills disagree. I pray this is not so because our new nation represents hope to so many.

In dark times I comfort myself by thinking of old friends who have found meaning and happiness in their lives here. You might try it when you are sad. Think of the Rawsons. They've raised the funds to build a new church, St. Augustine's in Troy. Then there is Rose, happy to be by the fire that she shares with her Danny in Glenns Falls. I speak often with Stephen Myers. He treasures his home in Albany and takes great pride in his role recruiting colored troops for the Army and getting them paid. Our dear Elizabeth, of course, never fails to astound. She and Susan B. Anthony are now preparing a women's suffrage petition to submit to Congress! Brother Michael is farming a grand piece of land in a place called Sandy Creek, and as you know, Jonah and Molly are expecting their third child and plan to buy a livery stable in Kingston.

Try resting your mind on those who live with purpose and joy despite disappointment and sorrow. Think of Leah's lovely songs, how she sings her melodies about the trials of her people while at the same time leading and comforting them.

Lincoln's murder tells me that the South has indeed not surrendered. Resentment toward the emancipation of the slaves may feed American violence for centuries to come. I pray not, and I hope with all my heart that a future President will bind Americans of good will back together.

I wish most of all, daughter, for you to have the blessings of a happy life. Those blessings –the sweet smell of grass in the morning, the touch of a good man on your skin, the laughter of an elder while recanting a tale of mirth—all come from doing meritorious work and being at peace in your soul.

The task is before you. Put your good mind, strong constitution, and sensitive heart to the task of making this a better land.

Your loving Mum.

The origin of the word "Iroquois" is a matter of debate. The term was universally used, however, among upstate New York native nations until the term "Haudenosaunee" grew to be more acceptable in the 20th century. I use the term "Iroquois" in "Dreams of Freedom" to reflect the era in which this story takes place. Courtesy of my friend, Doug George-Kanentiio, I also want to share with my readers some of the beautiful "place-names" provided by the Mohawk, Oneida, Onondaga, Cayuga, Seneca, and Tuscarora Nations to the landscapes of this story.

Saratoga:

Refers to a river by a hill

Schenectady:

Ska-na-ta-ti: the other side of the pines

Cohoes Falls:

Kahon:ios: canoe falls

Schoharie:

Sko-ha-li: driftwood

Niskayuna:

Koh-nis-ti-gi-oh-ne: corn fields

Mohawk River:

Oh-ion-hiio-ke: nice creek

Lake Champlain:

Ka-nia-da-la-kwa-lohn-de: bulging waterway

Hudson River:

Oh-iio-ge: nice river

Canajoharie:

Ka-na-jio-ha-le-: washed kettle

Lake Ontario:

Ka:nia:ta:ro:io: nice lake

Niagara Falls:

Oh:nia:ga:ra: big rapids

Skaneateles:

Ska:ni:en:ta:res: long lake

ACKNOWLEDGEMENTS

Foremost I want to acknowledge my writing and publishing coach, David Hazard, director of ASCENT, an international coaching program, who patiently, expertly, and with great kindness, showed me the way to accomplish this life-long goal.

My father's family were tenants on a farm poised on a hill just west of Green Lakes State Park and overlooking the old Erie Canal. His stories about descending that hill with a team of horses, cutting blocks of ice from the waterway, and packing them in sawdust for the winter are what sparked my life-long passion for the Erie Canal and upstate New York history. My mother, a woman who adored reading, and did so until she was 92 years old, gave me my appreciation for the written word. I credit the sparkling blue eyes of my grandmother, the former Anna Quigley, and the hilarious banter of her sons around the dining table in Philadelphia, with my strong sense of Irish heritage. I am grateful to my sisters, Carolyn and Pat, who discovered that the world knows and remembers the Erie Canal when they joined me in singing "I've got a mule and her name is Sal" with twelve German bowlers while vacationing in Garmisch-Parten-kirchen. Decades of "history conversations" with my two smart brothers, David and Marty, also motivated me to write this book, and my son Daniel and his wife, Elisha, guided me with kindness since the beginning of this endeavor. My niece Quinn Gardner, the family librarian, stepped in with her expertise and savvy on numerous occasions.

Every day, I thank my friend, the late Joanne Shenandoah, along with her husband Doug-George-Kanentiio and daughter Leah, for deepening my understanding of the wisdom and culture of the Oneida Nation. I hope I have honored that learning here. I am grateful to Anne Smith for convincing me to move to Canastota, my home canal town, and for Dot Willsey, President of the National Abolition Hall of Fame and Museum. She taught me that Peterboro is "second only to heaven" and motivated me to get this novel out to the world. Had I not read each of her husband, Ph.D. Historian Norman Dann's, marvelous non-fiction books on Gerrit Smith and Peterboro, this novel would have stood on considerably shakier ground.

My life-long friends Susan Reardon and Terry Greene contributed mightily to this effort, as did my principal cheerleaders Mary-Anne Schmitt Carey and Donald Carey. My friend Gregg Tripoli convinced me to start over, and I am endlessly grateful to him for doing so. I received useful, candid feedback from Linda Lowen, Carole Horan, Roxanne Bocyck, childhood friend Pam Holbrook and Sandra Swierczek, marketing ideas from Larry Mitchell, home-made Lebanese chicken and rice from Aminy Audi, encouragement from Linda Voss, Elaine Walter, and my cousin Joe Gabel. The marvelous image of Aileen came from Elizabeth Gabel. Without Cathi William's editing skills and Sarah Longley and Jen Farwell's marketing savvy this would not have made it to completion. The Erie Canal Museum in Syracuse was also helpful.

I also want to express my deep respect for the team at the Erie Canalway National Heritage Corridor. Thanks to former Congressman Jim Walsh, their outstanding work keeps the fire of history alive in one of the most gorgeous, important, underappreciated places in America.

Back Cover Images

Gerrit Smith—46 years old, oil on canvas. Courtesy of the National Abolition Hall of Fame and Museum, Peterboro, New York.

Native Woman—Photogravure of woman sitting for portrait, "Princess Eat-no-meat"; COMMUNITY—schitsu'umsh [Coeur d'Alene], Confederated Tribes of Warm Springs, Yakama, Séliš u Qĺispé, National Museum of the American Indian.

Frederick Douglass—John Chester Burns 1855, Engraving from a lost daguerreotype, published as the frontispiece to Douglass's *My Bondage and My Freedom*, 1855.

Interior Images

Map—The Journey of Aileen O'Malley–designed by Sarah Wiley-Joyce.

Page 12, Poster advertising a packet service to New York 1823–Wikipedia, Packet Trade.

Page 112, "The Shakers in Niskayuna–Religious Exercises". Courtesy of Communal Societies Collection, Hamilton College, Clinton, New York.

Page 190, Pamphlet by John Humphrey Noyes, "Sexual Relations in the Oneida Community". Courtesy of the Communal Societies Collection, Hamilton College.

Page 274, Image of Cazenovia Convention 1850 daguerreotype without the frame. Courtesy of the Madison County Historical Society.

MARILYN HIGGINS has spent her life loving and working in the cities, small towns and places of extraordinary natural beauty that comprise upstate New York. Her passion for the area's rich history and belief in its profound impact on America's national identity motivated her to write *Dreams of Freedom*.

As the chief economic development officer for National Grid (Niagara Mohawk Power Corporation) and later Syracuse University, she was told intriguing stories and saw the mysterious artifacts of upstate New York's Erie Canal communities. Her fascination with these places, where new religions were born and waves of immigrants, abolitionism, women's rights, and Haudenosaunee culture entwined in the 19th century continues.

A twenty-year volunteer with the Erie Canalway National Heritage Corridor, she is currently working with the National Abolition Hall of Fame and Museum and her home community of Canastota, New York, to promote the "Abolitionist Freedom Walk," a public reenactment of the storied 1835 canal journey and march of 104 abolitionists up a steep, nine-mile embankment to the Hamlet of Peterboro to form the New York Anti-Slavery Society.

Imagining the life of a young Irish woman in search of her lost family along the Erie Canal at a time when the area was a hotbed of dissent, and the critical last leg of escape on the underground railroad, energized her in the writing of this novel.

www.ingramcontent.com/pod-product-compliance
Lightning Source LLC
Chambersburg PA
CBHW040852010826
48978CB00013BA/994